HOT TYPE

HOT TYPE

America's Most Celebrated Writers
Introduce the Next Word in
Contemporary Fiction

Edited by JOHN MILLER,
with the editors of Equator magazine
HEIDI BENSON, CYNTHIA KORAL, RANDALL KORAL

COLLIER BOOKS
Macmillan Publishing Company • New York
COLLIER MACMILLAN PUBLISHERS
London

This is a work of fiction. Names, characters, places, and incidents are either the product of the author's imagination or are used fictitiously. Any resemblance to events or persons, living or dead, is entirely coincidental

Collier Books
Macmillan Publishing Company
866 Third Avenue, New York, NY 10022
Collier Macmillan Canada, Inc.

Library of Congress Cataloging-in-Publication Data
Hot type : America's most celebrated writers introduce the next word in
    contemporary fiction / edited by John Miller . . . [et al.].—1st Collier Books ed.
    p. cm.
ISBN 0-02-044701-9
1. Short stories, American. 2. American fiction—20th century.
I. Miller, John.
PS648.S5H68 1988
813'.01'08—dc19   88-17585   CIP

Cover illustration © by Karen Katz
Cover design by Lee Wade

First Collier Books Edition 1988

10 9 8 7 6 5 4 3 2 1

Special thanks to Tom Jenks, Oakley Hall, and Pat Towers

CONTENTS

FOREWORD
▪ Richard Ford

WHAT HELPS

What follows in these pages is straightforward business. Fifteen writers of fiction, myself among them, hand up the work of fifteen others, who for reasons of age, inexperience, or the damnable luck of the damnable draw, have not been widely read, or not widely enough, we think, but who should be. The backstage relations are no more than one might expect. We are acquaintances, colleagues, teachers, publishers, or merely distant admirers of the writers we bring to notice. This is often how excellent work finds a wider audience. And of course we share, as well, the same *polis*, as Auden said: we are "friends" in the broad sense that we practice the same vocation. And the fifteen of us believe that when anyone does well in this practice—as is the case here—all of us have reason to feel encouraged.

A familiar question arises, however, from such a shared undertaking as this. Simply, what can one ever do for someone else's work? It is a question that comes up—in this country, especially—for good reason, and often. At any stage in one's writing life, at any celestial point along the wide galaxy most of us occupy between celebrity and anonymity, we are often in contact and to some extent in context with other writers and their efforts, and are frequently in a position either of needing or being able to render assistance. Either we are beginners or old hands; students or teachers; exiles or well-connected-with-the-higher-ups; nobodies or luminaries; have-nots or (for a brief moment) *haves*. Nothing's to be rued, here. Giving somebody a leg up in the world, or (for goodness' sake) needing one, is neither a cheat nor a surrender to baleful networking. People simply need help sometimes, writers maybe more than most. Art, after all, is not a competitive undertaking if understood well; excellence should be encouraged; most of us know what it's like to be nowhere with nothing; most of us really do have time; the spirit of art, any art, is actually generous and inclusive, if occasionally severe, and always ennobling to its practitioners and their friends. So? Why not?

Of course there is little enough one can do, little that really avails. You can't teach anybody very much. There's no body of knowledge to master or specific skills writers must absorb. No particular work habit assures or condemns anything. No one background suits you best to be a good writer. Connections don't really help. No age is best to start or quit. No right attitude cinches it. Horace wrote, "Learned and unlearned, we all write." And wasn't he just correct? The lines toward truth radiate from us all and in all directions at once, higgledy-piggledy. Being born is all that seems to qualify you perfectly.

When I started to think of what to write here, I decided a list would help, a short menu of desideratums: *must-do's* without which the whole, old machine of writing would never turn newly or well, and ignoring entirely the Great Books, the famous tricks of the trade, and of course talent. One *must* learn, my list began, to take one's important work seriously; one *must* learn to create a "self" which is his writing self and who does his work; one must find friends who'll tell him the truth both when he does and doesn't like hearing it. One must not get discouraged, but must do his work even when he doesn't have the heart for it.

Or else, what?

Or else, I quickly saw, one does none of these things, whereupon one's work may become immensely better. Surely there are many things to learn about being a writer, but fortunately none of them is essential. Help may actually be palpable and near at hand—our teachers, our colleagues, our betters—but often there is simply no useful place we can make for it.

To be a writer in America is largely to float free, often apparently out of help's reach, in the charge of only ourselves, and often with little that's demonstrable to take heart in except, in a selfish way, the excellent work of others. Ours is a country with no vested *place* for most of its writers—old or new. Immense success, a condition in which many smart people read what you've written and feel their lives irrevocably changed for the good by it, is about the only satisfying *place* I can credit. Otherwise, no institution shelters us, no profession is there to join up with. There's no bar—except for the other kind, no AMA, no club ties. Universities occasionally extend a tepid, soft hand, but the grip's always weaker than we'd like. And anyway, no one first thought of being a writer without a moment of believing she or he could make it alone. And no one ever finished up without wishing it'd been that way. Add the unarguable fact that the numbers are against you, that becoming an excellent writer in any public way, outside one's room, with readers, is improbable—almost a perfect "empty set" in statisticians' language—and you arrive at the conclusion that becoming a writer is like trying to float a boat with holes in it in water that's too shallow to begin with.

Yet something feels hopeful, helpful even. We must like these working conditions—at least a little. No one makes us do it, and there are plenty of dignified chances to quit. Long odds, indeed, are always discouraging. But *no odds?* No odds are tart with possibility, with the brisk freedom that is commensurate with the task of making something excellent where, before, nothing was. What one needs to learn, what help's available, what encourages—all of that you have to make up on your own. And after all, making it up is the reason you're here, or should be. It's the writer's most inviting freedom.

With this in mind, one can accept help from without. Telemachus, after all, managed to make stodgy old Mentor into an eponym simply by concluding that his advice—"Few are the sons who attain their fathers' stature"—was, in fact, welcome news. And any of us can probably remember random instances of real help and the strange forms they took: a teacher I had in college, a small, bleak man with ashy-color flesh and a prisoner's crude haircut, who came to class each winter day dwarfed in a huge, fifty-ish bear's coat, a cruel felt hat, and an expression of profound disgust. Carl Hartman was his name, and he arrived to us every day, or so it seemed, fresh from some terrible fury of life that raged somewhere outside the classroom door, a fury of anger and sarcasm and permanent resentment against something—I didn't know what. But each afternoon he would appear, *suddenly*, five minutes late, slam the old oak door, bash his schoolbooks down onto the table, throw off that coat and hat toward the corner, scowl out at us all as we sat cemented in our own special dreads and woolly anxieties, and then in the softest, most compliant voice I had ever heard, say to us, "All right now. I'd like just to read aloud to you this wonderful passage Frank O'Connor wrote, and then we'll talk about your stories."

Frankly, I don't remember exactly anything else he ever said—about literature or writing or whatever our proper subjects were then. I'm sure he said important things. Only I remember that voice, a voice of alerting and imperiled sympathy. Sympathy for us, for literature and its wide, balming appeal, for himself, even. And to me here was the lesson and the help for a young writer: ferocity in vigorous contest with human sympathy was the stuff of life, indeed, of most human drama. Mr. Hartman came into our room twenty-five years ago to demonstrate that maxim, using his person as model. And that is what I still look for in what I read and what I hope to write each day: the real stuff. Probably I will look for it until I'm finished.

Sometimes, of course, help comes plainly: a phone call properly placed; a crucial word of praise. Sometimes it is in forms as ambiguous and frameless and seemingly negligible as not wishing ill to someone, or not having ill wished upon us. Sometimes help is being willing to explain to someone how luck makes odd turns and illogical jumps, and for that reason it—luck—is bearable. Sometimes help is cutting someone loose to the world at a crucial moment. Sometimes it is paying praise no one will ever hear.

Finally, what I like and admire about the relationships of encouragement that bring all these stories to notice now, is that such acts of help as are here seem to address directly an important if minor condition of any art—its local, ground-level circumstances, its ordinary beginnings. Art's spirit is serious in nature if not in demeanor, and at heart it is unselfish. If it could, it would always be a help. And here, in the stories that follow and in the words said about them, its needs are met, its requirements for survival generously, faithfully served.

—Richard Ford
May 1988

PREFACE

In March 1984, the editors of *Equator* magazine received this inspiring piece of advice from Malcolm Cowley, whose *Broom* was a mouthpiece for Modernism:

There is always a place for a magazine like *Broom* that sets out to print good prose . . . there was a place in 1921 and the place is still open in 1984. You are lucky to have a group to depend on. I hope they have new ideas and read a lot of manuscripts. New good authors are always hard to find, but often several appear at the same time. You ought to write a statement of belief. And you ought to make yourself some enemies.

And so, in a "postmodern" twist on an idealistic old formula, we set out to find great new writing for a commercial/avant garde magazine. To locate new fiction to stand with the magazine's reportage, we queried our favorite authors, asking that they introduce us to the work of emerging writers whose work they'd like to recommend for publication. This became one of the most popular features of the magazine, but it didn't stop there.

We were stunned by the enthusiasm with which authors (busy, private souls as they might be) shot back names and manuscripts. Soon the sheer volume of good new writing jamming our offices seemed to beg for book-length treatment.

We are pleased to be able to present here, under the Collier

Books imprint, the fruits of that overabundance: a group of stories by some of America's strongest new writers, recommended by top authors, evidence, we think, of the passion and generosity that joins the community of writers.

—The Editors of *Equator*
San Francisco, May 1988

GETTING OVER ARNETTE

■ Pinckney Benedict

One of the most heralded debuts of recent years was Pinckney Benedict's collection of thematically interrelated short stories, Town Smokes *(Ontario Review Press, 1987), presenting, as these impeccably crafted and unfailingly moving narratives did, men, women, children, and even animals (an enormous wild hog named Booze, an unnamed, doomed, rabid dog) of striking individuality. The stories were set for the most part in West Virginia, in a rural, though rarely pastoral, mountainous terrain. Reviewers commented upon the twenty-three-year-old writer's extraordinary maturity, not guessing that certain of the stories had first been written when Pinckney Benedict was much younger.*

Yet there is nothing of the prodigy about him—that vertiginous sense of a flaring-up, a meteoric rise (and possible fall), that sense of a talent bent on self-consumption. The stories were not quickly or facilely written, but intelligently, even shrewdly, rewritten. That is one of the reasons that Pinckney Benedict is so good a writer and why his stories, like few of his contemporaries', bear up under numerous rereadings. My familiarity with his work—I've read several of his stories at least four or five times—doesn't lessen my interest in it, but deepens it. One day, decades from now, Pinckney Benedict may reread these early, starkly brilliant, and seemingly effortless stories of his, and wonder how he did it.

Is there anything more mysterious than to be the bearer of a unique talent?

The word of Town Smokes*, while compassionately and sometimes wittily observed, is a world conditioned by tragedy, by violent acts, at least, happening to innocent or not-so-innocent people. There are savage beatings, there are shotgun murders. There are moments of merely haphazardly deflected cruelty. This new story, "Getting Over Arnette," is a distinct departure—lighter, funnier, more accessible to the reader. The narrative voice is direct, gently modulated. The humor is extreme but not disturbing. The good-natured irony discernible in the interstices of the drama of* Town Smokes *is here allowed its playful freedom: Loftus and Bone, the story's protagonists, are feckless, a bit foolish, and utterly likable. It is fitting too that Arnette, the chimera of the title, does return to her boyfriend—as casually and negligently as she'd gone off. And* *we are ready to believe Loftus's oddly complacent conclusion: "And he was happy in the saying of it and proud to live in that fashion, even though he knew that for his suffering she would never leave him for another man again."*

—*JOYCE CAROL OATES*

*L*oftus and Bone headed over to the Bowl*O*Drome to take in the women's leagues and see if they could get Loftus's mind off of Arnette. Arnette was the redheaded woman that had run off with some college puke a couple of days before and had broken Loftus's heart and shattered his life.

Loftus had had some time to think events through but still he couldn't stop running the final bit over in his head. The whole thing took just a minute to consider.

There was Arnette and there was this guy that looked like he was a fast tight end for some state school somewhere and there was skinny sad-sack Loftus standing watching them go off together. Loftus whipped a brick at them from the loose pile outside the cellar door but that was after the Pontiac was already in motion out of the yard, just too late altogether. The brick hit the trunk of the car and did some body damage, but Loftus couldn't find much satisfaction in something a couple of bucks' worth of Bondo was going to be able to fix.

So now Loftus looked at everything around him with a whitened mute expression on his face behind which that one scene played. It was with him when he stared at the half dozen spinning ceiling fans of the place and the way they kept the yellow bug-loaded fly strips going in some crazy helical motion from their wind. It just kept on unreeling even when little Sunny Tatum was on deck for her team doing her stretching exercises and deep knee bends in the shorts she wore to bowl in.

"Watch her go," Bone said and pointed at Alley 17, where she was. You could see just the legbands of her lemon-colored panties when she was in her squat. Loftus and Bone were sitting at one of the tables behind the lanes. They were the only men in the place and the women kept looking at them back over their shoulders in a suspicious and uneasy manner. Loftus chewed his underlip.

"Jesus Christ," Bone said. "It was a bad idea from the start and a sorry love affair. You never knew a single person that loved a redheaded woman like her and got away from it with a whole skin. Never happen."

Bone had been wondering what Sunny Tatum looked like naked since they were in high school together. Watching her make her approach to the lane in her shorts and team T-shirt, he guessed he could pretty much figure it out. The Rolling Pins was the name of her team, it said on the back of her shirt. The healthy wholesome bounce and heft of her was like a revelation to Bone.

"It might be that you could spend time in the arms of somebody made like Sunny Tatum and survive it okay," Bone said. "But a woman like that Arnette is all the time going off with somebody," he said.

"I imagine I'm the expert on that one particular issue," Loftus said.

"I expect you are at that," Bone said.

It was mainly a group of nicely cushioned married ladies that belonged to the leagues, which oftentimes encouraged Loftus and tempted him but tonight there was nothing for him. Grade-school teachers and beauticians and lonely housewife sherry drunks looked all the same, tired and slack, with no particular grace. He figured Arnette had taken that desirous chunk of him with her in the college puke's avocado Catalina.

"I told my future to you at the very beginning of it," Loftus said. "We was sitting over at Tiny's. That's the kind of woman that'll jerk the heart right out of a person's living rib cage, I said. I had my eyes open. I wasn't blind to the danger of it."

Bone nodded. "You did say it. You knew it was bound to occur this way, and still you're hurting anyhow. So I wonder what good is it in a foresight like that."

Down on the lanes, Sunny Tatum left herself a nasty split on the first ball of the frame. She was bowling with one of those colored plastic balls, swirled red and silver in a hazy pattern, with the holes drilled very close together to accommodate her slender grip. Loftus watched after the colored ball as it spun strange and lovely down the lane.

When she missed the tough pickup on the split, Sunny stamped her foot on the foul line and made the buzzer go off. She had on little ankle socks with pink pompoms above the heels.

"I'm dead, Bone," Loftus said. He gestured at the eight lanes of women before them. "I thought this would do it for me but I was wrong. I'm dead and just sitting here waiting for the rot and the worms to start in on me."

"You ain't dead," Bone said. "Just asleep or maybe stunned a little in your spirit is all. You'll wake back up to it after a while," he said.

Loftus wasn't listening. He watched Mary Teasdale as she put one right in the 1–3 pocket and dropped all ten pins. She was the dentist's good-looking wife and anchorwoman in the Rolling Pins lineup. A woman that could really put the speed on the ball usually got to Loftus one way or another, and Mary Teasdale had an arm on her that was taut with muscle and springy tendon. He couldn't find the interest anywhere inside of him.

"I went out with this girl one time," Bone said, "that was the daughter from a back-road rock-hard Baptist preacher's family and very difficult to get along with. She told me her daddy had give her a sharp old knife and said that she was to feel free to stick it in me if I so much as touched her on her tits or wherever. She showed it to me. Little bitty letter opener is what it really was, but plenty pointed."

"Son of a bitch," Loftus said. "That old man must of been somebody's gift to the world."

"Whether it was the old man give it to her or whether she just took it on herself I never did know," Bone said. "She was a real piece of work was that one. I took it off of her after we got out of the movies walking home and she only did manage to get it into me the one time." He pointed to a place on his forearm that could have been made by a BB from a Daisy pump gun or the lead of a pencil point a long time ago. Loftus nodded.

"So I'm bleeding like a pig down my arm and holding that knife and grabbing on to her while she's trying to get away from me back to home. She's gabbling and praying to God to take this cup from her lips or whatever. There we are out in the middle of somebody's empty back field, I don't know whose, the game is all mine, and guess what? After all that hoorah, I find out I don't want to touch her tits anyhow. The thing's just got no intrigue to it anymore."

"What do you know," Loftus said.

"Life's just funny like that sometimes," Bone said. "You never really do know what it is you're after at any given moment in time. Like that Arnette. She thought she was after you and what does it turn out that she wants? Not you, that's what. And there for a while you sure thought she was after you too. It's a fact and you got to admit it."

"There it is," Loftus said.

He sat back in his plastic chair and regarded the swaying backsides of the bowling teams. The Pink Ladies looked like they were having a hot night, all women that worked together at the Penney's downtown. The teams around them kept shouting out in shocked despair at their precision and continuing good fortune.

"You all ain't supposed to win," one of the nearby women called to them. The Pink Ladies had been up to then the absolute basement of the league.

"I guess you ain't so much now," one of the Pink Ladies said in the direction of the Rolling Pins. Mary Teasdale and the others ignored her.

"They's a lane open down there if you want to throw a couple of balls," Bone said. "Come on, you'll feel better if you get up and get going. Move around some."

Loftus had cash in his pockets to pay for a couple of games. He got up and started thrusting his fingers into the balls on the alley's racks, looking for one to fit him. Cool against the flesh of his hand, the balls put him in mind of Arnette. "She taints the entire thing when she goes, don't she," he said.

"I'll get us some shoes," Bone said.

Loftus found a ball that he could use. It was not one of the colored ones, but just a flat-black ball. He decided that was okay with him, swung the ball on the end of his arm a couple of times to get the feel of it right.

He went on down to the open lane and Bone came after him with the shoes. "Hey you, Sunny Tatum," Bone said in a loud voice, so that he could be heard over the clash of the pins and the rumble of the balls on the hardwood board lanes. They had the lane right next to where the Rolling Pins were.

The team turned to look them over with very little friendliness in their attitude, Mary Teasdale and Sunny Tatum and all, which embarrassed Loftus but which seemed to put a fire under Bone. "Hey," he said again when Sunny was facing him and couldn't ignore that he was talking straight to her.

"Hey back," she said to him in a way that was flirtatious but that Loftus figured meant at the same time, You, Bone, want me but won't get to lay a finger on me in this our lifetime. Loftus set his ball down in the return chute, hit the button to make the pinsetter lay down their pins. The contact in the button was corroded and Loftus had to jab at it a couple of times hard to get the thing to function.

"Looks like you guys ain't doing any too good," Bone said to the Rolling Pins. His tone was easy and his face was a shining invitation to all of them and to Sunny Tatum in specific. He held the ball he had picked out cradled in the crook of his arm like it was a football helmet.

"We're not guys and we aren't doing any too bad either," Mary Teasdale said to him. "So why don't you boys just bowl your game and get on with it like you ought to be doing. We're in league play here." Bone looked to Sunny Tatum to see what was up with her, but it was her turn to bowl and she was concentrating down the lane.

She released the ball smoothly, followed through with force. Bone noticed a tremor in one of her calves and an answering twitch in her stiffened forearm that he took as a sign of imminent surrender to the force of his personality. The ball slammed the head pin straight on and left her with another of her 7–10 splits, which was her greatest problem in bowling.

"Damn it," Mary Teasdale said to her. It just about made Sunny Tatum cry to be talked to that way, and it just about broke Bone's newly tender heart to watch it happen. The strain of the Pink Ladies' rise from obscurity was beginning to tell on Mary Teasdale and her entire team.

Sunny missed her pickup again, just sailed the ball straight down the lane and between the split pins. "Field goal," one of the Pink Ladies called out, and the rest of her team laughed.

"That's okay, honey girl," Bone said to her. "Everybody's got a down day." He still hadn't set his ball down in the chute yet. Sunny gave him a look that had a little bit of a smile in it.

Loftus polished his ball with a towel that somebody had left behind them at the lane. "Wayne" the black ball had inscribed on it in yellow letters just under the thumb hole. "I'm going to give it a shot now, Bone," Loftus said.

"Why is it you ain't giving me a hand here, good buddy," Bone said to him. He kept his lips in a grin for the women but his teeth were clenched together. "This whole entire deal is for your benefit after all," he said.

"Hey," Loftus said to the women, who weren't looking at him anyhow. He hefted the ball and stepped up to the line. The soles of the bowling shoes were slick and he watched his footing.

"My friend here not long ago underwent a very bad time is why he's being so unsociable," Bone said to the women. Mary Teasdale looked like she was ready to spit but ignored him as best she could. "Affair of the heart," Bone said, pressing his hands flat against his chest. He had to put his ball down to make the gesture.

"Some gal busted him did she?" Sunny Tatum said. She had sharp white even-spaced teeth and a voice like cotton candy.

Loftus rolled a gutter ball and when it came back to him in the ball return he rolled another one. "Your go," he said to Bone. He didn't care about the gutter balls. He didn't even mark them down on the score sheet. Scoring bowling was something confusing that he wasn't sure he remembered right.

"Tore him all up one side and down the other," Bone said to Sunny Tatum. "Used him for what he's worth and then left with somebody bigger and stronger and better-looking. He's not hardly a man anymore after he got his heart eat out like that, and I'm just here trying to help him get over it."

"Bowling help a man cure his love thing?" Sunny said.

"It ain't like that, Arnette and me,' Loftus said to Bone. To the women in the bowling alley he said, "For a time it was as good as good, until it went bad." They just looked at him.

"The attractive presence of such ladies as yourselves is starting to have a redeeming effect on him already I imagine," Bone said.

The Rolling Pins, all except for Sunny Tatum, had by this time had enough of Bone and of Loftus by implication and association, and Mary Teasdale went after the manager of the place to get the problem taken care of. She didn't even threaten Bone, she was so serious in her determination. She just went. Some women in a couple of the other teams cheered her as she steamed off.

"It'll teach them to strip us naked with their eyes," one big lady said to her friend. The friend crossed her arms over her bosom.

"That ain't all they was doing with their eyes," she said. "Poking and prodding like that, it's a sin," she said under her breath.

Only the Pink Ladies cared for the presence of Bone and Loftus at all and that was because they figured the men as potential good-luck charms. Also they had noted the distress they were causing among the other teams and they applauded that.

"I ain't telling nobody to leave," the manager said to Mary Teasdale when she complained to him. "I'm taking exactly nobody off them lanes." He was a little gray old man that sat on a stool in a storage closet behind some wire mesh. He handed out shoes and scorecards through a slot in the mesh and always took one shoe of the bowler's as security, even when it was somebody like Mary Teasdale, who came to the place every week practically and who plainly wouldn't walk off with the alley's greasy Lysol-smelling footwear. He had a cut-down baseball bat that he kept back in there with him and he swore he would use it when the occasion arose. Other times he kept to himself and minded his own business.

"You want to get them out of here, that's you," the old man said. Mary Teasdale clutched at the wire near the old man's face. "Me, I seen nothing thus far calls for that sort of handling."

"We'll make them leave," Mary Teasdale said. She was puffed like a toad with anger and poisonous emotion. "We don't have to put up with that kind of thing in here. Not by a long sight do we have to."

"That's you," the old man said, but he was talking to Mary Teasdale's back as she headed for her lane. The other women saw her returning with her complaint, which was their common complaint, unredressed, and they came together into a sudden single monumental resolve. It passed like a swift weather-bearing wind among them. They set down their bowling balls and squared their shoulders and moved in around Loftus and Bone.

Loftus looked at the stone faces of the women all around him. Bone was caught up in Sunny Tatum, who didn't seem to mind his attention and was not part of the general wave of resentment. Loftus tapped him on the back. "Bone," he said very softly. "Oh, Bone."

"Lord, lord," one of the Pink Ladies said. Her voice was loud and the only noise in the alley since all the bowling had recently and abruptly ceased. "Them boys had better get their ass in gear."

"What is it that you need from me exactly," Bone said to Loftus. Then Mary Teasdale moved into his field of vision in anger and fury and he knew something was up. She took hold of his forearms and another woman grabbed him at his waist and there were hands in Loftus's hair and twisted in his clothing. Someone jabbed a sharp elbow into his side and he could feel the press of bodies against him. He was held roughly up and could not fall.

"You need a lesson," Mary Teasdale called into Bone's ear. He jerked back but couldn't slip the grasp of a dozen hands. "You need to learn how to be like gentlemen," Mary Teasdale shouted at Loftus.

The women bowlers leaned hard against the men. They pushed them and shoved them and it was a painful progress but Loftus and Bone did not cry out as the women took them in hand and forced them to the glass doors of the place and through and on out into the dark.

"Hey, men," Eugene said to Loftus and Bone. Eugene owned and operated Tiny's, which was a saloon and pool and pinball place in town.

"Beer," Bone said to Eugene, climbing up onto a stool and pointing in front of him. Bone was smoldering like a fire that you have pissed on but not adequately.

"Me too," Loftus said. He shook his head, looking at Bone and wanting to laugh. It made him feel nervous and crazy, left by Arnette and then beat up by women and thinking it was a pretty hilarious juncture in his life. Bone hung his head down near the bar and swallowed without enjoying at all.

"You men don't look so good," Eugene said. "Always into something wicked ain't you."

Bone turned on his stool and looked out over the bar, which was quiet and empty except for one guy at a table near the back. "Who is it back there?" Bone said to Eugene. The guy at the table was somebody that he didn't know and that was unusual in Tiny's.

Eugene leaned close. "That there," Eugene said, "is a bona fide former member of the United States Armed Forces that fought in their secret war in Vietnam Republic of. At least that's what he says he is."

"Secret war," Bone said. "What secret war is it that he means?"

"I ast him that," Eugene said. "The one they tried to kill all the niggers with and the other unsociable undesirables, he said. Damn near worked, too, to hear him claim it. He gets all heated up over it if you talk to him. It's a subject you might want to steer clear of."

"Is he a nigger?" Bone said.

"Don't think so," Eugene said. "Light-skinned and passing if he is."

Loftus and Bone and Eugene looked at the guy just sitting back there sucking on the ice cubes of his drink and he looked at them sitting where they were. He sucked an ice cube into his mouth and crushed it with a loud noise and swallowed. Then he did the same again.

"What is it he is staring at like that," Bone said.

"Leave him be," Loftus said.

The guy pointed at their feet. "I am told that what you have there is a style of dress favored on many of the nation's better university campuses," he said. Loftus and Bone still had on the bowling shoes that they'd been wearing when they were ejected from the Bowl*O*Drome.

Loftus regretted the loss of his Durango steel-toed boots more than almost anything else about the evening. Bone had grabbed up the one sneaker he'd been allowed by the old man to take to the lane but it had been torn from him and carried off as a prize by some woman in a Pin Smashers shirt.

"But you don't neither of you look like something that might be going to college right away do you," the guy said. Neither Loftus nor Bone said anything.

After a time the guy spread his arms wide and said, "And for your unique footwear all this have I rendered unto thee." He was looking just at Bone now and had singled him out to speak to.

"This is my gift unto you. So come unto me and receive it unto thyself," the guy said. He was gesturing all around at the walls and chairs of the place and the liquor bottles behind the bar. He dumped a little of the ice over the edge of his glass.

"The hell you say," Bone said to him. "This here's Eugene's place. It says Tiny's outside on the sign but it belongs to this fellow Eugene all right."

Eugene gestured at him to be left out of it.

"I don't mean just the bar," the guy said. "I'm talking about everthing. The whole shooting match. The entire United States of America and the free world that tags along with it. That's what I'm talking about."

"And you give all that to me," Bone said. "I thank you for that," he said, and he laughed.

"Hell," the guy said. "I don't know if I would of done it if it had just been this little bar in this one little town. That might not of been worth it. But it was everthing and so I killed and died for it and just about everbody I know killed and died for it."

"Well sure," Loftus said. "I imagine we could set you up a drink through Eugene if you want," he said.

"I'd take a drink," the guy said. "I'd take a drink to the end of the world and have," he said. "You come over here and drink with me and tell me what is here to recommend itself in this tired town." He pushed out one of the other chairs at his table with his foot as an invitation. He had on a pair of black thick-soled jump boots.

Bone went and sat with the guy so Loftus followed him. The guy's name it turned out was Leonard Meadows and he was a big old boy from a town out in the desert of West Texas called Mankinville. "Even sorrier and littler than this place is if you can think of such a thing," he said.

Leonard Meadows had come up to work in the slaughter plant that was over near the railroad tracks and he knew a great deal about various cuts and varieties of meat. He was making pretty good money there and took to paying for the drinks after a time, which was good as Loftus's finances were quickly getting strapped and Bone never carried any money with him if he could help it even when he had any.

"I worked over to that plant one summer back a few years ago," Loftus said. "Man I don't remember so much about it except that it was nasty and greasy hard work and smelled just about worse than anything since. How is it you can stand it all the time?"

"I been worse places and done worse things than that, I am here to relay to you," Leonard Meadows said. "That there's a picnic is what that is." It was then that Bone and Loftus remembered about him being in Vietnam and they figured that was what he was talking about and felt bad for making him recall something like that. But when they apologized he told them not to worry.

He told them a mess of stories that had all to do with assault rifles and rice paddies and helicopter dust-offs and long-range patrols. He mentioned stuff like phosphorus rounds and grenade launchers and flametracks as if they were normal parts of the world and just setting around there in the room to be touched and handled and used on an everyday basis.

He talked to Loftus and Bone about guys that he had managed to kill successfully and about guys that had killed him only a little bit less successfully, and sometimes he knew the names of those guys or had found them out or just made them up. He talked about the Arvin which he seemed to bitterly detest and Brother Charles for whom he seemed to have a sorrowful sort of respect and a city by the name of Hue where he and some of his buddies had got into hardship.

"One guy I knew," Leonard Meadows said, "got jobbed with a phungyi stick and ended up with a hole about the size of a pencil in his leg. That thing dribbled and bled for the longest time and it never did close up. Something Charles did to the stick, poisoned it or puked on it or shit on it most likely. The guy that was stuck swore it was Ho himself shit on that stick, the infection was so evil and bad-smelling. They took him to Japan and everywhere with all the clean smart doctors trying to get that leg to close itself up but it never did."

"Jesus," Loftus said.

"Just another example of what the wily Southeast Asian can get himself up to when you come into his area, buddy," Leonard Meadows said. He finished up with his drink and gestured to Eugene to bring him another one.

"I got to shut it down soon," Eugene said. "Wife," he said.

"You bet, sport," Leonard said.

"You look like the kind of folks that can find some trouble when you want," Leonard said to Loftus and Bone. "So tell me about what wars you boys been fighting recently."

"We seen some trouble all right," Loftus said. "It was a bunch of women that didn't care for us so much."

"Lady-killers such as yourselves," Leonard said. "I find it hard to imagine."

"Well, him there," Bone said, pointing at Loftus, "he had this woman and she walked out on him was the start of it. Arnette. Turns out she's been stepping out on the town and it might even of been more than just one man. And he's all wore out because she's redheaded and good-looking and very stuck on herself in reality and if the truth be told." Bone glared at Loftus. "That's where the trouble lays," he said.

"Redheaded local girl name of Arnette and hot to look at," Leonard Meadows said, and he scratched at his head as if he was considering his past. "Sure, I do believe I've screwed her a time or two myself," he said.

Loftus knew it was probably just a joke but he grabbed Leonard Meadows's shirt collar anyway and started to drag him across the tabletop. He made the move before he knew what to do about it or considered the depth of trouble that would result. A wide piece of Leonard's shirt came away in his hand.

He never did see Leonard Meadows hit him or what he hit him with but he did see Bone go for the knife he carried clipped in an ankle sheath. He was lying on the floor and couldn't find a way to tell Bone not to do it. Leonard Meadows kicked Bone in the face with one of those big jump boots and shattered his jaw. Bone gave it up and lay down and bled on the board floor of the place. He spit a couple of times and then held his tongue out of his mouth. There were teeth on his tongue and they fell off and made a little clattering sound on the floor.

Eugene stepped out from behind the bar but stopped when Leonard Meadows turned and faced him. Leonard was standing in a strange way, erect but somehow curled like a snake ready to strike. Eugene figured he knew karate or some other kind of tricks that they teach in the military.

Leonard extended his right arm. "Do you crave to see your pancreas laying here in the palm of my hand?" he said to Eugene.

"No sir," Eugene said. "I got enough problems on my own already."

"I imagine you do," Leonard Meadows said. He looked around the room like he was sorry to have done what he had to do there and then he walked out.

Loftus reached a hand up to his head, afraid of what he might find. He was amazed when he learned that he couldn't really feel his head at all. He wondered if it was his skull or his hand that had something wrong with it, and what was it that could be wrong would make him feel like that. He closed his eyes so he wouldn't have to look at Bone lying down there next to him.

Eugene kneeled down by the two of them. "Oh my Lord in heaven," he said. Loftus didn't know which one of them he was worried about or whether it was both of them in dire trouble and need of a blessing. He kept his eyes closed and drifted away from the scene as best he was able, passing after a time into unconsciousness.

Loftus was not overly shocked when Arnette came back home alone into his arms and affections shortly after the fight. The college puke didn't even bring her back but made her take the bus for nearly five hours to get home and she was in a sore mood and tired from the dust and the heat and carrying her suitcase.

Loftus was still wearing a patch on his head but the stitches were coming out soon and that was good because the whole thing had started to itch like a son of a gun.

"You heard I got busted up, hey," Loftus said to her. She looked at him like she was surprised from where she was unpacking her case in the bedroom.

"No," she said. "I never heard a single thing about it." She shoved some more underwear in a drawer. Loftus was happy to see her woman things back in his place. He had missed the soft slippery look of them.

"I'm sorry it happened to you," she said. "Glad you didn't get your teeth kicked out like old Bone," she said when he told her the rest about the fight.

"I'm happy to have you back here with me," he said to her.

"You bet you are," she said.

He never asked her about Leonard Meadows or what he had said because he was pretty certain it had been a joke and he didn't like to think about that evening if he could help it. Bone had told him that he knew Leonard was now living out on the Ridge Road in Sunny Tatum's trailer with Sunny Tatum. She had taken him in out of love and affection to help cure his war injuries which were psychological and mental and difficult for him to deal with on his own.

"His injuries," Bone said through his wired jaw. "We ought to go after him. Get a gun and just go nail the son of a bitch."

Loftus hated to think of what might happen to them if they went out against Leonard with something so serious as a gun. Drinking soup and milk shakes and being silent most of the day, Bone had taken a grim turn somewhere inside of himself.

When Loftus finally did ask Arnette what it was that made her come back to him, she told him that it had just been a sex thing with that college guy and never serious at all. Loftus nodded at her like he understood and it was okay and acknowledged to himself that if he had been given a chance at a sex thing he might have taken it up in the same way.

"Don't ever do like that again," he said to Arnette one night when he got drunk and bold enough and the love he had for her welled up strong inside of his breast. "It like to killed me when you went," he said. There were tears in his eyes.

"No promises, you know that," Arnette said to him. Her eyes were blue and bright and her red hair framed her face. "Can't you just be happy with what it is that we have? That is one thing I learned from my time away, if not a single thing else, that you got to seize the day." She touched him on his bald stitched patch and smiled.

"All right," Loftus said. "I put no conditions on you." And he was happy in the saying of it and proud to live in that fashion, even though he knew that for his suffering she would never leave him for another man again.

THANKSGIVING WITH TRUDY

■ Anne U. Forer

There are some of us, here at the Exquisite Corpse *offices, who find it inordinately urgent to be human. Which is why, when Anne U. Forer's stories showed up in the mail, we fell all over our coffins with the urge to be grateful, even meet her, if not actually call her. We knew this gracious, slightly bristling, heartening but unsentimental optimist to be an indubitable human. Or so the voice of these stories tells us, sounding genuine. Ms. Forer is a bohemian of the old school. She lives on the Lower East Side of New York with complete faith in the glory of that historical bohemian nest. She exudes art like others exude ennui. Her friends, lovers, and forays are accepted a priori as the givens of her existence, and her prose sets out to defend them, as well as her friendly/ tender self subject to the cruelties of the epoch. Do not be fooled by the ease of her prose: Anne U. Forer is a dangerous radical. The conventional stories of our time are minimal, pinched, cold, lacking in spiritual largesse, ungenerous, and WASP. Not so here in the Forer world where sweetness and light is what it's all about. Defended, understood, by barbed street-wisdom, and protected, as I've said, by a tough bohemian history. This is prose in a blessed state of innocence as well, awaiting its baptism by fire, that audible crack in an autobiograpical writer's life when something huge and frightening becomes visible. It will come because writing is for Ms. Forer a vocation and, for better or for worse, the fates look out for true writers. They serve them Terror in all the dosage they can handle, hoping for exactly what Ms. Forer does: upholding the human against the monster machine.*

—ANDREI CODRESCU

*F*or some totally odd reason I don't know how to begin. It is the day after Thanksgiving and I did not spend it with my family. For some strange reason this Thanksgiving everyone seemed to do pretty much what they pleased, which turned out very interesting. Eddie and I had pumpkin pie for breakfast, then he went up to Michael's house to play his drums. Angela spent all morning making miso soup and listening to WBAI, preparing the miso soup for the vegetarian Thanksgiving she was invited to. At a certain point in the day she discovered that she did not want to leave her kitchen, did not want to leave listening to her programs on WBAI and she did not want to go to Thanksgiving dinner. Instead she arrived in my kitchen in the afternoon and we played chinese checkers. Her fifty-four-year-old friend Trudy for some reason, was it her cold, did not go to her relatives' Thanksgiving dinner on Long Island, did not go to the Thanksgiving of the girls who go with the Hell's Angels who live downstairs from her— and when Angela called Trudy from my house to wish her a Happy Thanksgiving and mentioned she was at Anne's house, Trudy said "I'll be right over," thinking it was an invite. So Angela, Trudy and I spent the whole Thanksgiving afternoon playing three-way chinese checkers, eating the rest of the pumpkin pie and having a hot discussion of our theories of nationality based on all our different boyfriends. This is the kind of conversation you have quite often with your girlfriends, but is the first one I have had three-way with a fifty-four-year-old woman who went to high school with Basha's mother in Worcester and is the same age as my mother. It is so odd to hear out of the mouth of a woman exactly your mother's age sitting across the table "and then there was this Italian I slept with" or "what about that German Jew I was in love with for ten years who never slept with me." Usually when they are your mother's age they seem to turn into another species. And it was extremely nice to sit around the chinese checker set chatting it up like three normal people, discussing who you slept with and making discoveries about nationalities on that basis. Trudy even said she loved being fifty-four because when you're fifty-four you don't get so hung up on men, if they don't like you back you don't drive yourself crazy about it. She said it was really freeing.

For me it was a little wonderful having Trudy here because in fact she reminded me an awful lot of me. I'd even go so far as to say I never met anyone as similar. After Angela lost at chinese checkers two times in a row, was in fact the big loser, I had such an urge to say "well, you can do other things, Angela" but I held it back. And Trudy said "well, you can do other things, Angela." And it was a little similar when she told her story about the German man she went out with in her late twenties. They went out but he wasn't interested in her. Then he called her after he got back from a two-year trip to South America (he was an engineer or something) and he told her that when he was in South America (in Colombia or Ecuador, Trudy couldn't remember) he went to a whorehouse and even though all the women there were very beautiful he chose the one that wasn't that pretty, but who had a sort of warm wonderful glow that came out of her. And he realized that he picked her because she reminded him of Trudy and that he must really like Trudy and that is why he wants to court her now. Trudy said: What a jerk—he has to go all the way to South America for two years and go to a whorehouse in order to discover that she was IT, how great she was. She said an Italian would have known in five seconds. And somehow, the way she settled back in her chair and flung out her arms when she said "to discover that I was IT" really reminded me of exactly the way I would have phrased it and expressed it when I used to believe that I was IT. Unfortunately I have lost that feeling of being IT but I remembered when I had it. And of course it seemed totally wonderful to me that you can go on thinking that way forever—unless, of course, you accidentally lost it somewhere along the line at age twenty-nine, or twenty-eight, or whenever it was that I started hanging out with Linda F. And I discovered that it's very interesting what life has in store for you when you're not IT, or maybe it's just a little more relaxing. But you can't help falling in love with someone a little who says that in your kitchen, and I guess I fell in love with Trudy at that moment, besides having a reminiscent second of what it feels like to be IT, the glory of it all.

It was such an inspiration having Trudy in my kitchen that now I have an enormous urge to talk to my parents and my Aunt Esther and my Uncle Paul as if they were normal people, instead of people from outer space, or relics from an earlier more innocent age, of trying to remember that parents and aunts and uncles can actually be normal people, instead of deleting everything from my conversation that you think they might find agitating. But of course Trudy lives on Third Street, across the street from Angela, and you just don't know if that is all the difference in the world, besides the fact that Trudy is a playwright. It's just completely nice to sit chatting over chinese checkers with your best friend Angela, and her good friend Trudy, both of whom live around the corner, it just happens that Trudy is your mother's age and her father pays the rent so she can be a playwright. "He just pays the rent and that's all," Angela told me. That Trudy is fifty-four and her father pays the rent so she can be a playwright just has the most blissful sound to my ear; I don't know why. Last year when Eddie was going to school my father said "of course I could send you a hundred dollars a month as easy as pie but I don't know if it is good for your maturity." You just have such an urge, if the subject comes up again, to mention that your new good friend Trudy gets money for her rent and she is fifty-four. I almost can't wait until my father calls up and we have another discussion about my maturity. And you think about all those family dinners Trudy had to go to, where they tortured her about her life, and insisted she was an oddball, or whatever they torture you about at family dinners: thinking you have problems or are not progressing properly in life. And yet she turned into the only normal fifty-four-year-old person I know. You think of all those peculiar fifty-four-year-old bosses you had, or executives, or peculiar fifty-four-year-old psychiatrists, or those elementary school teachers you met when you were a schoolteacher. It is really a great inspiration to meet someone who is fifty-four and not peculiar at all, although to be perfectly fair about it, you hardly get to know any fifty-four-year-olds when you are still thirty-three, except for bosses, and Linda maintains they're all lunatics.

THE WHOLE IDEA OF CINDY POTTS

■ Louis Beynon Jones

In the first Louis B. Jones story I ever read, the point of view was God's, and He was looking down on Marin County. Marin County was a-glitter. Its Porsches and Jacuzzis and malls had been set out in a cool, documentary light. Interested in a terrain that was strange to me, reading more Louis B. Jones stories, I found that the idioms, ethics, and whims of his Californians, with their snarled divorces and silky self-assurance, were always all in place, scrupulously so; but there were other characters who had achieved only toeholds in the great sleek cliff of Marin wealth, who were unconvincing sales reps or slightly lost real estate agents, or children, and he was on intimate terms with each of them. No intimacy colored his prose, however. Even when Louis B. Jones writes in a third-person less rarefied than God's, the point of view still passes with an unearthly and laser-cool lightness through the lives of his characters, resulting in sentences like this one, from "The Whole Idea of Cindy Potts": "The perfection of her handwriting bespeaks a blameless-ness in her that is, to her, heartbreaking." The little triad of pronouns balances in perfect compact comedy, and an emotion peculiarly adoles-cent, peculiarly convincing, is exposed. Let the reader read warily, however, for that irony comes hard on the heels of a "blamelessness" that not only Cindy but very possibly her author believes in. These creatures are Louis's own, and he would not be the marvelously funny writer he is if he did not find, deep down, their innocence.

—ELIZABETH TALLENT

*I*magine Cindy. Imagine Cindy on the mall. She looks like Tammy or Suzy or Kathy or Jenny. As they walk they move apart, or come together bumping hips. They are strung together loosely like a bracelet by the invisible thread of a question: What do you want to do? They could go to Radio Shack and look at stereos. They could go to Hungry House where the waitress hates them. They could go to the Emporium but they were just there. She feels most like herself when her thumbs are hooked in her belt loops. She shoves out one hip and flicks her hair. She and her friends are flipping through albums in the record store. She and Kathy and Jenny have together fallen in love with Johnny Risk, whose full-length poster is on the wall.

"If Johnny came in my room, you know what I'd do?"

"Something gross, no doubt."

"Oh, yeah, look who's talking, you're such a virgin."

"You're not, I suppose?"

"You don't even know the meaning of 'gross.' I'm talking *really gross.*"

"I think Jeff DeBono looks like Johnny Risk."

"I think Jeff DeBono is a fox."

"I think he's a dink."

"Jenny wants to suck Jeff DeBono's face."

"Shut up."

"Do you want to steal this?"

"You can't fit it under your shirt."

"*You* can."

"Not me. You steal it. I'm not stealing anything for you."

"Hey, I took those sunglasses for you."

"Sunglasses are easy."

"Shut up, you guys."

"Let's go to A&W."

"Let's go to Just Jeans, they have terrible security."

"Oh, God, I hate that place. I swear to God."

"I *abhor* that place."

"I'm hungry," says Cindy, and everybody says, OK, Let's go eat, I'm hungry too, though nobody will actually eat anything with calories, should we go to Shakey's or A&W.

Everybody waits for Cindy's cues, now that she will be getting an apartment of her own. She is incredibly lucky, everyone agrees. Her mom's new boyfriend, who hates her, will pay the rent on a place in downtown San Rafael to get rid of her, and she'll be able to do whatever she wants even though she's only fourteen. Her mother will be at the boyfriend's house all the time. She's incredibly lucky, her mom is so cool. Everybody else's parents are too old.

"Shakey's," says Cindy.

"All My Children," Tammy reminds everybody, referring to the wide-screen video at Shakey's.

"Or there's always Denny's," says Suzy.

"Oh, God," says everybody, "don't be gross."

They are already gone, hips bumping. Suzy gets jammed in the turnstile, but she catches up. They are walking across the parking lot, an expanse of blacktop as dark and smooth as a fresh lake of petroleum. The Shakey's sign is visible in the distance on stilts above the freeway overpass. These are the "Acres of Free Parking." Something about the thought fills Cindy with a tremendous sadness that sickens her like a drag on a strong cigarette.

"Oh, God!" she moans, stretching her arms. "I wish I had my apartment already."

"Really!" says everybody. "Total party."

"Invite over Jeff DeBono."

"Invite over both the DeBonos, and snort a lot of lines."

"Total beer in the fridge."

* * *

Imagine Cindy Potts's handwriting: careful, vinelike, with big fruit-shaped letters. Each "i" is dotted with a large seed. It's perfect. On standard notebook paper, she is composing a suicide note: "The sad part is nobody ever reconizes my star quality." She crosses out "reconizes" and writes "reconized," a small purl in the flow of emotion snagging on something deep. She is sitting in Composition, writing and doodling within the intimate arc of a guarding forearm. She can picture what would happen if she were to attempt suicide. Once, when her father was visiting, she feigned a swoon in a restaurant and lay on the floor listening to the dismay of her parents with a satisfaction so intense it made her ribs feel all warm and feathery.

Her mother would discover her in the bathroom or the bedroom with, say, a number of empty vials lying around. And Cindy would wake up in the hospital in one of those ugly string-tie gowns. They would make her stay in the hospital for a while, and her hair would get all limp and dark because she would be away from her shampoo. She couldn't accept visitors. And she would miss the party at the Weidners' that weekend. She would be sitting up restless in her hospital bed on a warm, sunny September afternoon, with breezes and birdsong outside, and she would *then* realize that this humiliating comedy of attempted suicide has an unexpected result: no one would want to get near her anymore, repelled by the new halo. At school, the glamor of death would be an aura around her that refracts the regard of her friends.

She crumples the note and begins to recopy it, this time with better handwriting, rounder periods, the same soft curves in each letter. The perfection of her handwriting bespeaks a blamelessness in her that is, to her, heartbreaking. She loves forming the rounded letters like a row of stuffed animals on a shelf.

Imagine Cindy at home. *Fantasy Island* is on. A few unpopped kernels sit in the bottom of an empty bowl. She is wading aimlessly off the patio into the darkness, where the somehow unfair smell of barbecues hangs over the neighborhood's backyards. Or she is draped sideways in the big chair like an overcoat, not really watching. She is lit violet by exploding grenades of light. Cigarette butts have been snuffed in melted ice cream. The telephone rings.

"Hi, Cindy."

"Hey, Mom."

"Can you do me a favor, Punkins? Can you move my stuff from the washer to the dryer?"

"Sure. Where are you?"

"I'm at Brian's. I'll be here again tonight."

"Will you be home tomorrow night?"

"Oh, Cindy, there's that heaviness again! All that gravity!"

"Well, Mom! I just want to know, like, should I thaw something?"

"Honey, don't you remember our conversation? Every time I talk to you this guilt trip starts. And it's a very subtle thing; I don't think you're really aware of it. You have to start experiencing your *light* energies. You remember our conversation, don't you?"

"Yes, Mom."

"You have to take responsibility for your own experience, remember? I love you, but I can't be responsible for your experience. You're a big girl now. You can put some lightness in the world."

"OK, Mom. I know."

"Love you, Punkins. And please move my stuff to the dryer? And set it on delicate? You'll melt my teddy."

"Yeah, OK."

"And do it right now. If you don't do it right when you hang up, you'll forget."

"OK! . . ." Her voice has the two-tone doorbell sound of exasperation.

" 'Bye."

Cindy waits until the dial tone returns, then hangs up. That's just the way her mom is, you can't fool her, she's incredibly smart. She has a master's degree in psychology from Sunset University, and for some time now she has had her own private practice in a small time-share office in the Northgate Industrial Park, furnished only with big pillows; and a quarter-column ad in the Marin County Yellow Pages: psychotherapy, healing, dreamwork, eating disorders. She has a sixth sense about people that is, for Cindy, unfairly omniscient; she always wins. There was a time, when Cindy was about ten, when her mom was a total wreck; she scarcely ever got out of bed; the check would arrive, and Cindy would be sent out to buy groceries. "Overcoming a resistance to abundance" was the crucial idea from her Overeaters Anonymous group in Berkeley. Now she's down to where she can borrow and wear Cindy's clothes, she's bought an actual Porsche, her boyfriend Brian is gentle and caring and generous, the kind of man you think you don't deserve. The familiar sound of her Porsche's engine, disappearing around the corner and heading toward the freeway, is the sound of abundance no longer resisted.

Cindy has wandered out onto the patio in the warm night air, kept in motion by the vague sensation that the new furniture repels her. The memory of a dial tone deafens her. She is looking down at the jars where her mother had tried to start tomatoes last summer, now just cylinders of hard gray dirt. A number of seeds are growing in the flinty earth beyond the railing at the edge of the driveway, where they must have fallen by accident. A tomato, bearing hard green fruit like peas, sprouts from the cinders at the crumbly gingerbread border of the driveway. Its seed, with its tiny speck of knowledge, is clutching gravel, sucking from it the necessary vitamins, or water or whatever. Everything on TV is boring, lunar. She goes back into the kitchen and dials the telephone.

"Hello?" says Brian's voice.

"Oh, hi, Brian. This is Cynthia. Is my mom there?"

"Hey, Cindy! How's my favorite girl?"

"I'm OK."

"Wow, hey, I was just thinking about you the other day. Really. I was at Record Factory in San Rafael, and you know, they have a BASS-Ticketron outlet there, and I *almost* bought some tickets for the Van Halen concert next month. There were just a few seats left, and they were really perfect seats for the money, and I could just picture you—front-row center. I mean, I came within *that close.*"

"Oh, well, thanks, Brian." She isn't sure how she's supposed to respond. "I mean, thanks for the thought and everything."

"Yeah, it's the thought that counts. I guess you want to talk to your mom, huh. She's right here. But hey, take it easy. Great talking to you. I hope I see you around."

"Yeah."

Cindy's mom says, "I don't want you calling me here."

"Yeah, but Mom? I've got a problem."

"Did you move my clothes?"

"Yeah, but Mom? I'm trying to make some of this macaroni stuff? In the box?"

"Yes."

"And I boiled the water and everything? But the thing is? I dumped the foil packet of cheese sauce in?" Why is she suddenly breathless? Why is her heart beating so loudly that she can feel it in her skull?

"Yes."

"No, I mean the packet. It's just sitting in there. Do I just fish it out? Or if water got in, it's probably ruined . . ."

"Is this supposed to be an emergency, Cindy?"

"Mom, I can't find any tongs or anything, and if the cheese powder is ruined I have to do something else with the macaroni. Because you can't just eat it plain, without cheese sauce . . ."

"My God, Cindy, it's so obvious what you're doing. Just look at what you're doing."

Cindy says, "What."

"You're a lot smarter than this."

"What."

"It's so obvious what you're trying to do. You ought to know how I feel about you, and you don't need to keep testing me. One test too many is just one test too many."

Her mother leaves a long silence, in which Cindy says nothing, implying that she has nothing to say in her defense. Her hands and face feel scalded, and she just wishes she could get off the phone.

Her mother goes on. "This is an important distinction I want you to see. On the one hand, you have to know I love you. But on the other hand, you have to be responsible for the quality of your own experience. I can't always be responsible for your experience."

"OK, Mom."

"Eventually we all have to grow up. It's totally obvious how inauthentic you're being when you call me like this."

"OK, I said."

"Did you move my clothes?"

"Yes," she lies hopelessly. "And I set it on delicate."

"Well, just in case you didn't, why don't you do it right now, as soon as we hang up."

"OK."

" 'Bye now, Punkins."

She hangs up and goes into the attached garage, to unstick her mother's sexy ghosts from the inner wall of the washer; and she transfers them in a strange escaping armful to the dryer, where she sets them tumbling, rhythmically clicking in the roar. The smell of lint is solace; the dryer is the house's faithful heart.

She goes back into the kitchen and takes up the packet of cheese sauce from the countertop, tears off the top to find the orange powder within, and wanders into the living room to see what came on after *Fantasy Island*, licking the tip of her finger and dipping it experimentally into the orange cheese powder. She decides that this feeling—of a tiny wheel spinning uselessly to a blur in her chest—must be boredom. She is watching a long string of commercials, licking her finger, dipping it into the orange powder, licking her finger, and imagining herself inert in the bathtub, wrists slashed, in the cooling broth of pink water, with stripes of blood running slantwise on the porcelain. She imagines her mother discovering her with her head thrown back on the rim of the tub, exposing a perfectly swanlike curve of the throat, her lips relaxed and parted in the gentle kiss of death. Those nimble once-restless fingers lie curled in total repose, holding an invisible angel's hand. Since her mother had not come home for several days in succession, Cindy's body had begun to putrefy, the water had turned from pink to brown. A light fur is already growing on her skin at the waterline, and over her mouth and eyes; it's like the cottony fur that fills old jars in the refrigerator. Her thighs have fallen parted in the water, and every muscle is relaxed in submission to the corruption. The linty kiss of the angel of death on her lips hangs suspended like a photograph of the escaping soul. The odor makes her mother gag. She calls Brian on the phone. Then she doesn't know what to do. She is too frightened and shocked to cry, to scream, to sit down, to move. She goes out and stands in the small front lawn amid buzzing tall weeds in the sunshine. The idea that her daughter is dead inside would not occur to a passerby. She could just be a woman standing on her lawn. Brian will be here soon. I'll get through this, she thinks. This will just be another of the many things in my life I'll have to work through. The grief will subside soon, and over the years I'll recover from the tragedy of having lost my daughter.

And in fact, that's just what would happen: Cindy's mother would recover over the years. She would join a group at the Center for Creative Growth in Berkeley, a holistic grief group composed of parents recovering from similar losses. There would be recognizable, predictable stages: shock; then guilt; after a while, anger at Cindy; then more guilt; she would make it her goal *not* to preserve the memory of Cindy; she would get clear. Brian would be at her side, gentle, caring, and gradually she would learn to embrace abundance again. Maybe there would be other marriages, even other daughters, she's still only thirty-four, there's time, the gorgeous horror of Cindy's putrefaction in the bathtub would fade. Time heals all wounds. Cindy dips her finger into the foil packet and it comes up coated with that tangy orange powder, and she sighs. The police or somebody would hose her out of the bathtub, and probably Formula 409 would take off the last stains.

When Cindy's mother comes home the next day, it just happens that Jeff DeBono is there. It's horrible. He had turned up unannounced in a Camaro he said he had borrowed from a friend. Cindy is surprised he has a driver's license. She is surprised he even knew where she lives.

It's horrible, excruciating. Cindy doesn't know where to put her hands, or how to stand. She and Jeff are standing in the front yard, facing each other, trying posture after posture. And Jeff is telling some complicated story about what happened last night when he and Mike and Eric got drunk in Novato and got stopped by a policeman on a golf course, where they were drinking wine out of a jug and one of them fell in a ravine. Cindy is so stupid, she can't think of anything to say, she just says things like "Wow" and "Really," and then thinks, *Oh, God, how stupid.* So when her mother's dusty purple Porsche pulls into the driveway and emits that familiar crunch of the parking-brake lever, Cindy seizes the opportunity to run inside and get away from Jeff, whom she had never even raised her eyes to. She leaves him waiting in the yard, slams the front door, and, once inside, almost *screams* from the sheer electrocuting embarrassment of Jeff's presence.

"Mom!" she cries.

"What." Her mother's voice comes from the kitchen, where she is plucking over lingerie she has extracted from the dryer.

"Mom!" Cindy runs into the kitchen, she is so excited that she is tiptoeing, her heels never touch the floor. "Mom, this boy Jeff DeBono is here, he just came over and everything, and he wants to take me for a ride in his car, he's sixteen, and he wants me to go for a ride, Mom, *please* say no. *Please please please* say no."

With a crease between her brows, her mom says, "Why?"

"Mom!"

"Tell him you have to do some homework or something. Why don't you want to go?"

Cindy writhes, braiding her thighs.

"Okay." Her mother smiles vaguely with bafflement. "I'm saying no. 'No.' "

"Thanks, Mom," she says, and she bolts for the telephone to—while Jeff is still waiting on the lawn—call everybody just for a second.

PAPEL

■ Mike Padilla

Mike Padilla is a young writer who seems certain to make a place for himself in our literature. "Promising" is the usual word, but in his case the achievement has already gone beyond promise. Padilla has a world of his own, an eccentric angle of vision on that world, and a language supple enough to carry his surprising movements from farce to heartbreak and make them seem not only natural, but inevitable. "Papel" is pure gold. Treasure it.

—TOBIAS WOLFF

*T*he big joke Tio Henry always told my tias was that old Eufrasia's house would go up in flames just like her burnt *chicharrones*. All that frayed electrical wiring that hung from the ceiling was too expensive to replace, she'd told them, though the government had offered to fix all the electricity in her village in 1958. I was careful never to laugh too hard, and a look from my mother always told me when to stop. When Eufrasia's heart gave out for the fourth and last time, my tio and tias drove south of the border as if a gun had gone off in a race. They came from Anaheim, from San Diego, from Glendale, from wherever they'd been waiting that late September morning.

On the bus from La Jolla my mother fidgeted with crochet needles, knitting a flowered pattern, unraveling it, knitting it again more tightly. She'd taken me out of school right when the first bio test was being passed out—the same test she'd locked me indoors to study for all week, even though the subject came naturally to me.

"When can I go back to school?" I stretched my legs and pressed my tennis shoes flat against the seat in front of me, flexing the calves that biking had begun to develop.

"Soon enough." She poked my leg with one of the hooks. She'd exploded into the classroom without asking the attendance office, had rushed past the biology teacher without looking at him, past the transparent anatomy model. *"Toma tus cosas, muchacho,"* she'd said. Some of the boys in back had snickered when she took my hand. *"Andale, tu futuro te espera."* If the words had been in English, the world might not have felt like it was slipping from under my feet as I ran after her down the waxed hallway.

Three days before, I'd met Jason and his friends at the reservoir on my bike. For the first time they hadn't spun off without me. They'd met me with a challenge, gripping their handlebars to intimidate me, but I out-biked every one of them, except Jason. For the rest of the week I'd spent lunch with them instead of eating alone. I'd started food fights, cornered girls in the hallway so they'd be late for classes, and gotten dragged into the principal's office twice. Even fat Charlie couldn't get into their group, and he was a fat white boy who got new rims and bearings when it wasn't even his birthday or Christmas. Tio Henry had been right: it's physical strength that gets people's respect.

"When we buy the new house, we'll have a swimming pool," I said, as if there were no question about it.

She pulled some yarn from her bag and nodded.

"And a pool table. Then I can invite the guys over on weekends."

"Tell me again what you will say if Señora Johnson asks."

"That my father called," I said. "That he invited us over for the weekend."

"Where?"

"Newport Beach. Wherever that is. What am I going to tell the guys in class?"

"Say nothing. And don't you let them influence you, *mu-cha-cho*," she said, pointing the hook at me with each syllable. "You're much too young for their bad ways. Keep to your school work so you—"

"So I can make something of myself." I'd heard it all before— the education, the money, the better life. What good was it if I had to live it alone, like my mother did, with only her knitting baskets and Bullocks catalogs for company?

"Can I call Jason tonight? If he thinks I've blown him off, I won't stand a chance with the group." Being one of only three non-whites in school left my odds at about ten to one, I figured.

She leaned over me, face to the glass. The bus had stopped at the border, and outside two patrollers in brown uniforms talked to each other. One of them came inside the bus, surveying us from behind mirrored glasses. My mother's hands flitted from her lap to her hair to the collar of her dress.

"What are you so afraid of?" I said.

"It's hard to put the past behind you," she said. She meant before she could afford to live in the outskirts of La Jolla, before she was a legal citizen.

I slumped in my seat and watched the next ten minutes tick by on my watch. My mother had promised that now the past wouldn't matter, that we'd begin a whole new life. No more shopping out of town, or saving bottles for their deposits, or secondhand space heaters in order to pay the La Jolla rent. But other things she told me about made her work her dress collars even harder: electrolysis for her legs, new designer clothes, wall-to-wall carpeting, and a silver tea service to entertain her guests, though I didn't know where they'd come from. As for me, I'd have a new dirt bike, and when I was old enough, my own car. A new La Jolla house seemed far in the future, though she promised it within a few months.

But for now my mind was on Tijuana. Though my mother said it was barren of opportunity, this time it would yield something for me. On the streets they sold firecrackers, the kind any boy in school would pay fifty cents a pack for.

Driving into the village, I pressed my face against the glass. There were the same squat, box-like houses, the same bulky, twisted fig trees up and down the road. My fingers gripped the vinyl armrest. "God," I said. "No telephone poles. No *phones*."

During the funeral the priest spoke too quickly for me to follow the Spanish. When it was over I took my feet down from the bench in front of me. My mother and I never went to the Presbyterian church she'd joined, but I knew it wouldn't have felt like this Tijuana chapel, with its burning incense and cold cement floor. The people moved slowly out the door. "Quickly, quickly," she said, but only I could hear her.

The women on the porches of the low, flat-roofed houses stopped washing and chatting to give us sad looks. I tried to imagine my mother crouched over a washboard in one of her designer dresses that she bought at the clearinghouse. But the picture wasn't even funny.

I stopped along the way to stamp the dust out of my shoes, but raised more, turning my ankles and legs orange up the knee. This road would be perfect for my dirt bike. I could see myself on my Bridgestone, head down, barreling into the wind, feet whipping around the crank, a long, thick stream of dust jetting out from beneath the back tire. Up the road, dry hills rose and dropped behind houses, showing off hollows, terraces, grooves, and steep inclines perfect for nose-diving and skidding. Even the rocky, pitted streets that never ran parallel invited good biking. If I could bring this home with me, I thought, instead of just firecrackers.

"It is like Tijuana not to have straight paths between places," Tio Henry said. I'd spotted him ducking through the chapel door five minutes before the service was over. "And look at their chickens on public display. An eyesore."

Short-haired mongrel dogs roamed the streets just as they had a year and a half ago, when old Eufrasia had fallen backwards in a chair just after my twelfth birthday. There had been fever, vomiting, and heart palpitations. The doctors said she wouldn't live, but she pulled through with us at her bedside. She wasn't even my grandmother, but my mother's grandmother. She was deaf, distant, and very wrinkled, and she talked of things that seemed to have happened hundreds of years ago.

"Don't let the old woman upset you," my mother had told me when we were out of her room. "Hers is not a sharp mind like yours." She had proudly smoothed my black hair out of my eyes. Still, though Eufrasia was deaf, no one ever said a disrespectful word in front of her, and not even the doctors touched her. And I can't remember, on any of our visits, that she ever put food to her lips or stirred a cup of coffee. She was like a spirit of the past that had chosen to remain in the world.

I walked a few paces ahead of my mother, Tio Henry, and Tia Margarita, so they'd know I was in a hurry to get this whole business over with. If I could get to a phone, I could call Jason. I'd tell him that the woman who'd yanked me from class was a maid, that she'd come to take me to the hospital because my mother had fallen down a flight of stairs. Maybe I could still go biking Sunday night at the reservoir.

"You'll have to tell these people to go away," Tio Henry said. "They're ignorant and must be told what to do."

"What difference will it make if Alicia is not there?" Tia Margarita said. She spoke in Spanish, as did all my tias. "She is the only one who knows where to look." Margarita, the tallest and oldest of the sisters, walked with powerful, masculine steps, her head steady under the tall black hive of hair pierced with a metal comb. The matching beads looped around her neck chinked loudly with each step.

"Alicia is a strange one," Tio Henry said. "But she knows what will happen if she doesn't come. Now think of what you will say to these people."

A bus without windows came rattling around a blind corner like in a movie chase scene, lifting its left wheels a foot in the air. I dodged the cloud of orange dust it made.

"My clothes," Tio Henry said. "Damn this afflicted place." When I looked back, he was shaking a rock from his shoe.

My mother slapped him hard across the back of the neck. "It's just a little farther, *hombre*."

"Speak to me in English, woman," he said. He was a dark, short man with tight muscles that twitched in his neck when he spoke. "How can I find an American wife with everyone always speaking Spanish?"

"Look around you, *viejo stupido*. Do you see any American brides blushing in these streets?" She tried to slap him again, but he was too quick for her. He grabbed her wrist so that she shrieked.

"*Hijo*," my mother said. I looked back, but kept walking.

Margarita stepped in front of them, threatening Tio Henry with the iron heel of her shoe. "Stop this nonsense." Because the street was too rocky for heels, she went barefoot, one pump clutched in each hand.

He jerked her loose. "Maybe soon I can buy an American wife," he said, laughing.

"Yes," my mother said, turning her wrist slowly in her hand. "Soon we will all have what we want."

* * *

When we reached the porch of Eufrasia's three-room house, Margarita punched one foot in each pump and mounted the sloping steps. Even if she hadn't stood at the top step, everyone in the crowd could have seen her high broad shoulders, her glossy mound of hair. She turned toward them, looking over them with her copper-green eyes. My mother, Tio Henry, and I went up the steps after her.

I recognized some relatives from across the border by their American clothes, but most of the people looked very poor. One man with a clean shave and neatly creased pants smiled at me. I tried to eye him down, but he kept smiling, until I had to look away. I moved close behind Tio Henry.

Margarita folded her heavy arms, and for the first time I saw how her upper body resembled Tio Henry's. She looked as powerful as him, with similar deltoids and upper back size. No sport I could think of could have given them both that kind of form.

At last she said, "Go home and work, or pray for your souls. You have no business here." They walked away, their feet crunching in the dirt.

"What do they want?" I said.

"They don't want anything. They only adored her." Tia Alicia stood in the doorway behind me. She led us into the bare front room of the house and lit the gas lantern. The yellow light flickered against the wall faintly.

She gathered her hair into a slick cord that fell almost to her waist. She was much shorter than her sisters, and so frail in the arms that she wouldn't have been good even at badminton. Just throwing her hair back seemed to require a lot of effort.

"You don't know anything," Tio Henry said. "If you did, you wouldn't still be living on this side of the border."

"You think like an American tourist," she said.

"I think like an American because I am one."

"Stop this," Margarita said, ducking into the bedroom.

"Give your Tia Alicia a kiss, *muchacho*," my mother said, nudging me toward her with her bony fingers. I kissed her cheek.

She said, "People have been stopping since three this morning. They come to the foot of the steps, but they do not knock. They try to peer in the windows, they loiter by the chicken coop. I keep the lights off and the blinds down."

Margarita emerged from the bedroom in a glittery, bright green dress. It looked cheap and fit tightly over her bulk.

"*Que vestido tan hermosisimo,*" my mother said. "Where did you buy it?"

Margarita gave her a long stare, then said to me, "There is a pickax in the tool shack." When I came back, everyone had gathered in a half circle facing the far wall. They looked like they might be posing for a portrait, only no one smiled.

Alicia pointed to the center of the wall and said, "There." She knew all the places to tap, for she had visited the woman weekly, bringing her groceries, clothes, and other things from the Zona Norte. Eufrasia would only have food from the open markets, and wouldn't accept anything that came from the stores downtown— "*los supermercados americanos.*"

I handed Margarita the heavy pickax, and she told me to stand back. No one moved. She spread her legs as wide as she could in her dress. She practiced swinging the pickax with ease, arcing it out from the wall. My mother clapped her hands together and said, "It is like the launching of a ship," but no one looked at her.

The end of the pickax slid smoothly into the soft plaster. A piece gave way, crumbling white and powdery to the cement floor. She swung again and again; the mound of plaster grew as she cleared the opening. She leaned the pickax against the wall and pushed her hand through the hole. I stopped breathing, almost expecting it to come out deformed. When she withdrew her white, chalky hand, her large fingers clasped a roll of tightly wound bills. With her straight, white teeth she broke the string that held the roll together and let the bills unwind and peel away, falling to the floor in dull green curls. Tens, twenties, and fifties in American currency. She pulled out another roll. Then another, and another, like magic, reaching deeper into the wall each time.

"We are wasting time," she said, and we began to work. She handed me the pickax and I started to tear away the rest of the wall, stopping only now and then to catch my breath. Some of the rolls had come untied, leaving money in hard-to-reach places. My mother examined the junctures of the house's frame, while Tio Henry held the lantern up to the crevices where loose bills might have fallen. They worked together, taking turns holding the lantern. Once, when my mother found a bill that had tried to escape her, she snatched it out of the wall and said, "This will be your making, *muchacho.*"

Margarita watched from the doorway, legs astride, hefty arms folded over her bosom. I wondered why I was working and she wasn't. Her face remained rigid, deeply carved with lines that were black in the lantern light.

After nearly an hour Tio Henry took the pickax out of my hands. "Don't kill yourself," he said, and began to swing at what was left of the plaster.

The cabinets in the kitchen were nailed shut. Tio Henry pried them open with the chisel end of the pickax, swearing all the while. The nails shrieked with resistance, then popped loose. Preserve jars lined the shelves in neat rows. They were so tightly packed with money we had to pry it out with sewing scissors.

There was no thought of sleep now, with morning bringing the dull green bills to light. I gathered them up and started to count. My hands had turned gray, and I tried to wipe the dirt on my shorts. At first I was slow at counting, but found that it was faster to separate the different denominations, then group them into stacks of five hundred each. I wrote on the floor with a piece of plaster to keep tally on the total.

With the scissors my mother cut open the mattress along the seam that had been opened and resewn with black thread. She brought armfuls of bills out and piled them in front of me. As I smoothed out the twenties, I found some personal checks that had been written to Eufrasia and signed with X's.

Tio Henry patted my head and said, "You're doing well, you're good at mathematics. Physical strength gets you respect, but no one wants to marry an idiot." I turned the checks facedown on the floor.

"Yes, he is the best in his school," my mother said, though it wasn't true. "He has many friends because he is so smart." Tio Henry laid his big hand on my shoulder and smiled down at me. "What would you like your uncle to buy you?"

"Firecrackers," I said, "for my friends at school."

He turned his face quickly toward my mother. "Have you been sending this boy to Sunday school? This Christian generosity sends people like us to the poorhouse." He looked back at me. "Think of yourself for once."

"I want them for myself," I said.

"Ah, modesty is a weakness! Think of something else, Christian boy."

"Firecrackers," I said.

"Firecrackers are dangerous," my mother said.

"Think harder," Tio Henry said, holding up a fistful of green. I felt the odds slipping. Twelve to one. Fifteen to one. "I want to call somebody."

"*Harder*," he said. His face began to wrinkle with laughter.

The blood was in my cheeks again. Margarita was watching me from the doorway. I saw myself eating lunch alone at the end of a cafeteria table. I could taste the cold lunchmeat going down my throat. "I just want to get to a phone," I said, as calmly as I could.

"The Christian boy has a weak imagination." He took up another handful of dollars. "This stuff is power, but you have to know how to use it." He put his hand on my shoulder again and squeezed gently. "You'll learn, you'll learn."

He went back to swinging the pickax. My mother stripped open the sofa and started pulling out the stuffing. Margarita was still watching me with her copper-green eyes, as if she were waiting to see me cry. I held it back as hard as I could.

Margarita said, "The boy should eat something. I will take him to *la tienda* for milk and *pan dulce*." She took my hand as if I were a child and led me outside.

"*Tu madre y tu tio*, they don't listen to you. *Pobrecito*." Her hand felt cold and dry, rock-hard with muscle. It was good to hold on to. "Forget about them, they are both idiots. Soon you will see how foolish they are."

"What are you talking about?" I said.

"Your mother is nothing, but she thinks she is something. Your uncle is nothing, but he thinks something of himself now that he has his citizenship papers. Someday you will find that you are nothing. Maybe your children or your grandchildren will be something." We stopped outside the store. Without looking at me, she bent down and gave me a hard kiss on the cheek.

"What about you?" I said. "What makes you think you're something instead of nothing?"

"Did I say I was not nothing?"

"Then you're nothing just like the rest."

"*No importa, muchacho.* You want firecrackers, am I right? I can get them for you." I looked up at her, but the sun blinded me. "Leave the back door open this afternoon when no one is in the house. I will put them in the wall behind the sofa. Make sure your mother doesn't see them."

She pulled me into the store and bought me milk and *pan dulce.* Then she pressed a fifty-dollar bill into my hand and said, "Say nothing."

Alicia dragged a *petaca* out of the bedroom. In it were some tarnished picture frames, old china, and some dresses. She held one of them up. "An unsightly thing, isn't it? Still, it can be restored."

"You can keep the artifact," my mother said. "The neighbors would think I was a maid come to do the cleaning."

"Use your imagination," Tio Henry said. He sprinkled a handful of twenties over Alicia's head.

"I think the diary is in the closet," Tia Alicia said. "But I can't find the key."

"What do you want with the old woman's scribblings?"

"She has many things written about the old ranching days."

"I'm not interested in her *historias.*"

"No one said you had to be. Maybe the boy will find it interesting."

"Don't go filling his head with ancient nonsense. He's an American. He has the future to look to, not the past."

"It is time," Margarita said. I knew what she meant.

My mother said, "I have a child, remember." She pulled me close to her side of the couch and wrapped her thin arms around my waist. "I know I can't demand anything, but—"

"Your husband in East L.A. sends you alimony. That's why you divorced him," Tio Henry said. "You're not so special."

"I only meant—"

"Don't forget what happens if the authorities find out. You won't get half what you're getting now."

My mother's eyes filled with tears, which she tried to wipe away before they spilled over. I tried to ignore her, but she pressed her face against my arm. I felt the moisture seep through my sleeve and couldn't move away.

"You should have been an actress," Tio Henry said. "Your tears might have profited you better."

She wiped her nose on my sleeve like a baby. "I want what is best for my son, not to have to live like *this*." She looked around her to indicate the room.

"You are far from *this*," he said.

"I want him to *be* someone."

Still in English, Tio Henry sang, "Somewhere, in the sometime, with that someone, I'll be someone at last . . ." He sang as if he were the only one in the room to hear it.

"See how your uncle treats his own flesh and—" A roll of money hit her sharply in the side of the face. Green paper exploded everywhere. The blood pulsed in my arms. She loosened her hold on me. I sat down to start counting again. Tio Henry leaned back on the sofa as if he were on a cruise to Acapulco.

"You must be sure never to grow up to be like your tio," my mother said calmly. "You must be sure to get a good education, make money so you can be somebody."

Tio Henry jerked himself forward. "And I'm not *some*body?"

"An old fool."

"Do you see me begging like a dog . . ."

I counted the money very loudly in my head. I saw him throw something at her. Two-fifty, two seventy-five. Someone screamed.

I counted. My mother ran to the bedroom. More shouting. Three-fifty, four hundred. Louder. Louder.

I ran out of the room and into the kitchen, took my books and went out. The screen door slammed behind me.

On the back steps I opened the book, but could barely see through the tears. Pictures of brains and hearts were blurred into odd shapes. As I thumbed through the pages of the later chapters, not reading them, hardly glancing at the pictures, the grayness of my hands came off on the pages. My hands were gray down to the pores, under the nails, in the creases of my palms, in the ridges of my fingerprints.

Alicia was stroking my hair. "Go back to sleep, *niño*. You need your rest." I sat up abruptly and she stopped. Her fingers were cold, but her firm voice soothed me.

"What are you reading?" she said. "Ah, *la biologia*. Show me."

The book fell open to the plastic anatomy pages. I pointed to the first page, a drawing of a skeleton with a wide grin and white, ghostly ribs. I wondered how long before old Eufrasia would look that way in her grave. I flipped the next page over. Now the skeleton had veins, now arteries. I kept turning the pages, adding muscles, organs, tissue, pink skin, and hair, until the picture became that of a complete person, shining pink and naked. I wondered what such a man would call himself. I wondered where he came from.

"You study too hard for such a boy," she said. "Your mama pushes you too hard."

"No," I said. "I don't care about school anymore." I closed the soiled pages of the book tightly and dropped it with the other books on the bottom step. "I need to call somebody back home."

"If that will make you feel better, *pobrecito*. I will take you." She started to run her fingers through my hair again, but brushed the hair out of my eyes instead. "We will go this afternoon."

When Tio Henry asked me to fetch some water, I went out and filled two buckets to the rim. I carried them in, trying to make it look easy. He set them to heat on the stove. Most of the houses had running water, but Eufrasia had refused to allow them to tamper with her house.

"Crazy old woman," Tio Henry said, as he washed his face in the water.

At noon a short woman in pants knocked at the screen door. Margarita filled the doorframe. The woman spoke in the kind of slow, distinct Spanish I could understand. "I'm Señora Lopez from next door," she said. "I wanted to offer whatever condolences I could." Margarita didn't invite her in. Finally, the woman said, "It's my daughter's birthday. You're welcome to come by for coffee and cake, if you have the time."

"Thank you," Margarita said. "We will be by for a visit."

Alicia was in the kitchen. "It would be nice if we brought a gift for the girl," she said.

"Remember our birthdays as children?" Tio Henry said to my mother. She turned away and said nothing. The roll of money had left a blue mark by her eye.

"Don't be angry with me," he said.

"A decent meal and a good bath is how we celebrated," she said, without turning. "And if one of us got a gift, we always broke it fighting over it. Why must you mention it?"

"I don't know," he said. "There's no reason to fight now, is there?"

She sat down and massaged her forehead. "I know. A better life."

He went out to the backyard and came back in a few minutes with two handfuls of eggs. "The birthday girl, her family is poor. She'll appreciate anything we can give them."

She straightened her back slowly, then looked at him. "It's a lovely gesture. Be sure they are the freshest ones."

Alicia turned away from them. "I will go to the Zona Norte and see what I can find." My mother and Tio Henry said nothing. Alicia looked at me. "Would you like to escort me on the bus?"

"Don't go depressing him with stories about the Old Town," Tio Henry said.

"Make sure he doesn't buy any *cuetes*," my mother said. "He'll blow his fingers off and not be able to hold a pencil."

"Keep your hands on your wallet," Tio Henry said.

* * *

In all the commotion of the *mercado*, I couldn't find anyone selling firecrackers. I had to be sure they would be here when Margarita came to buy them. I would tell her to bargain for six bricks and try to get some free bottle rockets in the deal. The people in the streets and produce stands shouted above the music of the mariachis—conversing, bargaining, advertising their goods to passersby. But nowhere did I hear the shouts of "*Cuetes!*" as I had last time.

Cars blew their horns to clear the streets of people. I walked fast in front of Alicia. She grabbed me by the shoulder. "How do you expect me to keep up, *muchacho?*"

I saw a man waving a red package over his head walking toward us.

"Now what would a girl like for her *cumpleaños?*" she said.

He got closer, but I lost him in the crowd.

"I always loved candy when I was a girl."

I spotted him again. He shouted in English, "Firecrackers! Firecrackers, cheap!"

"Don't get any funny ideas," she said. "Your mother will only take them away from you."

I looked over my shoulder as we walked past. He disappeared into the bright colors of the *mercado*. I checked the corner street sign. Madero and Seventh.

"Do you know who once stayed in that hotel over there? El Palacio, the pink one."

"Tio said not to tell me about the old days."

"Aye, do you think I care one way or the other what your tio *stupido* thinks? That's where the American fighter Dempsey stayed."

"Jack Dempsey," I said, straining to be heard over the market noise.

"He fought your Abuelo Lupe in the twenties. All the men in the family went to see your abuelo almost lose the fight in the first round, but come back with a knockout punch in the third. Not many men have done that."

"I don't believe it," I said. But Jason would if I could make him. "My mother would have told me."

"Your abuela's diary has the pictures of the fight in it."

"Did they have cameras in the twenties?"

"You are making fun of me," she said. She walked ahead of me, but I caught up with her.

I couldn't hear the man with the firecrackers anymore. I tried to figure my odds again—somewhere between twenty to one and fifty to one, if Margarita got me the firecrackers. The noise in the market made it hard to think.

At the bus stop we couldn't sit down. There were too many people with souvenirs on the benches.

"What will the diary tell us?" I said.

"Everything."

Everything. How much longer was I going to have to wait for this slow bus?

"I'm going to buy firecrackers," I said. "I don't care what my mother says." I turned to run back into the crowd, but she grabbed my arm.

"Your mother will cut my throat, *niño!*"

"Then can I make my call now?"

She hesitated, then took out a handful of quarters and dimes from her pocketbook.

Under the awning a man in a print shirt was dialing a number over and over again. I clutched the change, jangled it loudly, kicked at the dirt. "No one's *answering*," I said to him.

"*Muchacho malcriado,*" he said, hanging up.

I dialed the operator. "Person to person. La Jolla, Estados Unidos."

"*Momento . . . diga.*"

I gave her Jason's name, then the number, half in Spanish, half in English. She said something too fast for me to understand.

"The bus is here!" Alicia was waving her arms at me.

I shoved some quarters into the slot until the operator stopped talking. I'm at the hospital, I thought. My mother has fractured her collarbone in two places. If these operators talked slower, I could understand them.

One ring.

"*Esta sonando.*"

A second ring.

I hung up before it could ring a third time.

On the bus I leaned my head against the window. My faint reflection disappeared in the sun, reappeared in the shade.

"Is it true that we're nothing?" I said.

"Ah." She nudged me in the ribs with her elbow. "Those are questions for the educated. Don't ask me about *la filosofia*."

I watched the Old Town fall behind in the orange haze. "The diary will really tell about the fight?"

"With pictures signed by both fighters."

"Can I keep them? My friends won't believe me. I was supposed to bring firecrackers, but this would be better."

She put her hand on my knee. I was glad Tio Henry was not there to see it. He would have called it a spectacle.

When we got back to Eufrasia's house, Margarita had put the money in the *petaca*. I tried to lift it, but couldn't even slide it across the floor. I believed we'd never get it out the door, and the thought of a new life became just as unlikely. Margarita told me to close the back door. I stepped through the kitchen and slammed the door shut. Then I opened it quickly, just a crack.

We found Señora Lopez helping the children play pin-the-tail-on-the-donkey. When she saw us, she gestured for us to join her by the fire.

"Who is the birthday gift?" my mother asked.

"Imelda, *la bonita* in the yellow dress," she said.

"Yes, she is very pretty."

Tio Henry slumped in his chair, large fingers clasped around the mug between his legs. He stared into the fire. My mother stretched her leg under the table and kicked him. He sloshed beer into his lap, looked at Alicia, and sat up straight. Margarita sat a few feet away from the table, her arms folded.

Señora Lopez brought out coffee and cookies on a tray. Only my mother took coffee.

"Have you lived here long?" she asked.

"Yes, I knew Eufrasia well. And were you close?"

My mother stirred her coffee briskly. "We tried to keep in touch. We were out for a visit a year and a half ago."

The shouts of the children filled the next few minutes. I'd thought that knowing Eufrasia would have been enough to start us talking. I hoped Señora Lopez would tell about Abuelo Lupe, but no one mentioned him.

"It is a shame we didn't know her well," my mother said.

"She wasn't an easy woman to get to know."

"I must go," Margarita said. We watched her take long, pounding steps toward the street, her green dress glimmering in the last of the sunlight.

"She fought hard to save the school so the children wouldn't have to bus to town. Not even the government crossed her."

"She was important to the district," Alicia said. "She knew it and wasn't modest about it."

My mother sipped her coffee and Tio Henry said nothing.

"Why was she important?" I said. My mother tried to pinch my leg under the table, but I squirmed out of her reach. My heart beat faster. I thought, let's see what else you've kept from me.

"You see how the houses sit in bunches throughout town?" Señora Lopez said. "That is where the ranch hands lived. When ranching died, many of those people needed help to keep from starving."

"And Abuela gave them money?" I watched my mother's hands.

"She helped with food and laundry and children. The children hated her because she was so strict."

"Why did the tourists start coming?" I said.

"You have such a pretty girl," my mother said. "Such lovely hair."

"Because of the San Diego Exposition in 1915. They came by steam dummy."

"Steam dummy?"

"*Hijo*," my mother said. "Do not bother the señora. It is his schooling. They teach him to ask too many questions."

"A kind of boat?" I said.

My mother grabbed me, digging her fingers into my arm. I decided not to ask anything else. Señora Lopez looked at her with wide eyes and Alicia blushed. "Thank you for everything," Alicia said, "but I'm afraid I must go."

Señora Lopez got up to refill my mother's cup. Tio Henry said he would take some tequila if she had any. My mother watched her go into the house, then turned to the fire. Her face flickered with red light and shadows. "She has many tales, doesn't she? She seems quite happy."

"She is too ignorant to see her condition clearly," Tio Henry said.

She smoothed out her collar. "We were lucky?"

"Lucky our parents escaped Tijuana before they died."

She folded her arms against the cold and gave him a long stare. "I was only thinking of the lies I tell the neighbors." She looked at him as if he were the cause of every bad thing that had ever happened to her.

An older child blindfolded the birthday girl and put a sawed-off broom handle in her hands. Tio drank the last drops of beer from the mug and placed it firmly on the table.

Señora Lopez set a bottle and a glass in front of Tio Henry. The children had gathered around the piñata. One child bobbed it by yanking on the clothesline. The girl swung at the air, grazing the burro. Tio Henry drank shots quickly, refilling the glass every few minutes.

The piñata broke with a crack, and the children scrambled in the gravel. I remembered the *dulces de leche* Alicia had left for the girl and handed them to Señora Lopez.

"We must go," Tio Henry said. He stumbled as he got up, tucking his shirt in at the back of his pants. His drooping eyelids shot open as he heard one of the children scream. Two girls were fighting for one of the prizes. His skin flushed in the firelight. "Margarita." He ran out of the yard, falling once, scrambling, rising again. Señora Lopez went over to the children.

"The old fool," my mother said. "Too much tequila. Go after him."

I found him in the front room of Eufrasia's house, standing among the dust and chunks of plaster.

"*El dinero,*" he said softly.

That was all he said for a long time. Through the window I could see that the hills in the distance had turned from orange to red.

I went into the bedroom after Tio Henry. Alicia sat on the bed, smoothing the pages of the diary. She looked up. "Margarita is the strongest of us. She always gets her way. You should remember that from our childhood." She handed me the diary and I paged through it.

"How?" he said. "How could she cheat us?"

"I caught her just about to leave. She threatened me with her shoe."

I flipped through the pictures in the diary. A wedding ceremony. Some children posing on the sidewalks of Tijuana. And the fight, with signatures on the backs. The actual knockout. Everything I needed.

Alicia brushed her hair back. "*Niño*, how was the girl's party?"

"All right." I was looking at one of the pictures. Abuelo Lupe sending a blow to Dempsey's head.

"I had better go before your tio loses control." She lifted her hand to my hair, but then stopped. "I see you've found what you wanted."

I thumbed through the pages to find more pictures. Three of the actual knockouts. I could probably give one to Jason. And one of Dempsey with his arm around Abuelo Lupe. Probably before the fight. And some others that weren't as clear.

When I looked up, Alicia had gone. I tried to read some of the Spanish in the book, but didn't understand most of it. I saw the checks where I had left them. They were all that Margarita had left. I put them in the cover of the book.

I found Tio Henry at the señora's table again. My mother clenched his arm as he poured another drink. "What is wrong with you? Why must you be so rude?"

When he put the glass to his lips, the rim clicked against his teeth. "We have lost everything," he said. He swirled the drops of liquid at the bottom of the glass.

"No," she said. Her voice was almost cheerful. "You were right. It will be worth it in the end."

"No, *hermanita.*"

A few seconds passed. She watched him with a very small smile on her face. Tears came to her eyes. "Everything?" she whispered.

He leaned into his hands. The muscles in his arms never seemed bigger.

I stood between them, put the book on the table. "We can still cash these." I opened it. "About a thousand dollars."

Tio Henry took the checks. He laughed very quietly. "Worthless, *muchacho.* Just like the old woman's scribblings." He closed the book and tossed it to the fire with the checks in it. I jumped up and reached into the flames. I pulled my arm back, waved my empty hand in the air. Tio poured another drink and watched the book burn. My mother stared at him, her smile nearly gone. The book went black in the flames, and out of the pages a black smoke rose like a ghost escaping.

We sat without saying anything, watching the fire burn low. The torn piñata twisted back and forth on the clothesline. When the sting had left my hand, I felt my pocket for the fifty-dollar bill. It was there—safe, crisp, and neatly folded.

TERMINAL ISLAND

■ Stephen Cooper

The short story brings the news, it has long been realized, and the news is not good. Life is short, cruel, shot through with beauty, and we move bewildered through it. This is a very short story, but the journey it makes is long. It brings to mind Yeats's lines

> *I must lie down where all the ladders start,*
> *In the foul rag-and-bone shop of the heart . . .*

The rag-and-bone shop of the heart becomes emblematically and literally real in Stephen Cooper's "Terminal Island." I like this story very much. It gives us the moment—takes us into that moment—that squalid place with the heartbreaking view from which one can see and hope blindly, forever.

—JOY WILLIAMS

On the Friday after the preinduction letter came I drove my mother down to Long Beach. She had to see the doctor about her eyes, which were going bad. She had been going every week, though it didn't seem to be helping much. I would wait in the waiting room to drive her home. The waiting room was always full of old people who wore dark glasses and held on to their canes. I would skim magazines or nod off if I was loaded.

I wasn't loaded though on this day. I'd been staying straight since getting that letter. I didn't want to show up for my army physical all loaded out. So I found a *National Geographic* with a colored map folded up inside. The map went with an article about this country up in some mountains. The old men there marked their birthdays riding horses through the fields. You could see how fast they galloped by the way the pictures blurred away. These people lived to be a hundred and ten or even twenty and they took great pride in riding as fast or even faster than when they were young.

I was turning the page to read to the end when the door to the waiting room eased open. My mother was feeling her way out along the jamb with both hands. She had skin-tone patches over both her eyes held down with perforated tape. I put the magazine down and gave her my arm to guide her out.

"You get her home and draw those drapes," the doctor said from behind the reception counter.

He was shuffling papers, not even looking out through the glass partition. He was a credit doctor and he worked fast, through lots of patients, in and out. Most of his patients were old. But my mother was still young, only forty-two that summer, even if she was a widow with only one son left, and failing eyes.

"Your hand's so cold," my mother said.

I got her around the plants and the jutting canes and the coffee table, then down the cement stairs outside, one at a time. Out in the parking lot the wind was kicking papers and rocking an empty half-pint back and forth.

"You know what they say about cold hands," she said. She drew her legs inside the car. "My, but it's boiling in here."

We drove then for a while without her talking, which was strange. She usually talked an awful lot with those patches on her eyes. She would talk about the weekend, or the weather, or her book collection of Blue Chip stamps, anything, just to keep from saying nothing. And when we got home I would draw the shades and let her rest. The doctor was putting drops in her eyes which he said might make them burn. But she never said a word about the burning, then or after.

At the railroad crossing near the Edison plant we had to stop for the flashing light. The bell was ringing and the arm was down but there was no train. A gust of wind hit the car broadside. You could feel it lift from the rocker panels.

My mother said, "Raise the roof back home in Texas, that old wind would. Plywood ceiling. You'd see it give, then suck away, like it was breathing."

As if to show me, she took a breath. She held it in for quite some time. When she let it out the bell was ringing and still no train.

"This wind out here, it's pretty stiff but not so gritty," she went on.

"Less dirt out here to blow," I thought to say. "All this black-top everywhere."

The bell stopped ringing and the light turned green and the arm finally hoisted itself back up. I eased my foot back off the clutch and we crossed the tracks.

"There's plenty of dirt out here," she said. "How many thousand acres of Signal oil?"

She must have smelled the oil fields coming up then. The road went along the fields for quite a ways with the working wells and the gumdrop tanks. The air always smelled like they had just repaved the road. Of course they hadn't repaved anything, not one crack or jagged hole. High above the refinery buildings the giant chimney flames burned slanting, pale and almost smokeless against the sky. The air around them shimmered. My mother rolled her window up and folded her hands on her blue print dress.

"Is it true you've gone and joined up in the army?" she asked.

I hadn't told her because I didn't think she'd want to know. I had joined up on the 120-day plan 118 days before. We hit a pothole. The whole seat jerked.

"They got this program," I tried to explain.

"They got a program," she said back.

"It's this deal they got for joining. You learn a trade."

A fancy tank truck cut in front of us. We appeared in its curving, shining chrome. My mother was facing straight ahead with her face held tight that way of hers.

"I told them I want to learn a trade. They said there's no better place to learn. Building bridges. That kind of thing."

The tank truck pulled ahead. Our reflection disappeared. I don't think I believed any more of what I was telling her than the recruiting sergeant who had told me did. He had sat there with his cigarette burning while I figured how I was going to die for joining up. But it's what he had told me and I had listened and now I was telling it to my mother. She sat there by the window taking it in behind those patches. I guess she'd heard it all before, from Pat and Jamie.

"So when's the swearing-in?" she said.

"Not till next week," I said. "Monday morning is the physical. They give you time to get all ready and stuff."

We drove then for a while not talking about that or anything else. For once I wished she'd just go on the way she usually did after the eye doctor. The oil fields stretched a long distance behind the razor-top chain link, a thousand wells all pumping steady in the wind.

Finally, she raised her hands up in the air and folded them tight in front of her mouth. She held them folded there with her knuckles against her lips.

"I've got an idea," she finally said. "Let's don't go straight home just yet."

The fact was that we were already getting pretty close to the projects. I could see across the oil field to the smudged gray line of cinder block. I was pretty sure my mother knew exactly where we were.

"Your eyes don't need the rest?" I said. "You know you're supposed to rest them."

"I've got all night to rest my eyes," she said. "Don't you feel like going someplace different for a change?"

"Sure," I said. How could I blame her? There were just the shades to draw at home. "We go straight home all the time. Today we'll go someplace different."

"So where do you want to go?" she said. "Is it your pick or mine?"

"Anywhere!" I said.

"Then let's get away from these fields. Too much of that tar smell and you just can't think. We'll go someplace with a view, as dumb as it sounds."

So I turned around and drove us past the last of the Signal fields. The smell thinned down in the gusty heat. Sidewalks reappeared with walking people. There were discount houses and barber shops and places that would cash your paycheck with no ID. We passed the shot-up arrow pointing out to the prison on Terminal Island.

"That's better," she said. "I know! Let's drive up the hills there in Palos Verdes, past where all the rich people live. I'll show you a special spot I used to know." She sounded better, not so tight or now-or-never.

"A special spot for what?" I said.

"Where you can see across to Catalina," she said. "Clear to the world-famous Avalon Ballroom. They turn those lights on and when the night's clear you can really see it."

I said, "Fine." The Avalon Ballroom was where you sailed across to dance cheek-to-cheek. It was one of those places from back in the old days, nothing I cared enough about to see its lights. And Catalina was just an island. Nothing special. But I was doing this for my mother, what little I could do, her youngest son. I turned off the boulevard up the winding hill toward Palos Verdes.

The commercial district fell behind and the air turned sweet with eucalyptus. The open hillsides were gold and yellow in the slanting light. We passed some stables and a tile fountain misting rainbows in the wind. I realized how often I must have driven past that fountain and never seen it. My last year in school I would drive up nights to park with girls I hardly knew, Mexican girls who kissed me back and one or two who even let me touch them, though never once did I do what I bragged of back at the projects. That was the other thing I thought would happen in the war.

The last of the guard-gate fancy houses gave way to rolling open country. We turned a curve and the ocean sparkled into view. You could see the whitecaps angling in and a big black tanker steaming south, and when I looked back down at the side of the road there was a peacock.

"We just passed a peacock," I said to my mother. I had seen peacocks at the zoo. "Standing right back there by the side of the road, up on a rock."

My mother sat forward in the seat, as if she could see its folded colors.

"Oh!" she said. "That's lucky. Was he spreading?"

I said, "It was just standing there, looking back."

"Even so," she said, "it's something. Wouldn't you say? I'd say it was."

I was glad I had told her, for it seemed to please her some way deep.

"You know my daddy kept a pair of peafowl back in Texas," she went on. "You didn't know that? Those noisy buggers. They'd keep us up nights with their singing, but he always said they were worth the trouble, just to see."

She was talking easy now, as if she had something to look forward to on the way home later on. She touched the tape around her eyes and then my shoulder with the same two fingers, then she put her arm up on the seat behind my head.

"We're getting warm now, I can tell," she said. "We're almost there."

"You'll have to tell me when," I said. "You're the one who knows the way."

"It's where I used to come out with your father back on Sunday afternoons. Back before you were born, if you can believe that. Pat and Jamie were little boys. We'd bring them along and they would play like crazy. We'd been out from Texas long enough for your dad to find some work. He was working swing there at the tire plant, six days on, Sundays off. We'd come up here different Sundays when we could. I'd pack a picnic, thick ham sandwiches and soda pop for your brothers, and chips, and Pabst Blue Ribbon beer in cans for the two of us. Ice cold. Your father would drink most of the beer himself and I'd drink a can or maybe two and the boys would play and we would take a nap out in the sun."

She leaned back against the seat with the sun now full upon her face. The sun was striking the ocean, making it shine like broken glass. My mother had never spoken much about my father or about her own life, how it was, and so it was strange to hear her talk now as we drove. My father had been killed in an accident at the Goodyear plant when I was two and when Pat and Jamie were seven and six, and she had raised us on her own there in the projects. She'd had some boyfriends but none for serious.

"Tell me when you see the lighthouse coming up," she said. "It'll be to the right, off on a point. Where the U.S. Coast Guard used to have its rifle range."

"If it's tall and white, I guess I see it," I said. "A couple miles, two or three. I didn't think the Coast Guard had to shoot at anything though."

"Now find the place where the road dips down."

I slowed down so I wouldn't miss it. The lighthouse was coming up, no work to do on such a bright clear day. I started thinking my mother must be remembering things all wrong. Then the blacktop dropped from under us, sharp and sudden, so your stomach felt it.

"We're here," my mother said. "Now you can park, just anywhere. It's just a stroll to where I mean. You'll see."

I parked the car down off the road and cut the engine. It was quiet. A bird chirped off somewhere, then another, higher pitched. A whirring bug noise rose and fell upon the wind. My mother opened her door and started to get out. I went around to give her a hand.

"Now," she said. "The wire. There's still wire, isn't there?"

A three-strand fence ran between the road and an unworked field. The field sloped down toward a jagged cliff. After that the ocean stretched for miles.

"There's wire, and a little path," I said.

"You hold the wire and slip me through."

I pressed down the middle strand with my foot and held the top one with both hands. She felt for the top strand and hiked her dress and in one quick down-and-up smooth motion she was through. She stood there for a moment holding the dress up in the wind, waiting for me to climb on through the same way that she had. She seemed different than I was used to seeing her back at home. She looked younger standing there with her long legs bare and that waiting look. Maybe I had never looked at her very close before, but now I did. With those patches on her eyes I could look, and I stood there looking, for a minute, maybe longer, I don't know. I think she knew what I was doing but she didn't say. She just kept standing there.

"Come on," she finally said. "We're almost there."

I climbed through the wire, nearly snagging my shirt. She let go of the blue print hem as I stood up. The wind pressed the flower pattern against her thighs and flung her hair.

"Can you see the island?" she said.

"It's out there."

"You know that song. Let's sing that song."

She took my arm and we walked together down the brushy slope. She sang, "Twenty-six miles across the sea, Santa Catalina is a-waiting for me." The ocean sparkled and a rabbit jumped and a bunch of quail smacked the air breaking cover, and for a time there I almost forgot about the war.

"One time your father brought up his little .410 pump and shot a quail when it flew up in front of us. It flew right straight up in front of us and he shot it down with one good shot. But it was too little to do anything with. The boys they had to touch it and when I got it home it was just nothing, this little shot bird. He never brought his .410 with him after that."

Burrs were catching in my socks and on my mother's dress around her knees. The edge of the cliff was coming up off to the side. It curved around in a wide half-circle above the dark blue of the bay. You could hear the breakers down below and the wind.

"Now wait," my mother said.

She held me back. The edge of the cliff was still ten yards off. A wheeling sea gull banked and held upon the wind.

"To the left is where it should be. Down level with the ground. It's dug in deep so they couldn't see it from on the ocean."

"Who?" I said. "See what?"

"Our place."

To the left was just more brush, a bed of cactus, a slashed-up tire, broken bottles, rusting beer cans. There was a circle of dirt with heat-cracked rocks made black by years of matchbook campfires.

"I don't see anything," I said.

"Look for concrete."

She let go of my arm. I took some steps off to the left. The sea gull's shadow hung in front of me, then veered away. It crossed something light-colored, flat and solid—a slab of concrete, I finally saw. It was overgrown and almost hidden in the brush.

"You mean this thing?" I said. "This concrete slab down here?"

"You found it!" She seemed excited. "Help me over."

"Watch that cactus."

"There's a ladder we used to use."

There was an opening, three feet square, near one square corner of the slab. I kicked a tumbleweed out of the way and saw some numbers. It was a date formed in the concrete, *1942*. I leaned over the opening and saw an iron handhold leading down.

"This is it?" I said. "Your spot?"

"Not up here. Down inside. The view's in there, what you see by looking out."

I could see the space beneath the slab. It was a bunker, square and dim. There were rags and cans and bottles on the floor.

"You go down first. Then you can help me down."

She had one hand behind her head to hold her hair down in the wind. With the other she was clutching at her dress. I wished we'd gone straight home and pulled the shades like we usually did, back to the projects, where there wasn't any view. I was going to the war and I was going to end up getting killed. But I didn't want to touch those rusted rungs down in that hole. Below the cliff the ocean crashed. Another stiff-winged gull streaked by. I was full of fear all of a sudden. The wind felt cold even with the sun. It's all for her, I told myself, and clambered down.

As soon as I climbed down there it was cool and almost damp. I stepped off the bottom rung onto a piece of glass and felt it crack. What light there was came mostly from the slit in the seaward wall. You could see through the slit how thick the concrete was, and then the ocean, a hard bright slash.

"Okay now, help me down," my mother called.

She was standing at the edge of the hole in the low slab ceiling, holding her dress down against the sky. She felt forward with the toe of her sandal until it touched the edge. Then she sat down and swung her legs. She was quick even with those patches. I held her waist while she climbed the rungs down next to me. I could see what the rags were on the floor now, rotten blankets, cast-off underwear. I could barely control the trembling starting up inside.

"What is this place?" I said. "It says 1942."

My mother said, "It was for the war. The Second World one. They built these places to keep an eye out."

"An eye for what?"

"For the invasion they thought would come but never did."

She stood there just in front of me. The wind sifted in through the concrete slit. I didn't know one war from the other. She touched her throat.

"Let's go look out on the view," she said. "You can tell me what you see."

I cleared a way and walked her over. The slit ran right about the level of her eyes. A band of light cut across her face. Her hair tossed back and forth in the shining light.

"Are we there?" she said.

"We're here."

"Then tell me what you see."

I had to stoop. The light was blinding.

"Okay. I see the sky. It's really blue. There's not a cloud. And I see the ocean. Mostly ocean, no invasion. Not today."

She squeezed my hand and said, "Go on. But don't be silly. What else do you see?"

"I see Catalina," I said. "Clear as a bell and long and dark."

She stood there listening while I went on. But I wasn't looking out there anymore. I was looking at my mother, her streaming face in that band of light. In all the years I could remember I had seen her cry only twice before. Once for Pat and once for Jamie, when they were buried. They were buried a year apart but she stood there crying by each one's grave when everybody had left the V.A. cemetery but her and me. Now all I could see were those flesh-tone patches flooding tears.

"You can see it as clear as if we were almost there. By boat—by the Big White Steamship. You can see the mountains, and the town of Avalon, and I'm pretty sure you can see the Avalon Ballroom."

"Without the lights even?" my mother said. "It's not dark yet. Is it, Johnny?"

"No, it's not dark. It's awful clear."

"Oh, baby," she said. "Oh, Johnny. We made you here."

I didn't know what to make of that, or how it mattered, or if it did. But this was her day. We'd come out here instead of going home. I put my hand around her waist and kissed her eyes where they would have been and she didn't turn or take my trembling hand away. I remembered Pat then when we were young and he was the biggest, playing war, and how he and Jamie always ended up in bloody fights. I would stay quiet where I'd been killed while they would argue over whose side won and come to blows before my mother could come rushing out. She would come rushing out and pull them apart where they were rolling around in the thick green ice plant and say "No moaning" to whichever one was crying loudest.

The ocean echoed on the walls and the wind blew in like my brothers' ghosts. My mother kept saying, "I loved you all so much. I loved you all." Even when it got dark she kept on saying it, and when we were in the car again driving home, past the Signal fields with the giant chimneys jetting flame. The sky was orange. It rolled and pulsed, the color of night where I'd always lived. I thought of that peacock staring back at me with its feathers folded. I was going off to war. I thought I was ready for anything. I got us home and pulled the shades and started packing.

THE PIZZA

■ Rebecca Stowe

Rebecca Stowe's "The Pizza" is an account of the last melancholy days of a decayed marriage; it is also a first-rate illustration of how comic symbolism can intensify a narrative fall. "The sauce has separated and formed hard red mounds. The mushrooms have a furry white coating; the pepperoni has curled up into little greasy brown balls"—the pizza disintegrating in the sink is a way into Janice's emotions that is far more assaultive than any direct exposition would be. That dying pizza in the sink—which makes us laugh—is how Stowe's story of the breakup of a loving couple of goodwill gets to tell itself, as if, in fact, there were no author on the scene.

Stowe's story is "modern" in another sense; it belongs to the age of casual divorce, the triumph of ennui and discontent over the lost ideal of permanence. And it is plaintively American in its notion of the available (though receding) bright horizon, that frontier land of the free and easy—one can always push on, leave one's ruins behind, and set out optimistically for, as Janice remarks, "I don't know. Down South. Out West. Maybe even Mexico." Pizza by now is more American than cherry pie—cherry pie once required hot toil within one's own secure hearth, but pizza walks in the door in the cool arms of a delivery boy who doesn't care who you are. No malice, only malaise.

Becky Stowe was a member of a graduate writing seminar I presided over at City College some years ago. Here is her charming, sad, jaunty, painful—and very well-made—"Pizza."

—CYNTHIA OZICK

*W*e are starving.

Fred and I are sitting in our living room; he's in his black recliner, with his legs stretched out, his pants leg dangling over the broken metal frame, hiding the signs of dilapidation. His Marlboro box is on the end table, next to the brass lamp my father's lawyer gave us as a wedding gift. Fred's hands tremble as he reaches for his cigarettes.

I watch from my corner of the couch, my feet wriggling impatiently in the crack between the cushions where the orange slipcover sticks. Fred blows smoke in the air; it forms a curtain between us and we're safe. I too light a cigarette. I tap it in my blue ceramic ashtray: Parco di Principe, Sorrento. I run the white tip of the cigarette along the bumps of the words, molding a sharp white ash. I had wanted to steal it, stick it in my suitcase with the rest of our honeymoon souvenirs, but Fred wouldn't let me. Stealing is stealing, he said, my honorable bridegroom, even if it was only an ashtray. He said he'd buy it for me, but that took all the fun out of it.

I tap my cigarette in the ashtray, clicking the filter against my fingernail. It's the only sound in the apartment—my brazen clicking, echoing off the gray walls.

Fred is annoyed. He peers at me through his smoke. "Well," I hear him say, "are we going to eat or not?" He turns his head and glances out the window, as if the darkness outside is a silent call to dinner.

"I could eat," I admit.

"Make something."

"No."

I am tired, too tired to cook. Fred doesn't want to cook either so we smoke instead. It grows darker and darker as we sit silently smoking; centuries pass before Fred crushes his cigarette and turns his face from the window to me. I don't like to look at him without the smoke; I can't bear his soft brown eyes, his mouth, his goofy lopsided grin. He smiles at me and I look away, across the room to the ugly old console hi-fi, sitting against the wall like a brown packing crate.

"How much money do you have?" he asks.

I count the number of cement blocks from the top of the hi-fi to the ceiling. Eight.

"Eight dollars," I tell him.

"Jesus," he moans, "is that all?"

I don't answer. It's none of his business and I'm sick of fighting over money, sick of him telling me how extravagant I am, sick of his warnings of rainy days, sick of him accusing me, like some Grimm Brother, of being a reckless grasshopper rather than an industrious ant.

"We could order a pizza," he says.

"We could."

I hear him reach for his Marlboros. My Macho Man. He taps the box on the table; without looking I know he takes one, twirls it between his thumb and forefinger, looks at it, cups it in his palm as he reaches for the matches. He'll hold the matches and read the advertisement before he strikes.

"Well, do you want one?"

I wait till I hear him exhale. "I don't care," I say, Fred's little lying wife. I'm so hungry I could eat ten pizzas, a thousand. "I don't care," I tell him again.

"What do you want on it?"

"The usual."

Fred's hands begin to tremble again. He has forgotten "the usual," and he's trying desperately to remember. He knows better than to ask. It doesn't matter, even if he remembered, I'd tell him he was wrong.

"You call," he says, clever Fred. He thinks he's solved the problem but I'm not willing to let him off so easily. "Life can be so easy if you just let it be!" I used to say, but Fred has no trust in things that come easy, even Life itself. And I too am becoming suspicious, although I would never admit it, not to him.

"No," I tell him, "I'm too tired to call. You're closer to the phone, you call."

"Janice," he pleads, "you know what you want. You call."

I turn and smile at him. "But I want *you* to call."

He frowns and crosses his arms over his big chest. I look past him, into the tiny kitchen, where his closed books are piled on the chipped Formica table. There's a notebook there, blank. Fred and I don't discuss them, but neither of us move them. We leave them there to gather dust and silently accuse us.

"I'm going to quit med school," he announced one night, out of the blue. "Why?" I asked, lighting a cigarette. He said he didn't think he wanted to be a doctor, he felt no real commitment. He thought perhaps he'd like to be a writer and I said fine, that was an interesting choice. Was there anything in particular about which he thought he'd like to write? He wasn't sure, but he felt this *need*. Well, I said, I certainly can understand *those*. He slit his eyes and glowered, preparing himself to accept my sarcasm. But I smiled and told him I thought it was a wonderful idea; he should switch over to arts and sciences and get a master's in English, no use wasting all that grant money. He lit a cigarette and dared to smile at me. "Then you don't mind?" he asked and I laughed. "Of course I don't mind. *You're* the one who wanted to heal the sick, not me." He watched me, trying to discover whether I was being serious or sarcastic. "Bitch," he spat, deciding on the latter, and I shrugged.

"Call Dominic's," he says again.

"No."

Through the smoke, Fred's mouth tightens. I look at his scar and remember when I used to sit on his lap and run my finger up and down his chin to feel the tiny lumps between the soft skin and his jaw. "Did it hurt?" I would always ask. "I don't remember," he would murmur as I traced its outline with my tongue.

"If you want a pizza," Fred is saying, "pick up the phone and call."

"You suggested it."

"Do you want a pizza or not?"

I shrug and light another cigarette. "You were the one who wanted dinner," I remind him.

I see his hands shaking and I turn away; I don't want to look at those big hands, so gentle, shaking now with anger, with frustration, with excitement, the excitement of a fight. He always talks about how calm he is; but see how his hands betray him? I say I'm nervous but my hands are steady, except my thumb, which clicks the filter of my cigarette.

"What is the *matter* with you?" Fred demands, but I don't answer. I don't answer *any* of them: my parents, my friends, my colleagues, all of them asking the same question, over and over again until I'm ready to scream. How can they be so stupid? Do they think that I *know*? They tell me I'm ungrateful, they remind me to count my blessings, they tell me how lucky I am. When that doesn't work, they blame themselves: "What have I done?" "Are you mad at me?" No one has done anything; I'm not mad at anyone. "What have you got to be so miserable about?" my mother used to ask and I didn't know then, either. What *does* a ten-year-old have to be miserable about? "She wants to be Queen of the World," my mother once told Fred and he laughed as I stuffed my mouth with a handful of raspberries, raspberries picked especially for me, with my mother's own hands, picked for me because I love them, even if they are hellish to pick, what with all those thorns. "That's right," I told them, savoring my difficult berries, "that's exactly what I want to be. Queen of the World."

"You don't want to call," I finally say, "because you've forgotten what I like on my pizza."

"Oh, Christ," he moans, although the little red blotches are forming on his cheeks. The corners of my mouth begin to twitch.

* * *

I always want to laugh when Fred is angry; when we argue I feel elated, alive, the adrenaline begins to charge through my veins, reminding me of the danger; I could hurt him with my vicious tongue, my little pink saber. I begin to giggle, thinking of myself as Janice, the Saber-Tongued Tiger. How I long to run across the room and jump in Fred's lap: "Look at us!" I would say. "This is ludicrous! Let's be happy!" I look over at him, but he is still glowering, no chance of his finding any amusement in my Tiger pun. I feel my own face grow warm and although I try to hold my mouth firm I'm afraid Fred can see the glee in my eyes.

"Mushrooms," he says softly. "You like mushrooms on your pizza."

I roll my eyes; the defiant adolescent. "That was difficult. I like mushrooms on everything. What else?"

"Onions." His voice is hard and dull. Soon he'll jump up and stand in front of me, shaking his fist threateningly, and I'll have to try not to laugh.

"Very good. And one more thing, Fred. I like *three* things on my pizza."

"Meat."

I exhale and am surrounded by smoke. "What *kind* of meat?"

"Goddamn you!" he screams as he jumps from the recliner. "Goddamn you to hell!"

As he stomps past, he waves his fist at me. I smile up at him, his sweet little wife, and he groans in frustration. I feel the couch sag as he grabs his thick winter coat from the other end. I hear the door slam. As I listen to the sound of his boots crunching away in the snow, I lose the desire to laugh.

I've called Dominic's. It's amazing to me that I can pick up the yellow plastic receiver of my telephone, speak into it, and within half an hour my desire will be granted. It delights me, this magical power, but Fred says I'm just plain crazy.

"You're spending too much time with your students. You're beginning to *act* like a second-grader." "So?" I asked, pulling the cellophane wrapper from my cigarette pack. "I *like* seeing the world through a child's eyes. It fills me with wonder." Fred's sarcastic laugh burned in my ears as he leaned over to light my cigarette. I thanked him. Coldly. "Maybe you should spend more time with people your own age," he suggested, but I'd rather not. I loved my students, I loved all the children in the school. And they loved me with an absolute, unquestioning devotion no adult could possibly give me.

I don't want to think about where Fred has gone, so while I'm waiting for the pizza I count the cement blocks that make up our living-room walls. I count only the whole ones: there are 256. We've lived here two years and I've never washed the walls. Thick, heavy dust lines the crevices between the gray blocks.

The battered linoleum floor is covered by a braided rug, a gift from my mother. We don't have a vacuum cleaner so once a week Fred sweeps it. I sit on the couch with my lesson plans and my books spread on my lap and watch as he pushes the broom across the rug in short, swift strokes. His straight hair falls over his eyes and every few strokes he wrinkles his nose and tosses his head, but his hair falls back over his eyes and I laugh with silent delight, dumb love.

"You should follow him one night," Robin always says, but I have no desire to know what happens to Fred once he leaves our apartment and disappears into the dark void outside. "What if he's seeing another woman?" she asks and I say, "Good, good for him." She too thinks I'm crazy. "Aren't you curious?" she asks and I tell her no, no I'm not curious about what goes on outside my apartment, outside my school. "What is the matter with you?" she asks, reminding me of how much "fun" I used to be. I shrug, despising myself for being a wet blanket, wishing I could crawl out of this hole and go back to being lighthearted and frivolous. She reminds me of how daring I was: "Remember the time you did the cartwheels down the bar at the Alibi?" She recites a list of schoolgirl pranks: the time I marched with the Kiwanis, twirling an invisible baton through downtown North Bay; the time I stole the fetal pig and walked it through the halls on a leash; the time we all piled in my car and started to drive to Tijuana, to find out if there really *was* a woman who fucked donkeys. The time I climbed the lighthouse and couldn't get down and they had to call the fire department; the time we drove to Croswell to enter the Miss Michigan Pickle Contest, and I won; the time we drove to Canada and ended up at a Polish wedding by telling them I was the singer with the band and I sang "She's Too Fat for Me" all night. "I was a real card," I tell her and she's hurt, she wants me to laugh with her, but I can't, not now. "I'm sorry," I say and we sit on the couch, silently holding hands, like a pair of little girls waiting for something to happen.

I walk over to Fred's recliner and sink into the black leather, hiding until the pizza arrives. I pull my legs under myself and cuddle in Fred's chair, still warm from his body. Where is that damn pizza? I laugh, thinking it's funny that I should wonder where the pizza is and not Fred. I tell myself there's probably something significant in that and remind myself to think about it—later.

"If you're so miserable, why don't *you* leave?" Robin asks, levelheaded Robin, but how can I leave him when I still love him, despite the arguments and coldness and the barriers we've built between us. "I love him. He needs me." Robin, levelheaded Robin, says nothing, she simply squeezes my hand and sighs for me.

Why? I might as well ask God as ask myself: Why would God give me love and then make me realize it's not *enough*? "You greedy little bitch," God would say if He were speaking to me, "I give you love and you're not satisfied." He'd shake the heavens with His scorn for me, His hungry child, crying for more. "What *do* you want?" He'd ask. "Well," I'd tell Him, "my mother says I want to be Queen of the World." "What?" He'd thunder, enraged at my grandiosity. "Do you want to be ME?" Hell, no, I'd tell Him, I don't want to take responsibility for all those suffering souls You created, I just want to be happy. "Is that so much to ask?" I would brazenly question. "Is that unreasonable? What kind of a lousy job have *You* done, to create a world in which asking for happiness is asking too much?" "That's not My job," He'd say, shaking His head and turning His back on me. "I gave you life. It's up to *you* to do something with it."

Fred has forgotten his cigarettes. I take one from the box and light it, inhaling Fred's smoke deeply. I watch the tip glow brightly as I suck in the smoke. I bring it close to my palm and feel its heat—I'm so empty, if I touched the hot ash to my palm, I'd ignite like a dry, sun-parched bush; I'd go up in flames and everything in our apartment would burn with me. Fred would come home to find nothing; the cement walls would be all that remained of our gutted life.

"You're so mean to him," Mother says. "Your father would have a fit if I spoke to him the way you speak to poor Fred. I don't know how he stands for it." "Neither do I, Mother, neither do I." She wants to know what he's ever done to me to deserve such treatment. "Nothing," I tell her. She thinks it's disgraceful, but I am Queen of the World and Fred is my servant, my page boy. "Get out!" I command. "Why don't you just *leave* me, Fred, find some nice girl who'll do your laundry for you?" And he goes away, into the void, but he always comes back.

The doorbell is buzzing. The pizza, at last. I get up and slowly walk to the door, wondering if I should run away with the delivery boy; grab him and pull him into our apartment and make love to him on the dusty braided rug. And could he love me, this delivery boy, this bearer of pizzas, could he give me what I need?

I open the door and there he stands: a mere pimpled teenager, the pizza in his arms held out like an offering. I look into his eyes: Could you love me, little boy, could you satisfy my ravenous hunger? Look at me! I silently command, but he's staring at the pizza box, shoving it toward me—Take it, lady, will ya? All right, all right. Run off to your life, little boy, to your football games and proms and drinking parties, have a good time. I hand him a twenty-dollar bill and tell him to keep the change. He finally looks up, confused by my generosity, and I close the door in his face.

I sit in the middle of the rug and open the box. I tear the pizza in half—one for *you*, one for *me*. I've lost my appetite, but I know I have to eat, my grumbling stomach tells me I'm hungry, hollow, but I no longer care about food, about eating. I look down at the pizza and I'm filled with disgust. "This isn't what I *want!*" I scream and my voice echoes off the cement blocks, all 256 of them.

I force myself to pick the mushrooms off my half. "Eat," I say, but the mushrooms taste like rubber and I have to spit them out. I take Fred's half and carry it into the kitchen. I place it in the sink and run the water over it. I leave it there for Fred.

Upstairs, I open his drawer and take out a T-shirt. I take off my own clothes and toss them in a heap in the closet. Fred's T-shirts are huge on me; the sleeves come to my elbows and the bottom comes almost to my knees. I love the feel of the smooth, cool cotton on my naked skin. I climb into bed and giggle—it's Fred last clean T-shirt and he'll be furious. "I thought I told you never to wear my T-shirts to bed. You put lumps in them."

Lumps! I love it! "I'll give *you* a lump, on the head," I teased and he picked me up and carried me up the stairs, but we started laughing so hard he couldn't make it and so we stayed there, laughing on the steps, tickling and teasing and loving one another.

I curl my legs up to my chest and stretch the T-shirt down to my toes. I pull my arms through the sleeves and wrap them around my waist, hugging myself to sleep, covered by Fred's soft T-shirt, his last.

I haven't seen Fred for three days. He comes home at night; I feel him get into bed, but my face is tight against the cold, grainy wall. Sometimes, he reaches out and touches my stiff back. I moan softly and shift position, as I think sleeping people do and I suddenly realize that I've never watched Fred sleep. I wonder, sadly, if I had taken the time to watch him, to see him while he slept, his defenses swept away, whether things would have turned out differently. I watched him only when he was awake; I saw him but I never really looked. I didn't need to. I saw what I wanted to see and that was enough for me.

I left a note for him. "Your dinner is in the sink." Every morning I go downstairs to check to see if the note is still there and it is, untouched, unanswered. We used to leave each other notes all the time, happy newlywed notes, tender, silly love notes left on the kitchen table. I'd get up early to go to school and write Fred love letters as I sat at the table, drinking my coffee. Sometimes,

I'd put on lipstick and kiss the paper—a kiss for sleeping Fred, my sleeping prince.

The pizza is turning white with mold. The sauce has separated and formed hard red mounds. The mushrooms have a furry white coating; the pepperoni has curled up into little greasy brown balls. There's no other food in the apartment. I pick up my dinner on the way home from school: a Big Mac, Kentucky Fried Chicken, a hoagie from the Village Bell. I don't know where, or if, Fred eats. He leaves no clues, no telltale chicken boxes or hamburger wrappers, only the cigarette butts in his ashtray to indicate he's been here.

At night, after I've finished my lesson plans, I go into the kitchen and watch the pizza, waiting for the mold to grow and grow, to devour the pizza, to cover it in a thick mossy blanket. When it's completely covered, so that every single inch of the pizza is white, then I can go.

I pack slowly, carefully. I fold even my underwear. I take two of Fred's T-shirts and place them with my own clothes. I take the suitcase and hide it in the study closet. I'll come back to get the rest later—the wedding gifts, the silver and the crystal. Fred won't want them; he'll be happy with the everyday china and the stainless.

I have called in sick, the first time ever. I drive out to the Arboretum and trudge my way through the snow to the hill overlooking the river and find my way to "our" rock. I'm suddenly overcome with the desire to lie down in the snow, to roll around in it like a dog rolling on a sandy beach: heedlessly, crazily, senselessly, rolling out my aching fury. I look at the naked trees, barren now, no sign of the buds that will pop out soon, surprising us all. I think of how sad it will be this spring, when I come here without Fred, when I have to be surprised alone.

I brush the snow off our rock and sit down and light a cigarette, watching the ice float by in the river, waiting for Fred to leave our apartment, to disappear again.

* * *

Fred's car is gone, but he isn't. I'm surprised, upon entering the apartment, to find him standing at the sink, watching the pizza. When I close the front door, he turns and looks at me—he's been waiting for this. "I'm such a shit," I think, "trying to sneak out like a weasel." We stand staring at each other, knowing this is our last chance. I look at him and I'm so filled with love for him. I can see his love for me in his eyes—so much love for one another, so little for ourselves. Maybe, I think, maybe later. Maybe after . . .

"There's a rotten pizza in the sink, Janice."

I look at him, dumbfounded. Slowly, slowly, I begin to understand and I'm overwhelmed with love for him; relief and love wash over me and I understand.

"Where will you go?" he asks and I shrug. I'll stay here until the end of the school year; find a place in Ann Arbor, stay with friends, something. Then, then maybe I'll take off, go someplace warm, someplace where I don't have to watch things die once a year.

I smile. "I don't know," I say. "Down South. Out West. Maybe even Mexico. Someplace where I don't have to scrape my windshield every morning."

Fred laughs and we stand apart, not daring to touch one another. His hand moves and I think he's reaching for me but instead he opens the drawer next to the sink and pulls out a pair of tarnished silver tongs, another wedding gift from another rich friend of my father's. I don't need to watch. I go upstairs and retrieve my suitcase and when I come back down, Fred is gone, the pizza is gone, even the tongs have disappeared.

I walk into the living room and sit on my corner of the couch, lighting a cigarette and rubbing the match along the bumpy words on the ashtray: Parco di Principe, Sorrento. I pick it up and look at it before I hurl it at the wall. It shatters into a thousand blue bits, falling on the hi-fi like little chunks of sky.

He should have let me steal it.

ONE BLOOD

■ David Walton

This year is the twentieth year that I've been reading Dave Walton's remarkable stories. His distinctly persuasive writer's voice, the florid colorations of his imagination, the instructive irony with which every sentence is charged were well established in me from the time I began writing my own sentences, and have stayed with me—essential—as his work has thrived: two fine books of stories—one of which, Evening Out, *won the first Flannery O'Connor Prize for fiction.*

Here, in "One Blood," he is, as always, telling us how we talk and what that means; how the words we choose, or that choose us, somehow skew and refract, reverse, undersell, even make mockery of what we want to say—what we long to say in order to be our best selves. Everyone in Walton's stories is always trying his best to be good, trying to do right. Such an intelligence is, of course, innately political (what we say privately, in fact, we often address to an implied public), and in this gently, Swiftian epistle to the world, the politics are those of our domestic phobias, those fears and mass dreads that are incompletely controlled by the over-savvy protocols and cool lingo of the family unit, the "cluster," as the story has it. Walton's targets are all clearly marked here. Yet because he is so full of mirthful compassion for us, for our predicament as humans, no one is maimed or even wounded. This is a funny story, after all, even if it's dark at the edges and completely serious. He wins us with his precisions, with the surprises of his invention, with his own peculiar savviness about our life. If you ask me, we should pay attention to this man. He is doing what we want him to do, what we need: he is telling us about us, and in that endeavor he is listening very, very carefully.

—RICHARD FORD

*T*o You Who share Our Concerns—

You will be surprised to see a second letter arriving within a week of the last, but, as you who are used to reading between the lines of our holiday bulletins have no doubt already inferred, this has been a year of changes in the Clark-Nickey household.

We have already written you that Lara Claypool has become unduly modest, not allowing anyone into the bathroom with her and not letting her mother see her undress, which we'd put down to her having to share a room with Lourie Nickey. And even before you'd written us, we had discussed with the girls these blood-sharing cults—which, if you've been following the news lately, have cropped up in New Jersey and one in Memphis that sounds very much like the same thing, so that you should not believe these are exclusively a Pittsburgh phenomenon.

"They are not blood-brother ceremonies," Lara told us then, in that pained-patient way we've all observed ever since Lara Claypool took on for herself the obligation of improving her elders. "And they're not cults, either. They're a demonstration of freedom from that kind of thing," and she seemed so weary with the whole topic that we saw no need for pursuing it.

The Utley boy who we've all been so curious about, by the way, and who Lara keeps referring to as a "workingman" and a "wage earner" and who we've been afraid might be a school dropout, turns out to be a boy from her class, who tells us he picks up a little extra money as a helper for his uncle's construction firm (which sounds like not much more than a pickup and a couple of toolboxes), and who Lara doesn't appear to be all that interested in after all.

One other thing that we need to tell you, which we didn't think to mention in the letter we mailed you last week, is that a boy from the school has killed himself two weeks ago, by cutting his wrists, Carey Solomon was his name. We don't remember Lara ever having mentioned him, and didn't think then it had made much of an impression on her. "He was a weak individual," was all she would say at the time, and shrugged it off, and again we didn't think to pursue it.

Late last Thursday afternoon—which would have been the day after that last letter was written—Mom walked into the girls' room too quick after knocking, or thought there was nobody inside—there's some disagreement now on this point—while Lara was dressing from her bath, and instead of covering her front Lara pulled the bathrobe over her left shoulder, which struck her mother as unusual, and she asked to have a look at that arm.

Lara immediately started complaining about people all the time barging into her room, and pulled the closet door open and tried to move in back of it, but Mom held her ground and insisted on seeing what was on that arm—which turns out are five very deep and carefully made cuts, each one about an inch long and lined up underneath each other about half an inch apart, from the curve of her shoulder to about halfway to the elbow. The top three are healing into welts, the two bottom ones still have scabs on them. None of which Lara would offer her mother any explanation for whatsoever.

It wasn't until late in the evening the two of us were able to discuss this privately, Lourie and Tim were around the house all evening, and initially we'd hoped to resolve this without either of them finding out about it. Strange to say, too, we didn't immediately draw a connection to the stories about the blood cults, which we thought of as fingertip-slice, oath-taking kinds of things, but imagined that maybe there'd been some sort of accident, maybe involving the Utley boy, that Lara had been keeping from everyone.

And, too, at the time only one of us had an actual picture of what these marks looked like, and that one only after a struggle and over the loudest of objections, and when we finally were able to get Lara by herself, she absolutely refused to bare herself to a man not her father, and would not answer any questions we put to her.

All day Friday and all Friday evening Lara and Lourie Nickey and for a time we thought Tim Nickey were sticking together—so we never had a chance to talk to any one of them alone.

Saturday morning we grounded the entire crew, until we could start to get to the bottom of all this.

First of all, Lourie Nickey refuses to bare her arms to either one of us. Lourie has always shown a good deal of reticence in this house around Mom, and we think now that a portion of the distance that has grown up between Lara and her mother develops from Lara sharing her room with Lourie and Mom not wanting to intrude on their privacy. And we had, by the way, noticed that both girls were in long sleeves and wearing sweaters even on warmer days, but again, there's only so much you can react to in family life.

Most of Saturday and Sunday we spent trying to arrange for Sandra and Stuart and then just Sandra to come by the house and talk with Lourie, you will appreciate us not going into all the details of what that finally entailed.

Around 2:00 Saturday afternoon Lara and Lourie locked themselves inside their room and apparently barricaded furniture across the door, refused to answer anything we called in to them, and wouldn't come out until they left the house yesterday morning, that's Monday morning, to go to school. So that most of what we've known up until now has come from Tim Nickey, who at first didn't want to uncover his arms, either, apparently out of loyalty to the girls, but who it turns out hasn't any marks on him at all; and in many ways it's the effect of all this on him that has us the most worried now. None of this has been made easier, we have to tell you, by all the stands we've taken with the children against strip searches in the schools.

According to Tim, who professes to have only the haziest information about them, these groups—there are apparently several different ones at the school, they don't appear to operate under any specific names, or use insignias or any regalia, and loathe the term "cults"—meet every two or three weeks, depending on when they can find a place. We haven't been able to determine if they've ever come here while we were out, but Tim gives his word they've never been to the house while he was home, and says he thinks but is not able to confirm that Christopher Nickey has not been involved.

"That is something I'm not able to confirm," is an answer he keeps giving, but Tim's Old Dad thinks he hears what sounds like a fine line being drawn.

There are five or six members to each cluster they seem to call themselves, boys and girls both, but definitely not couples, and after the cuts are made each one presses against each of the others in turn, so the bloods can mingle. We gather that the limit to how many can belong to a cluster is determined by how quickly the bleeding staunches, and how rapidly they are able to move into place—Tim tells us he "thinks" Lara and Lourie's group has now "worked up to either seven or eight people." It sounds too like part of the procedure is for everyone to be stripped to the waist.

We're anticipating, of course, the kind of impression a great part of this will be having on you, but feel we need to present you with all the information we have, so that at least you will be able to see what we have had to deal with here.

Yesterday—Monday—morning Sandra came by and picked up Lourie and Tim, and while we anticipate that Tim will be back with us in another day or two, for the time being Lourie will be staying with the Lachmans. Sandra's reaction, typically—at the offset at least—was that we all needed to be more "understanding" and "try to see these things more from the child's view of things."

Before Lourie left we sat both girls down and explained to them that while we've always encouraged them to trust in the integrity of their own feelings, right now there are dangerous infections circulating in the bloodstreams of some people in our society, that are by no means confined to those people alone, and while we wouldn't want to ostracize anyone or feel we needed to cloister ourselves, these blood-sharing activities were an unwise and probably unnecessary risk to be taking.

Oh, yes, yes, they both told us, they knew all about that, they'd heard about all that in school, yes, they understood perfectly. Then after Lourie was gone we sat Lara down again and tried to get her to express her own feelings on any of this. We both understood, we made sure that she knew, that at her time of life she might be drawn into associations she might think we might disapprove of, maybe as a way of asserting her own individuality—

Lara snorted at this.

"Like some kind of *club*, you mean? Some sort of peer-group bonding ritual? Is that what you think I'm into?"

Something we learned about by phone from Sandra earlier this afternoon is an incident that occurred on the way back from the courthouse trip in December. Coming down Swissvale Avenue, the bus passed an elderly woman lying on the sidewalk with the side of her face bleeding. This was on one of the first snowy days, along a part where the houses are set up on a bank and have steep steps leading up to them, and she'd apparently taken a fall. There were a number of people standing by, there was no suggestion of her just lying there, but the bus slowed down long enough that all of them got a good look.

Then, coming through Regent Square, they went by another old lady being loaded into the back of an ambulance, her head all bandaged, and when they got back to the school, the teachers, probably wanting to quiet any uneasiness anyone might have experienced, talked to them about calcification and the aging process, and it seems that in this Social Dynamics class they're all taking they go through the whole history of the organism, know all about life stages and body chemistry changes.

A lot of that ties in now with the kind of talk we've been hearing from them lately about "hormonal restlessness" and "outsipid role-model emulation," that up until now we'd been writing off as their typical drollery, like telling us they feel "gruntled" today.

We also learn from another phone call from Sandra just a while ago that Lourie Nickey has only two of these scars and that she dropped out of the group after the second time because she couldn't bear the knife, which sounds like a kind of woodcarver's gouge, and in fact may be. In that Laws and Customs cluster the girls had last year the books had photographs of decorative mutilations in African and aboriginal tribes, and some of that seems to have got caught up in this, too. (Clearly someone is going to need to go down there and conference up with these people about some of their curriculum choices.)

It was on this last point, on Lourie Nickey having abandoned the group, that we were finally able to get a rise out of Lara. Was she trying to show she could be braver than Lourie was? Or did she think she was taking over from where Lourie had failed? Was this, as we've believed on other occasions, Lara Claypool trying to live out the resentments of Lourie Nickey?

This latter notion seemed especially to rile Lara, "I don't need to do for anyone else anything I wouldn't do for myself," she informed us, in that withering tone.

It was Dad who then thought of the Solomon boy, who cut his wrists two weeks ago. "What about him? Is what he did braver? Is that something you'd approve?"

That boy was nothing but a weak individual, she told us again. "He was too small of a person to deny himself. It was his admission of failure, what he did."

A call back to Sandra has confirmed what we were already starting to suspect, that this Solomon boy was part of their same group, and had defiled himself, or believed that he had, and did what he did out of atonement—in a hot bath, Roman style. Every member of these groups Lourie tells Sandra pledges to be and to remain a virgin, to use no needles, to exchange no body fluids with anyone not belonging to the group.

Then what if one of these people has a hereditary or spontaneous infection, Sandra wanted to know, and Lourie is supposed to have said, "Then all will share in his fate."

At the time though it was Dad, always so quick to intuit on these lines of feeling, who said, "And he cared too much about the rest of you to risk contaminating you in the way he thought he'd contaminated himself?"

Lara was nodding and had started to cry, and we gathered her in close to us. And that's why, we told her, though we'd always told her we would support her in whatever choices she made in her life, and were ready to support her in this if this was truly what she needed and wanted for herself, we hoped that first we could all sit down and she would try to tell us exactly how she did feel, and maybe would allow us—but then she started pushing back from us, getting almost frantic and shouting out terrible things, contemptuous things, and ran back up to her room and has barricaded herself in there again. This was two hours ago now, though just in the past half hour or so she's started talking through the door again, first just with Dad, and just in the past few minutes to Mom again, though she's still saying she's getting a bus first thing tomorrow to Cincinnati and living with you two from now on, which the two of us are starting to be reconciled to as the best option, for the time being at least, and maybe as a necessary first step toward healing this breach.

We've been taking turns writing this, on floppy disk, and Dad will have it on CMAIL to you first thing when he goes into the office tomorrow morning, so there will be no surly and belligerent young lady arriving on your porch tomorrow afternoon without prior explanation. And we would suggest that you deal there with Lara and with the things we've been telling you for a day or two, before you try to get back to us with your feelings about all this.

We would suggest, too, that this might be a good time for us to remove the strictures against phone contact we agreed to last summer, which then helped to uncomplicate a situation that was fast becoming insolvable, but this time may well make insolvable a situation that is already complicated enough.

What she yelled running up the stairs was, "You—you can't even contain your secretions," we both agree is what it sounded like, pushing away from us, her mother says, as if she didn't even want us breathing on her.

Lara's mother feels this is the most serious kind of breach, and one likely to endure for years to come—though both of us agree we eventually will have to, and will, find a way of bringing her around. Eventually she'll have to come out of that room, and face us, and say something to us. We who are of a generation that won an entire nation over to bell-bottom cuffs and the metaphysics of truckin' know a thing or two ourselves about life processes. Eventually we'll find a way to make her hear us. Of course we know that in the course of it we may be ourselves the ones who have to change, but we're prepared for that, it's possible we would even welcome that now.

"Possibly it's a time for a change," we've been saying to ourselves for weeks now, in various ways, and possibly this is the way it'll have to come.

But of one thing we're both convinced, and that is that we need to keep a common mind in this, if we expect to have any effect at all.

We look forward to your reply—

IRIS HOLMES

■ Sibyl Johnston

"Iris Holmes" is a story about a damaged child. It is also a story of transformation. Iris herself is transformed by circumstances from what she might have been. Her parents' lives are completely shaken. The author is charged with telling the story "so that Iris will say it's the truth," and the reader, led into this potentially frightening narrative by the calm, utterly trustworthy tone of the prose is changed as well. Sibyl Johnston's fictional account, which alternates between conventional narrative and journal entries, is gentle and uncompromising. Its very clarity seems a gesture of respect for the human dilemma. There is always a sense of the author as stranger to a familial love whose strength is both debilitating and miraculous, yet her perceptions are permanently altered by an attempt to understand and a willingness to feel. In "Iris Holmes," Sibyl Johnston creates four distinct characters and touches on the mysteries of accident and fate, on identity, on the meaning of suffering, on redemption. It is an unforgettable story, and its publication marks the debut of a promising and unusual writer.

—JAYNE ANNE PHILLIPS

*M*y mother, who is an artist, decided once to capture a spiderweb she found on our back porch: a huge, hexagonal, nearly symmetrical one. She wanted to make a painting out of it. She stained a board black, carefully knocked the spider out of its web, and succeeded in trapping the web on the board. Then she sprayed the whole thing with varnish and the web vanished, melted.

Notebook, August 24, 1982. I'm writing out on the patio today, watching Iris while Carolyn bicycles up the canyon to the lake and back.

It rained last night. Damp air swells the cottonwoods like a long breath, fills them with movement and sound. The trees are breathing; the sounds—of them bending in their highest parts, three times higher than our cabins' roofs, of the wing-shaped leaves touching one another—are like rain. And out on the river there is the visual silence, the motion and stillness of dragonflies over the water, their gray reflections coiling on its surface. (I think they shed their wings sometimes; I find broken ones like small tear-shaped windowpanes, all over the ground.) Deeper, the river darkens into vague colors that seem to be more than an effect of light. I can smell and nearly taste the water, leaves, soil, and now and then a rank breath or two: Carolyn and Robert's goat or the Jerseys from the Madsens' farm down the road.

Iris is propped across the table from me in a lawn chair, just sitting there. She's wearing her pink topsiders today, her cords, and the rose-colored T-shirt Robert printed for her—"I Wear This Shirt, Therefore I

Am"—and she's wrapped in one of Carolyn's hand-stitched quilts to ward off the canyon breeze, the river, and a relapse of pneumonia. My notebook, extra pens, and Diet Pepsi are on top of the table; from its round edge, between Iris and me, a spider dangles. It dropped several inches a minute ago—an almost free-fall, an elastic pause like a yo-yo about to ascend. Now it twirls slowly, legs flexing like the fingers of a deaf-mute.

Carolyn and Robert built this patio themselves from rocks they gathered farther up the canyon. The broken edges are fitted to other broken edges; the surface is uneven, and I wonder if Iris's chair would tip if she slid to one side. Carolyn has wedged her in pretty tightly with the quilt, and left me three phone numbers in case anything happens. Iris is easier to watch than most one-year-olds—she doesn't run away, break things, or fall in the river—but then she's also more difficult. She just sits. There's a scar by her eye where one of the chickens ran over her once, just about the only time Carolyn ever left her on the ground.

The spider is building a web between the table's top and leg. It's one of many translucent orange spiders, the kind with round bellies like glass eyes, that make their webs in our windows and across our open doorframes. The Puritans used spiders as metaphors for God. I'm a little afraid of them. When I moved out here I had my cabin fumigated—pointless. The next morning I found the first of many typed spider poems from Robert stuck on my front door:

> *What but design of darkness to appall?—*
> *If design govern in a thing so small?*
> *—Robert Frost*

Now I just brush their webs away with my fingers or let them stay.

The spider gropes across the surface of the table like a blind hand.

Once, a year ago, Robert said he thought God surrounded himself with paradox to keep us from approaching him in any way but by faith.

The day Robert said that was in August of 1981, about a month after Iris's birth. I was in the university bookstore, a modern flat building in which the shapes and proportions of things are noncommittal: neutral colors that leave no memory, fluorescent lighting that casts no shadows, a pale tile floor. And, behind the random noise of several hundred students buying fall textbooks, bland, aimless Muzak.

Across the room Robert was leafing through last week's *New Yorker*. He saw me and began walking toward me. Robert is sturdy and angular, with wiry auburn hair, slate-blue eyes, and a pink-and-white face he doesn't move much. He always speaks precisely, lingering a little on the consonants, which makes each sentence sound simple and self-evident.

We talked about our summers: I had visited home in Illinois; Robert and Carolyn had bought a goat; I had almost cut my hair; Carolyn had had her baby a month early. "How did it go?" I asked him. I hadn't seen them since she was seven months pregnant.

The morning before I'd left for Illinois we'd sat together under the trees, Carolyn laughing, dangling a stick in the water with one hand, the other hand returning now and then near to her middle. I leaned toward her and placed my palm on her; through her flesh I felt pressure, an independent lump. I pulled my hand away; Carolyn smiled. "You're funny, Sibyl." We talked about names, labor, the advantages of natural childbirth; we watched the trees, the river, the dragonflies dipping suddenly, violently, over the water, halting, then dipping and swinging again into motion. Carolyn yawned, stretching, her arms strong and dark, the color and sheen of pecans, the edges of her hair shining white for an instant in the sunlight. The trees slanted out over the river, their bark twisted like elephant's skin around the heartwood. Shadows of the bright new leaves blurred and gently changed the light on Carolyn's arms, her face and hair. She took a deep breath and sighed. The baby had begun to press against her lungs, she said, making her short of breath. Carolyn and Robert had not planned on a honeymoon baby; Robert was unemployed and they had no medical insurance. "I don't know, Sibyl," she said that morning. "I yell and yell at him about getting a job and he just sits there and takes it and then I'm even madder. I've decided to stop worrying about it. We're getting by, I guess. We'll just have to keep getting by after the baby comes." She leaned back in her chair, looking up at the trees and the Kodak-blue Western sky, one hand shading her eyes.

From inside we heard the sounds of Robert fixing breakfast. Carolyn smiled, leaning back in her chair. "Robert's a good cook," she said softly, her fingers caressing her belly. "And you get him between the sheets and he is the best."

The screen door slammed; it was Robert with the breakfast tray. He placed it on the table between us, then pulled out a chair. "I have been remembering, Sibyl, the first time that Carolyn and I visited our midwife. The midwife put an electronic stethoscope on Carolyn's abdomen and we listened to our baby's heartbeat." He poured Carolyn some goat's milk. "At first we heard only Carolyn's body, but after a moment we heard a small sound that reminded me of a train. And this was our child's heart." He was silent for a moment, the white pitcher tipped in the air above his glass. "I could feel it in my soul. I think Carolyn had hoped I would react more visibly, and she might have felt disappointed."

"Well," Robert said now, slowly, "the birth was rather difficult." He stopped, swallowed, glanced down at the floor. Then he continued. "Well, it seems the umbilical cord was wrapped around the baby's neck and she nearly asphyxiated. In fact, when she was born she had turned blue and her heart was not beating. Her Apgar scores were one and four." He paused, looked at me. "Do you know what an Apgar score is?"

"What?" I felt a dull chill. "Did—is she all right?"

"Oh, she lived. In fact we took her out of the incubator today. She was in a coma for two weeks. Our doctor didn't think she would survive. The nurses asked us whether we wanted to change Iris's name so we could save it for our next baby. But Carolyn kept seeing her move. And now she's breathing on her own." Robert took a breath. "One of Iris's doctors told us earlier this week that it looks like Iris's brain was damaged during the birth. So we think she will probably be mentally retarded." Robert cocked his head to one side, tapped two fingers against the wooden stair rail.

"But—Robert, that's awful."

Robert nodded. The skin around his lips and nose was white. Behind him, someone pushing a dolly of books was trying to get past us. Robert turned and we started down the stairs together.

*　　*　　*

Notebook, April 30, 1982, nine months later. Carolyn, Robert, Iris, and I are sitting by the river, on the patio. We are drinking lemonade and I'm taking notes. I have permission to write about Iris: Carolyn said, "Just tell the truth. Tell it so Iris will say it's the truth." She believes we'll all have to face Iris someday.

Robert's garden is beginning to bloom: clover and herbs between the patio's stones, patches of ferns, forget-me-nots, pink impatiens. Fuchsias in hanging baskets and begonias in two cut-off wooden barrels; marigolds and snapdragons around the house, creeping jennie, basket-of-gold. He's built a roof on the chicken coop to protect his garden (and Iris) from the chickens—but now Carolyn's dogs and my cats are warring through the ferns. Carolyn picks up the hose and squirts them, accidentally spraying Robert and me. "Carolyn!" Robert says. He's next to her, holding Iris. Iris flushes, moves her hands, and arches her back. Carolyn turns off the water and bends over them. "I'm sorry, Iris." Then she glances up at us. "See, she knows." Iris is wearing the little bikini Carolyn tells me she surfs in, and the soft terry jacket Robert got her for an early first birthday present.

A bluegill hovers in the shallow water near the bank. The river is full of fish—mostly carp, though. Carolyn is fishing now, trying to catch us breakfast. She can't cast out very far because the trees hang too low over the water and the lines get tangled in them. She wears a loose Mexican dress, bright white with red, blue, and yellow flowers embroidered on the yoke. She's gotten overweight since the birth. Her face is heart-shaped and freckled, her eyes sage-green, her lashes invisibly blond. Her hair is straight and short and blond.

The bluegill flickers in shallow water, seeming to wait, now and then flicking to a different angle. Its shadow wavers on the sand. Robert drops a pebble into the water; the fish vanishes. Robert talks about planting anemones next year, about making a rock garden. He bounces Iris gently on his knee—an exercise designed to teach Iris how to hold up her head, or that she has a head. "Iris is a very strange child," Robert remarks— although, since last summer, Robert and Carolyn have learned more about her: she is blind, her doctors informed them soon after the birth. She is quadriplegic and cerebral-palsied. She now receives Dilantin and phenobarbital several times a day to control otherwise nearly continuous epileptic seizures. Carolyn puts it in the food that she Osterizes and then, four times a day, pours into a plastic syringe with a long, thin tube attached. Then she carefully slides the tube down Iris's throat and into her stomach—since Iris can't swallow, she doesn't gag—and slowly, bit by bit, pumps the food into her.

And one day last fall Carolyn said, "Iris is deaf," and clanged together an iron skillet and a Revere Ware pan till the windowpanes rattled against the sills; Iris didn't move. And—though there may never be a way to test this—all of Iris's doctors now believe that her mental retardation is much more than moderate; that only her brain stem functions. Robert and Carolyn have to control her body temperature, covering or uncovering her to keep it stable.

I closed my notebook as Carolyn began reeling in her fishing line. The water wrinkled into a V, which jerked toward us. "I still can't get a picture in my mind of how she's going to be ten years from now, or twenty years from now, if she lives that long," Carolyn said. The red-and-white bob swung in a shortening arc, flinging water on all of us. Carolyn's hand followed it back and forth, then grasped it and moved along the line down to the hook. She leaned over to pick up a worm from the can by her feet. "Iris's first neurologist just asked us how much she'd changed in the three months since she'd been born, and we said not at all, and he said, 'Well, that's the kind of thing you can expect from her—how she's grown in the last three months is a reflection of how she's going to grow.' " She put the worm on the hook. "Iris's neonatologist just said, 'It's all a question of time, how much time will pass before you find out for sure.' " Carolyn cast out again. The fishing line gleamed, a long, silver bow like the strands of spiderweb that float by randomly sometimes when the sun is out.

"Well, I think we've found out for sure," Robert said, shifting position. The aluminum chair squeaked.

"We don't think she'll progress now," agreed Carolyn. Supporting the fishing rod between her knees and leaning her free arm on Robert's shoulder, she played with Iris's hair, flattening a lock between two fingers and pulling gently. The sunlight turned it silvery-white. Carolyn looked up, her voice quickening. "But you just never know; you just never know how much control she's going to get with her hands, or with her swallowing, or

with anything, because it's just all time. That's the hard part."
She raised her eyebrows apologetically. "Iris is just Iris and that's
how she's going to be, I guess." Her hand followed the curve of
Iris's cheek, gently, to her delicate chin. "The first months, we
were always looking for things that were going to show that she
was going to come out of it—for her all of a sudden to respond a
little to sound, or to us visually . . ." She smiled quickly, touched
a fingertip to Iris's wrist. "She does respond tactilely, though—if
you touch her, she knows, and she wakes up." She trailed the
finger up the inside of Iris's arm; Iris's expression changed: she
blinked slowly, her mouth moved a little—almost a suck—and
her arms flailed toward her face. Carolyn straightened and picked
up the fishing rod again. "That's the hardest part—because parents always try to get answers and doctors don't give answers.
They just say, 'Well, you have to give her a little time, just give
her a little time.' "

She stared steadily at the plastic ball on the water, her face still,
and rested the fishing rod on her knees. Robert shifted Iris on his
lap and put a hand on the back of Carolyn's chair; she turned
away from him to tell me about the specialist they had visited the
day before. Her voice was a little uneven. "Sibyl, a perfect Apgar
score is ten and ten. That doctor said a score of one and four is no
accident."

Robert and I looked at her. "What do you mean?" I said.

"I mean, twenty minutes before Iris was born the nurse couldn't
find a heartbeat . . ." Now her voice was slipping, falling across
sharp edges, diminishing. She paused, then said quietly, "She
was born in secondary apnea—no pulse, no heartbeat, no breathing . . ." She ticked it all off on her fingers. "The cord was
asphyxiating her all that time. Now why didn't somebody do
something?" She sat still for a minute, then leaned back in her
chair. "That doctor says he doesn't believe in the 'brotherhood of
doctors.' He says he thinks we ought to sue."

Robert jiggled Iris some more, looking out over the river,
his face expressionless. Iris sat like a thin Buddha cradled on
her father's lap, blond brows gleaming in the sunlight. Her
pupils seemed to focus, then slid over to one side; doctors had

said she could perceive some light. She grasped Robert's fingers—a reflex.

Maybe they just want to blame someone, I wrote in the margin of my notebook. "Well, I guess you're lucky she didn't die," I said. Carolyn and Robert looked at me for a moment, like they hadn't heard me. "She did die," Carolyn said. *Maybe they need to blame someone.*

I spent much of that spring with Carolyn and Iris, lying across Robert and Carolyn's bed, eating creetchies (Carolyn's name for Rice Krispies Treats, on which she and I binged every week or so), looking up through the windows at the trees and the changing sky, talking, putting off other things, taking notes for my book.

The bedroom walls needed replastering; this was the unfinished, usually unseen, part of the Holmeses' house. The walls were lined with cardboard boxes full of books, stored foods, and back issues of the underground Mormon newsletter Robert edited.

"I had a dream about Iris," I said one day. A water spider moved on the wall behind Carolyn and Iris, and another up in one of the corners. Carolyn had moved the canary in his three-storied bamboo cage over near the window. I pulled off a piece of creetchie, twisting it to sever the gooey strands of marshmallow. "I dreamed she learned to talk. And I remember, I thought, who would ever have expected her to do that?"

Carolyn shifted from her stomach to her side, leaning her head on her arm and stroking Iris's hand. "People dream about Iris," she said. The pitch of her voice drifted down as she spoke, like a sigh or a sound dying out, or something falling. "One time Robert dreamed Iris smiled at him." She propped herself up on one elbow and her face and voice became animated, as if her words were weapons against something: Iris's newest physical therapist, she said, told her Iris's arching her back and stretching when she was uncomfortable was not a cortical brain function—not any kind of communication after all, "Because as far as we know, Iris's cortex doesn't send out any signals"—but a reflex that should have come and gone and come again by now.

"So maybe she doesn't know we're out here, after all?"

Carolyn shrugged, shook her head, smiled a little. "And the latest theory is that this reflex will block her from developing other reflexes—like swallowing—and it will overbuild her back muscles so sooner or later, if we can't stop her, she'll be stuck that way."

Like the older C.P. victims you see in wheelchairs, their backs curved the wrong way like bows, I thought. That would be bad for Iris: her prettiness was an asset. Any person, therapist or not, would be warmer and more patient with a blue-and-silver baby like Iris than with those who looked as bad off as they were.

Outside, the cottonwoods stirred and glittered. The sky was white. A few raindrops hit the windowpanes. I got up and closed the windows; the canary hopped from one perch to another. Carolyn sat up, leaned back against the headboard; she took Iris under the arms, supporting her head so it wouldn't loll, and arranging her in her lap, talking to her in a lilting, penetrating voice. Iris's hearing aid whistled; Carolyn adjusted it. The canary began to sing, an intense, quivering coloratura. Carolyn watched it absentmindedly. "I'm supposed to hold her like this to keep her from extending, for as long as I can every day." She smiled and shook her head again. "Poor Iris. But I feel guilty whenever I'm not doing it . . ." She folded Iris's legs up tailor style, holding the ankles with one hand, then gently pushed Iris's head forward with the other hand. Carolyn's fingers were long and straight, her palms wide. Her hands looked delicate and strong. Her wrists were fleshy. She had gained about forty pounds in the year or so since Iris's birth; now she moved like a pregnant woman again, aware of extra flesh that, in some way, was not part of her. I could see the outlines of bones in the back of her hand as Iris tensed and strained against her palm. Iris's neck reddened. Her arms came up and flailed slightly. Carolyn grabbed them, then hugged her close. "See? She hates it!" She sighed and leaned back against the headboard, still holding Iris like that, trying to hide her hopefulness. We watched the rain for a minute as it washed over the window, bending the landscape. "I think when I go visit my mom this summer I'll get a permanent," Carolyn said. "You know—curly all over?" She laughed. "Robert says I'll look like Harpo." She tilted her head a little to one side and smiled at me again. I thought of Robert smiling across the table at the Humanities banquet this past March, discussing Camus's *The Stranger* over lime meringue pie and twirly vanilla cookies: "The meaning of the cliff is in not jumping." Meticulously, he had scraped the meringue off the lime jello with his fork.

Carolyn continued: she was not happy with what I'd written so far, she said. "You make it sound like I don't love Iris." She handed her to me, showed me how to hold her, then talked about her dying, watching me. "I just can't think of Iris's body being without her. Can you?"

Can I? I thought. "I don't know."

"You should spend some time with retarded children—do some volunteer work or something. It would help your book a lot." I smiled; she reached over and took Iris back, then laughed. "Boy, Sibyl, it's a good thing we're friends."

I agreed politely. "I guess it's hard for me to really feel a lot of these things," I said. At home I had three books of index cards filled with details and ideas about Iris. I had been putting off sorting them because every time I tried, I wound up overwhelmed, in tears. Now, the thought crossed my mind again that maybe I had better just toss them all. This isn't fiction, I thought.

Carolyn reached over to the old trunk beside the bed and picked up a glass picture frame containing photographs of Iris right after she was born. "You might be interested in these," she said. Irony? I looked down at the pictures anyway as she handed them to me; I wrote in my notebook:

Iris in intensive care, lying in a small white plastic box—isolette—ventilator taped over mouth, feeding tube up nose, pins in either side of chest to monitor heart, umbilical catheter in navel for testing oxygen in blood directly from heart. That must have hurt. And did anyone know if it hurt? Nameplate on isolette: Iris Holmes; 7/20/81, 4:29 A.M.; Reg. No. 1020127; Weight: 5 ½; Feeding: B; pink-and-blue cartoon of stock with baby sliding down one leg. Carolyn holding Iris; Robert masked and holding Iris for the first time. Iris's eyelids are lavender. Her fingernails are transparent, like little bits of waxed paper. Carolyn and

Robert touching Iris through an opening in the isolette; Robert's father holding Iris.

When I looked up Carolyn was still staring at me. "It wasn't easy holding her, because of all those tubes," she said. "She was hard to hold."

Carolyn leaned to one side and looked out the window at the river, which was fifteen feet from the house and rising. "If this rain doesn't stop, our landlord says the river is going to overflow its banks and wash us right out of the canyon." Behind her the spider minced delicately along the top of the headboard. The landlord had advised all of us to get some sandbags for that spring.

Carolyn talked on: a box of fifty unreusable plastic tubes for feeding Iris cost $75. Robert had a job interview with Mervyn's that week—a promotional writing job that could take them anywhere in the country, but probably to Texas. Carolyn didn't want to go to Texas—"But honestly, I don't know how we're going to put food on the table." She's asking for something, I thought: What? Robert had been job hunting off and on since before Iris was born. Carolyn, Robert, and Iris lived off the Social Security checks Iris got because she was blind. And nearly every week someone—an acquaintance from church or a friend of the family— left groceries on their doorstep. Carolyn was grateful. "When Iris is not alive we'll be able to do anything we want, but right now we have to find a job with a good insurance policy." She tilted her head, touched her forehead lightly with one finger, then stroked Iris's hair again.

Everything was blurred green through the wet glass. Crocuses were shooting up in the lawn. We both hoped Peg, the Holmeses' German shepherd, wouldn't destroy them before they bloomed. Carolyn jiggled Iris, who was breathing hoarsely, then pulled a plastic tube out of Iris's diaper bag and slid it down her throat. I imagined the pain of something hard and foreign in my throat, my chest. The tube was attached to a plastic vial, from which protruded another tube, which Carolyn put in her mouth and sucked. There was a sound like the dregs of a milk shake, and the vial began to fill with mucus. Carolyn held the vial carefully upright to avoid getting a mouthful. The mucus trap was one way of preventing pneumonia or strangulation. But I still couldn't use it; the last time I'd tried I'd gagged because of the way the air tasted. Carolyn had smiled: "You're not much help, Sibyl."

"You know," she said now, looking up from the tube, "before, whenever something really bad happened, I just figured it would work out, you know, it would get better." She carefully pulled the tube out of Iris's throat and stuck it back in the pink canvas diaper bag. "Iris is a bad thing that didn't get better."

She touched the thin strands of white linen thread in the bedspread, tracing their small repeating square pattern with one finger. "A friend of Robert's mom crocheted this as a wedding present."

"It must have taken her years."

Carolyn leaned forward to look at the pattern. "You know what, though?" she said. "It seems to me more and more that I'm not a normal person." She looked up. "Iris is my salvation from normalcy." Suddenly the spider dropped from the headboard onto her hand. She jerked, shook it off, releasing Iris, who began to arch backward. Carolyn turned her onto her stomach, folding her arms so her face wouldn't press into the bedspread, then took a magazine from the trunk that sat by the bed, aimed, and smashed the spider. "They bite Iris," she said, replacing the magazine. "I pick her up in the morning and she's got red marks all over her and I feel awful."

There was not much anyone who lived near the river could do about the spiders, though; in my cabin one crouched permanently in the corner above my typewriter—every time I got rid of him, he came back again. I usually picked them up in a glass and took them outdoors; Robert left them; and Carolyn smashed them. And at night when I turned out my lights I would usually see three or four more silhouetted at my bedroom window, spinning. Their webs were always empty in the morning, and by afternoon had been blown apart by the breezes.

Carolyn got up to go mix Iris's dinner.

* * *

Notebook, July, 1982, a few months later. Carolyn bathing Iris, Iris's body long, her limbs long and soft and undeveloped. The muscles in her back and abdomen hard, defined. Her feet new, pink and white, never-walked-on, their soles soft and puffy like little pin cushions. I take hold of one and it feels like a hand.

Carolyn lays her naked on the kitchen counter with a folded towel for a pillow, rests one hand on Iris's chest and turns to close the window. Carolyn wears one of Robert's flannel shirts. Her hair, which is longer now, is tied back with a scarf. Iris's arms are bent at the elbow, her hands in fists moving a little in the air around her head. Her legs are crossed at the ankle, her long toes clenched like fingers. (With her clenched toes, Iris can wear thongs better than a lot of one-year-olds, and she owns several pairs, which she often wears with her bikini.) I try to imagine cool ceramic tiles on my back, no sight, no sound. No conscious-ness? Not sounds or colors or shapes, certainly. Tastes? Smells, sen-sations—and a little light. And does she know she perceives that much? Carolyn says blind people are not more sensitive in other ways—they just learn to do without. Iris's eyes, cloudy, impenetrable, slate-blue, are fixed—focused?—and half open. Carolyn strokes Iris's palm with her finger, gently calls her name. Then, slowly, she caresses each limb and Iris's chest, first with burlap, then with a piece of rabbit skin, then with ice. She hopes to teach Iris that she has legs, arms, a face. Iris pulls away from the ice, but with her whole body—possibly a reflex. Her face reddens and contorts. Both arms stiffen and she seems to look slowly around. "Oh . . . !" says Carolyn, her hand in the air near her cheek. "Is she going to do it?" She waves her hand. "Robert!" Iris's mouth opens and she cries—a short exhalation that sounds like a backward gasp. We all applaud her in the morning sunlight. This could become a problem for Iris; everyone loves it so much when she's displeased.

Carolyn squeezes her, touches her cheek to her belly, kisses her on the navel. "You are Ms. Cute!" She picks her up. "Oooh"—through clenched teeth, squeezing her—"what a chunk!" Iris tenses at the water, her back rigidly curved, and Carolyn continues talking softly to her.

Carolyn's kitchen faces east, so now, at ten in the morning, it's filled with light. The water shines on Iris's body and in the air, where it falls like another form of light when Carolyn lifts her hands out of the sink. She lathers up each of Iris's legs, then turns her over. "Look at this," she says. "Iris has the best bum." She squeezes it, rubs the soap over the soft pink skin. Iris tenses, then relaxes. Carolyn turns her around again and sits her back in the water, cradling her head with one arm. Iris's face reddens. She scowls.

After the bath Carolyn pours olive oil on her hands and rubs it into Iris's skin. It works better than lotion, she says, because it's not clammy. "Besides, I really believe the body can absorb things through the skin. It makes sense, doesn't it? This has got to be good for her!" She holds Iris's arm up by the hand, wraps her oily fingers around it, and massages it. She bends the arm at the elbow, the wrist, the finger joints—an exercise to keep Iris's muscles from atrophying. The doctors say Iris is beginning to get contractures in her elbows, her wrists, her hips; Carolyn must exercise her to prevent her limbs from folding up like little birds' wings. "See? She loves it! Look how loose she is!" Again she leans over her. "Mmm, smell her now!"

"Give the girl a pimiento," says Robert.

Robert pushed open my screen door one night that August, letting in several big moths and—I hoped—no spiders. "Carolyn has just returned from her visit home and we were thinking, wouldn't a Reuben sandwich be nice? And I said, well, we must get Sibyl. She'll never forgive us if we go for Reuben sandwiches without her. Want to come?"

Wells Drive Inn was looped in cursive on a pink-and-aqua aluminum sign outside the restaurant, *Reuben Sandwich* printed in black beneath it. Wells' was a loose arrangement of brown-and-black obtuse angles. Inside, the walls were pine, stained to look like cedar and hung with twine macramé owls and planters.

"Diefenbachia," Robert observed.

We ordered our sandwiches and picked up our Cokes from Mr. Wells, and Carolyn, carrying Iris, made for the Ms. Pac Man machine in the corner near our table. She placed Iris in her carrier on the floor, then turned to the machine, deposited a quarter, and began jerking the lever up and down, back and forth, guiding Ms. Pac Man through the iridescent maze on the black screen. "So what kind of a job are you looking for?" I asked Robert, snapping the plastic lid off my Coke. A thin woman in an orange coat pushed open the door behind him, followed by two little boys.

"Well," Robert said, watching them as they crossed to the counter, "I interviewed with a company the other day who wanted to hire an advertising copywriter."

The thin woman leaned across the counter, talking to the cook as he grilled our sandwiches. Her children twisted the knobs on the Rubik's Cube machine near Carolyn.

"M-m-my name's not Mike!" said one. "W-we changed names."

"Okay."

"He's sixty pounds now," the woman told the cook. "I don't think either one of us wants to carry that around—"

"M-my name's Matt, y-your n-n-name's—"

The woman looked around. "Matthew. Michael." She glanced down at Iris.

One boy leaned away from the other, arching his back to look upside down at his mother. "When I grow up I'm going to change my name to Stan-ley." Robert watched the little boy, almost smiling.

Carolyn's postcard the week before had asked me whether Robert had found a job yet. That was the deal—he was supposed to be working by the time she and Iris returned from visiting Carolyn's parents. I had never relayed the question. Robert had spent the week gardening, fishing, taking Peg for runs and the little boys from church for swimming lessons, visiting me, closing all the doors and windows and listening to classical music full blast. In a way, I didn't blame him—with a résumé that included a B.A. in Humanities, two years of assisting in the university's international film program, five years of raising orchids, and the additional skill of goat milking, the only jobs he could get were the ones that would make him most miserable. And Iris's bills were insurmountable anyway, unless he found a job with insurance—again, the kind of job he didn't want. He had swum up to my back porch the day before and hung there, talking about Carolyn's visit home, writer's block, the English department, his hair glossed flat and burgundy-gold in the streaks of light that fell through spaces in the trees and made shadowy light places on the river, places where you could see into the water. The sharp, pale little freckles on his arms and shoulders looked like they were being washed away, and the skin on his nose and his shoulders was turning pink. "One redhead to another," I had said, "you're going to burn."

After a while the porch had gotten all wet where he hung on, there were goose bumps on his arms, and his lips looked purplish. He pushed off from the porch, treading water. His chest looked whitish-green under the water and seemed to bend off at an odd angle before disappearing into the river.

Peg had gotten twisted up in her leash by the back door and started to whine. "Margaret, are you grieving?" said Robert, and began a sidestroke toward the shore to save her.

Ms. Pac Man bleeped and blurped. The freckled woman walked over to look in Iris's carrier. "Pretty baby," she said to Carolyn's back.

Carolyn glanced over her shoulder, then turned quickly back to the machine. "Damn! He got me!"

"When I grow up I'm going to change my name to Stan-ley."

"So you'd be writing newspaper ads and stuff?" I asked.

"Well, yes, and probably composing letters and working on ad campaigns, that sort of . . ." After a moment, the rest of his breath came out in a sigh. Robert looked around the room. "Oh, hell," he said. "I'm not looking for a job."

"About four months?" the woman persisted, her finger in Iris's hand.

Carolyn let go of the lever and shifted her weight onto the other foot. She looked up but did not turn around. "She's a year."

"Oh . . ."

Carolyn didn't wait for the inevitable next question. She turned sharply from the machine and told the woman, whose face was now slack, as if waiting for a punch line or the end of an unfinishable sentence, "Cerebral palsy."

Robert smiled calmly, his lips closed and his eyes wide open, looking at the woman and at Carolyn, who looked back at him. Mr. Wells called out our number and Carolyn picked up Iris and went to get the sandwiches.

"Robert tell you we're moving south?" she said after she put Iris down on the empty chair, distributed the sandwiches, and sat down herself. "Our lawyer says the case will be stronger if we can get it into a federal court, but the only way to do that is for one party to be living out of state. So we have to go by March first."

"If we decide to move," said Robert.

"Robert doesn't want to leave the old homestead."

My sandwich was oily, tangy, rye vapors in my throat and nose. I moved my straw around in the ice of my drink. "Why would federal court be better, Carolyn?"

"Oh, you know, he just thinks it'll be more professional and quicker. And the county where the federal cases are tried is more liberal than this one, and he thinks a liberal jury'll be in our favor. Besides, if we file here we'll be attacking one of the city's main employers and one of their most prominent doctors, and a good lawyer would use that against us. That's why we have to move, basically."

And because here, Carolyn never wanted to take Iris out alone, she wanted to take a vacation from church and other people's questions, she wanted to leave. In addition to the strangers who asked what was wrong with her baby, there were old friends she couldn't face without breaking down; the welfare representative who wanted to see Iris because—we could only assume—she suspected Carolyn of child abuse; Carolyn's obstetrician, who interpreted Iris's problems and their causes differently than Carolyn did; and a long line of well-meaning visitors who almost invariably told Carolyn and Robert what special people they must be to have been given such a responsibility—to which Carolyn had begun responding as she had to me: "You can be special too. Why don't you go volunteer to hold some little retarded babies for an hour a week?" There was Iris's doctor, "the meanest pediatrician in the state," who took one look at Iris and told Carolyn, "That kid's brain is rotten." Carolyn had had to find a place to pull over and cry on her way home from his office. There was Robert's younger brother, just home from being a missionary in Argentina, who asked in complete innocence, "Well, why haven't you healed her?" And there was the day Robert, in a sentimental mood, asked Carolyn, "But would you really want her any different?" Carolyn stopped what she was doing, stared at him, and then gasped, "Yes!" and started crying and couldn't stop for half an hour. "I thought I'd finished that," she apologized afterward.

On the other hand, there was the pharmacist who filled Iris's prescriptions: "She just looked at me—like she knew everything about Iris—and said, 'You take good care of that baby.' I guess she might have known a lot by what drugs we needed. But I don't know—I wouldn't be surprised if she had a baby like Iris." And there was Carolyn and Robert's lawyer, "the toughest, most ruthless lawyer around—that's why we got him," who Carolyn had disliked until once, when she couldn't answer a question about the birth, he had said, "There's no hurry. I lost a son last year in a plane crash." There was Carolyn's childbirth instructor, who had taken herbs and seen doctors and prayed throughout her pregnancy because—again—she was hemorrhaging, and whose baby had been born, brain-damaged, the same day as Iris, and then died. She had buried him where she could see the grave from her house, and now brought Carolyn a big bag of groceries once a month—always "anonymously." There was Carolyn's bishop, who had handed her a check for $1,600 to cover Iris's latest hospital bill. And there was the fact that, when all Iris's other doctors had given up, her insensitive, unsympathetic pediatrician had pulled her through six bouts of pneumonia and never billed Carolyn.

My Coke left watery brown circles on the gold-flecked Formica table. "So you think for sure you want to leave?"

Carolyn glanced at Robert, who said nothing. "We're not sure." She pushed her chair back suddenly and walked toward the ladies' room. "Back in a second."

Robert placed both hands flat on the table and closed his eyes. "I would like to write a story," he said, "about a couple who have a baby, and the baby is retarded, and so the parents wonder why, if God is omniscient and omnipotent, did that happen? But then they come to realize that it was the doctor's fault. So, they start believing in God again, and attending church, and praying that they will win their malpractice suit so they'll be rich the rest of their lives." He opened his eyes and looked at me. Behind him, on the plate-glass window across the room, we were reflected in faint, colorless lines and planes, like ghosts on the night outside. *Breakfast Is Coming*, said the sign on the Hi-Spot across the street. *Entrance* was painted backwards on the door. Don't bother, Robert, I thought; I'm already writing it.

Carolyn was back. "Rob, does Iris have dreams?" Robert moved his eyes to look up at her. "No, really—what do you think she dreams about?"

"Angels," said Robert.

Notebook, August 30, 1982. Carolyn has returned from her bike ride. She bends over, shakes her head and arms out, reaches for her toes. "Ohh," she says, straightening. She pushes her hair back from her face, twisting it up off her neck, then lets it fall. The permanent is starting to grow out now; her hair is smooth and brown on top. Her face and neck are flushed, her freckles invisible. Her skin is damp, silvery at the edges in the late summer light. She picks Iris up, carrying her with one arm, and I follow her up the bank and through her back door. Inside, the air is still, warm, human-smelling. The phone is ringing. Carolyn's Adidases scweech on the gray-painted floor as she turns on the cold water. "Don't answer it," she reminds me. She has been too exhausted lately to want to talk much. It keeps ringing. The water splatters on the porcelain, glassing around her fingers. When it is cold enough she fills two pewter mugs and hands me one. Then she walks into the living room to get Iris's wheelchair—a fancy, $1,200 model with seat belts, a back that adjusts to her shoulder height and leg length, a footrest to keep her legs bent, pads to hold her back and head straight, restraints to keep her legs from scissoring. Two of its parts were especially made for Iris. The wheelchair was paid for by welfare, is described by Robert as "the most expensive thing we own, practically," and is rarely used because Carolyn is embarrassed by it: "I feel like putting a sign on the back: 'Yes, she's retarded.' " But the chair does hold Iris in the right position so Carolyn doesn't have to, and she will be able to use it for years—maybe all her life.

Carolyn wheels Iris into the kitchen, then sits down across the square oak table from me. Its surface, waxed and unvarnished, is cool and smooth as skin. It absorbs and diffuses light rather than reflecting it. The phone stops ringing and Carolyn unplugs it. "Some woman from the Children's Hospital called last week to ask for a donation," she tells me. They got to talking and the woman told Carolyn that her little boy was born with spina bifida. "She was so . . . cold," Carolyn says. "She just rattled on and on about how her son would learn to control his bowels. And I'll never forget—just before she hangs up she puts on this testimony-meeting voice and she says, 'Carolyn, God doesn't make mistakes.' "

Carolyn leans her elbows on the table for a moment. Then she whispers, "I wish somebody knew how I feel." I think of Robert reading aloud by the river: "Behold, I cry out of wrong but I am not heard; I cry aloud, but there is no judgment."

It is beginning to get dark. Fragments of the sunset float on the water, amorphous but stationary. Dark, vivid twigs, leaves, branches tangle against the sky. A heron passes, flying low along the water, slow-winged in the way that very large things are slow, legato, wing feathers gilded with sun. It follows the river, bending with it into the trees away from the road. Half of Iris's face is in the light; her mouth is a small curved shadow; her brow, her cheekbone, her chin cast shadows. Her legs, slender and swollen at the knee, are bent; she sits like a grown person in her chair and for a moment I feel time passing; I can see Iris five, ten, twenty years from now—in this room, in this chair. She is nearly silent, her eyes half open and glaring sideways. We can hear her breathing. "People don't see Iris," I realize suddenly. "They only see what she means to them."

Carolyn's face doesn't change. "What does she mean to you?" she asks. She leans forward, rocking back and forth on her elbows. On the window behind her the spiders are beginning to spin.

Robert has said that Iris more than anyone is a prisoner of her body. Sitting in the darkening kitchen, I think, What does Iris mean? Her image on my retina? The bite she takes out of my vision of things? What should I make of her? "I guess Iris . . . embodies questions I can't answer."

Carolyn glances up at me, then takes a quick breath and looks around the room and down at the table, running her fingers gently over the cool pewter mug. "Embodies questions?" she whispers.

I look at her hands, white on the rough metal cup in the last sunlight. "Carolyn, we're just trying to protect ourselves—that's really all."

"But I can't protect myself—I live with her." She looks at me. "Have you ever tried to know?"

It is nearly dark in the kitchen; there is only the faint gleaming of Iris's wheelchair, the mugs, the windows.

Carolyn pushes herself tiredly up from the table and turns away from me, to fix Iris's dinner.

THE SLEEVES

■ Lynn Grossman

I can tell you all about Lynn Grossman. I have never had a drink with her, nor a coffee with her, nor shared even as little (as much?) as a subway ride with her, but I am still willing to keep my shoulder to the assertion that I know all about Lynn Grossman. But you must not think that I think that it is because she has been, and still is, a student of mine that I think I know all about Lynn Grossman. You see, I am not that kind of teacher and Lynn Grossman is not that kind of student—meaning that for each of us the object is the story and not the person. Yet I am still offering you my claim to complete knowledge of Lynn Grossman. Indeed, the reason I am so insistent as to the necessity of your hearing my claim is this—to wit, there is for me no way to pay a higher compliment to the force of a story. I mean that when a story does its work, there issues from it the hard mark of its maker. I mean that when Lynn Grossman made "The Sleeves" the force it is, she disclosed her heart for the singularity it is. I mean that I am glad to receive the exception of that heart—and to have the teacher's honor of passing it along to you.

—GORDON LISH

*T*his all starts when my Wednesday cuts me back half-day from full-day.

Half-day's not time for doing a whole house right plus laundry, so I ask Mavis if she knows another Wednesday, but Mavis is looking for a Tuesday herself.

And just when I'm working up the nerve to quit my Wednesday, my Wednesday says forget about the shirts.

What do I care? Mavis says. A job's a job.

First half-day, my Wednesday's got soap suds coming out the top of the machine.

Second half-day, I smell the burn from the iron when I come to work.

I ought to see it coming.

Next half-day my Wednesday comes up to me real sweet and says, "Help me with the shirts, will you please, Ida?"

"Sure, sugar," I say, "Soon as I finish the house," and then I work real slow, so by the time half-day rolls around, I'm only just through the upstairs bathroom.

My Wednesday buys this new laundry soap. On the box it says Love Smells Like Fresh Laundry. "That means love smells like work," I say to Mavis.

"Let his new one do the no-good shirts," I say.

Mavis says half-day's a half-day more than no day, so next time my Wednesday asks, I say okay about the shirts.

* * *

My Wednesday's got the shirts emptied onto the kitchen counter. The shirts are all rolled up tight into themselves like big fists, and the sleeves are knotted around the rolls—double knotted, some of them.

"Oh my, sugar," I say to my Wednesday, "that's no way to treat a shirt," but I know that's the way she gets them.

We set about freeing the sleeves.

The pre-soak's just some bleach in hot water for the white ones.

I count five shirts, including a knit one we throw in with the sheets.

The wringing we do at the sink. We split it up sleeve and tail, sleeve and tail. I stand still and my Wednesday twists the shirt around and around, loose at first, to get rid of most of the water, then tighter and tighter until the drips coming off the shirt are almost as small as nothing.

"No time for vacuuming, all this wringing," I say to my Wednesday. "No time for dusting, too."

Pre-soak's too good, if you ask me.

The thing about other people's laundry is it's got a certain smell.

This time it's three shirts.

This time I get through the dusting.

This time my Wednesday wants to scrub the collar and the cuffs.

"Oh, sugar, won't that look extra fine," I say to my Wednesday.

"When it comes to men, some women are dumber than others," I say to Mavis.

"When it comes to men, you ought to know," Mavis says to me.

The shirts come out of the machine twisted into things that do not look like shirts.

When I change out of my working clothes in the bathroom off

the kitchen, my Wednesday's got the shirts hanging out to dry on the shower curtain rod. When I open the door, the shirts wave in the breeze like somebody's already in them.

The dirty smell is not the smell I mean. It's the people smell I mean.

Each of the shirts he gives her smells different, flowers and sweet things, and smells like that. It's not hard to tell on the shirts. Three smells, three women.

"You hold, Ida," my Wednesday says to me. "You hold and I'll twist."

She twists and she twists the shirts until I have to tell her to stop twisting.

"Not much cleaning time half-day," I say to my Wednesday, "what with me helping with the shirts and all."

"For a man like that," I tell Mavis, "I'd just as soon eat those shirts as wash them."

My Wednesday's got a shirt on the ironing board and she's pushing down real hard on the iron like she is going to strangulate the shirt.

"Here, sugar, let me do that," I say. "It's the heat that ought to do the work, not you," I say.

The sleeves on the shirt are hanging limp on both sides of the ironing board like a man giving up.

"No thank you, Ida," my Wednesday says to me and keeps pushing the iron, so I start in on the kitchen.

I'm doing the stove when I hear the spray starch sound, hiss hiss hiss.

"Jesus on the Mount," I say to myself, because it sounds like a lot of starch to me, and I turn around to say out loud, and that is when I see what I see.

I see my Wednesday spray the shirt with her perfume, and then I see her iron in the smell.

I mean to tell this to Mavis, but when I see Mavis, Mavis tells me she's got a new Tuesday, thirty full-day plus bus fare, so I forget.

* * *

The sleeves are what is tricky on a shirt.

For the sleeves, my Wednesday's got a different board shaped like the big board only smaller, and skinny enough to fit a sleeve on.

My Wednesday sets the small board on top of the big board and then she slides a sleeve on, and then she irons and turns, irons and turns until the sleeve is done all the way around.

When I did the sleeves I used the tip of the iron around the button part. The way my Wednesday does the sleeves is flat iron all the way.

Today what my Wednesday's got is one shirt.

We wring it out over the sink, and this time I give her twist for twist. We twist this one until we ache. Until I ache, at least.

My Wednesday pre-soaks and scrubs and twists and does the machine, then when she's done, she does the whole thing all over again.

Second time through, I won't do the twisting with her.

It takes my Wednesday a full half-day to do the shirt.

The way it ends is I tell my Wednesday I'm sorry but I've got a full Wednesday starting next time.

And when I tell Mavis I need a new Wednesday, Mavis says I'm a bubble-headed fool to quit when it's down to just one shirt, because now that it's just the house and one shirt, half-day's not bad time at all.

WE FIND HARRIS AGAIN

■ Michele Owens

Michele Owens tells "We Find Harris Again" in idiomatic American English, with its familiar cadences, its homely colloquialisms, as provincial and consoling as a kitchen. Her characters "had to laugh" and are "just as glad," unmistakably marking them with a time near our own. The narrator is a perplexed and oddly endearing mother, following her hard daughter's romance with a man named Harris. But it is Owens's gift to show us a Harris and a Cindy who are not only the boy next door and the pretty girl who, in high school, was "the balls," but also figures as emblematic and mythic as those in Sam Shepard's and William Wyler's America. And all their larger-than-life adventures are followed by the weariless and pitch-perfect mother, who tells us "Well, this was definitely no cowboy" when we meet Harris in King City, California, under a hot sky, a "shaggy factory."

We come to know a suburban America where the boy next door bangs out dented fenders and washtubs in backyards and falls in love with Cindy by "hilariously setting ice cream afire" at four in the morning in her family's kitchen.

Our narrator is a guarded romantic, with endless capacities for generosity and expansion. She owns a small personnel agency. "I liked placing secretaries," she says, "getting them to tone down the eye makeup and delusions of grandeur and showing them how to please a boss." She uses phrases like "weak-handled love" and "distended daughter"; dares statements like: "No one can steer a course by a baby, which offers the most variable of destinations. But Cindy never gave up the wheel. No, you have to live for the smell of a fresh-powdered bottom and for the sudden drizzly smiles against your shoulder. At the root of all that is womanly, it seems to me, is a deep appreciation for the inadvertent." She tells us, "I was tired of King City, but I believe in love, which is why I left my husband and why at forty-nine I am still a pretty woman."

But the story is not about the narrator's romance, but about her ideals, which change, watching her daughter's life with Harris. Owens's language, full of quirks and economy, rings with authenticity and humor as these romantic figures fall in their more dimensional and humane mother's eyes.

In a small garage apartment with a baby, Cindy "made the day into an endless breakfast."

Harris's broad hands worked "restorative magic on the ancient toasters and gummy steam irons and irregular clocks he'd saved from abandonment."

I especially like Owens's dialogue. "Look, Cindy, I was not a one-man show of a mother," Harris says.

"You can't take that Frankenstein car of Harris's," our narrator says, always the mother.

"It's like the day before you were born," someone says, of the salty, slick, unclear Mexican Pacific.

While Owens writes in a nuanced, crooked, distinct American voice, her story is finally not about style or timbre, about any gentle emotional shift. It is bigger than that, more risky. The narrator takes on romanticism, in its peculiar American movie shadings, and changes by the story's end. Though a romantic, our narrator finally tells a moral story. We close on the end of a promise.

"The two of them looked pretty grand as they walked off into the King City sun," she says. "The sight of it made me sick."

—MONA SIMPSON

*A*fter three weeks on the road in a tiny car, our limbs were in rebellion. So when Harris's elderly landlady looked up from her hose and said, "You're going to have to go looking for him. He's probably got his head in some garbage can in town," we were just as glad. Keeping the most casual eye out for Harris, my grown daughter Cindy and I stretched our legs. We walked and walked, long past the quaint Western center of King City, California, far onto the ugly blacktop of local industry. At the back side of a pipe factory, I saw a man scramble down a fence, large sections of blue tubing under his arm and in the way. "Honey, that's him," I said.

Cindy squinted. "Yeah, I guess."

Well, this was definitely no cowboy who dismounted the factory. Blue shorts drooped and red Keds stumbled. It was Harris all right, with the same dopey style and powerful chest of old. He saw us, too, and he came towards us with a face that hadn't seen a razor in a few days, with dragging blue shrink wire and a powerful sweat in the mighty western summer.

"Harris," Cindy laughed.

Harris just flicked the toothpick in his teeth, and it seemed like a warning that even if he did look stupid, she wasn't going to get off easy. She'd once been pretty crazily stuck on Harris.

"Surprised?" I said.

"Well, I woke up this morning and when I thought I'd do a little trash digging to start the day, you ladies were the last thing I expected to come up with," he boomed. Harris rubbed his hands across his T-shirt as he broadened his chest. Then he lifted those arms high and stretched that back wide and chewed that rakish toothpick. Although there was a lot of sad history to remember, I just had to laugh at the sight of him. He was as attractive a young man now as he'd been six years ago when he was my daughter's lover. I'd liked Harris more than I would let on then as he'd lie on his back in the den, toes wiggling above him, conversing calmly with my incensed husband. Now Harris has a little baldness on top, but that, like his awful clothes, only points to the preeminence of his legs, his arms, his back, and his beautiful, beautiful eyes. Harris scratched his head and then kissed my cheek. "Good to see you, Mother."

He and my daughter had had a child, long since out of the picture for Cindy. It was an awkward meeting for the two of them. Cindy's usually direct gaze was scattered upon the hot sky, the shaggy factory, and the various points of interest of the Harris before her. It had been my idea, before we started our vacation, to call Harris's parents and get his address. Cindy had given her grunt of an okay to looking him up and I not only hadn't tried to discuss it further, I let it take us three weeks to get from Connecticut to California, I was making such a point of not making a beeline. Harris invited us for dinner, I suppose to give himself time to figure out what to do with us, and then drove quickly off in that patchwork car of his.

"Jesus," Cindy said, tears advancing and retreating on the syllables.

"Harris looks good," I said.

"Harris always looks good." My daughter has prominent teeth which bite her words and give a calcified validity to her meaning.

My daughter met Harris when she was a senior in high school. In those days there were always big boys in our kitchen who thought she was the balls—she had square shoulders, she was honest and dignified, and she dressed just like them. I think before Harris, though, they admired her more than romanced her; her adventures until then seemed more boy's life than true love. A very steamed policeman once brought my red-eyed daughter home from smoking and making out on the golf course. Cindy's buddy had run off into the woods, but Cindy was more interested in antagonizing the policeman than in wondering what happened to the boyfriend. "Don't you have any traffic violations to take care of?" was the first thing she said after the officer shoved her into our foyer. At 5 A.M., in my bathrobe, I had to sweet-talk the man out of my house. Sometimes the curl of Cindy's lip was bratty, sometimes it was full of the God's honest truth. When Cindy would lean in the doorway of my bathroom as I stabbed myself in the eye with mascara and she'd say, "Your husband's totally confused out here. He has no idea what's wrong with you," she'd make me ashamed of my entire everything.

We lived in a comfortable house in Storrs and Harris was a junior at the University of Connecticut. They met each other at some bar and suited each other well, long strides and laconic tones. With more backbone than a parent could wish for in a child's love interest, Harris wasn't too happy at school. He was a fine arts major and when I'd ask him about some famous art history professor, he'd drum his fingers on his sternum and say, "That fucking guy knows all the big sweeps and nothing about painting."

"School teaches you nothing you couldn't learn better on your own," he'd say as he banged out dented fenders and washtubs in our backyard. It was particularly difficult for my husband to watch Cindy's frowns grow harder, the more of Harris's do-it-yourself rhetoric she heard. Her father has a great sense of the dangers of unreasonable behavior and a restricted sense of what's reasonable. Shuffling above the oil-stained, grease-brown, and ever-handy Harris, the poor man was caught between beholdenness and dislike. So when my husband came into the kitchen at four in the morning to find the pair hilariously setting ice cream afire, all he could do was nod and scratch his head. A little scalp under his fingernails was not much satisfaction, for he thought he was watching the sloppy wreck of his daughter.

Harris troubled me, too, as he carried baskets of wet leaves off my lawn, though I liked Harris in secret. I was not sure it was so bad for Cindy to have a little jolt to her veteran and unsurprised bearing. My feeling for my daughter is a constant struggle between empathy and concern. I liked Harris, but I wished he would disappear when I saw how thoroughly Cindy had lost her mind. Cindy has marble eyes so blue that she frowns because the pitch of light they grab is hard to bear. They are so bright, it hurts me sometimes to see the sun in them. There was a lot to look at in the fall sun, leaves rolling around and spectacular half-lit clouds, but Cindy couldn't take her eyes off Harris. As realistically as she walked, she was blind in love.

After Cindy graduated from high school, she moved into Harris's apartment, got a job at the school pub, and shrugged off the idea of going to college. Harris never offered adequate explanation for getting a degree himself. I can still see my short husband, fists wearing out the pockets of his khakis, wandering the hallways after Cindy left. I hate to even think about him, the dumpy stoic; I would kiss his jowl and tell him that it would be okay. "She's ruining her life," he'd say, trying not to make too much of it.

"Of course not. It's a long life."

I owned a small personnel agency, which I sold after I left my husband. I liked placing secretaries, getting them to tone down the eye makeup and delusions of grandeur and showing them how to please a boss. My work was a wry island in a sea of skinned knees, runny noses, and overcooked rice. One windy spring night, I was locking up the rattling glass doors of my office when behind me I heard, "I'm pregnant."

I jumped. Cindy was at my shoulder, her hands in the pockets of her jeans and her straw-colored hair blowing in her face.

"I said I'm pregnant." She headed right for my reaction, not stalling in my confusion.

"Oh." Well, unlike her father, I believed experience was good for the young, but at the idea of my daughter pregnant, I'm afraid I was rather disgusted. "Well, that's too bad. I can't think of any reason why you should tell me."

"Because I'm not going to get rid of it."

It was appalling, her mistaking Harris's zygote for everything that was lovely about Harris. It made me cry. "Didn't you get enough love from me?"

"Look," she said impatiently, "you're not the point. I just wanted to let you know that I'm going to be having a baby," she said and turned to step like a trooper down Main Street.

I called her on the telephone and pleaded with her. I'd had a weak-handled love for her father, but I'd grabbed tight when I found out I was pregnant. It seemed as if there were fewer possibilities in those days and at twenty-three I'd married for the license to discuss loudly my baby's being premature. In consequence, for twenty years I turned out the light on a man who never kept me from envying the large loves of literature and television. I never got what I wanted, which was a love as big as all outdoors and nonetheless a tight circle of two.

"So why the hell have you been lying to me and Daddy all these years?" she said. Reasoning with Cindy was like one of those dreams in which the knife you wield winds up in your own belly.

"You can't saddle Harris," I warned her, for by this time I had high respect for Harris's ability to buck anything anyone tried to put on him.

Harris called her an idiot, and Cindy moved morosely home. Let me tell you, it was not easy to look at my distended daughter; she was just too young for all this. I couldn't understand it. It seemed like a sentimental decision, and Cindy was not a sentimental girl. Harris surprised me too. He visited every night. I could hear him through the ceiling, still telling her she was a fucking idiot, but when the baby was born, he decided to move them to Oregon and his parents' garage apartment. Harris was not, however, bowed enough to work at a desk. He shoveled dirt for a landscaper and gave me the benefit of a lot of long-distance sarcasm. "Look, Mother, you know you couldn't possibly love me any better."

My daughter was soon twenty and in a panic to discover what it's like to care for an infant. I think motherhood must be tougher on someone like Cindy, who was too willful to be prepared for the casual and constant tenderness required. She couldn't find anything to say to Harris's sweet big-boned mother, and the rap at the window was a constant reproach, so Cindy asked her not to come around as much. With the wounded grandmother out of the way, Cindy made the day into an endless breakfast. Harris would come home in the evening and find her still sitting in her bathrobe, drinking coffee, with Cecilia howling beside her. After the baby was in bed, Harris would sit in his dirty overalls at a picnic bench in their living room. He sketched or painted or his broad hands worked restorative magic on the ancient toasters and gummy steam irons and irregular clocks he'd saved from abandonment. Over his shoulder, Cindy would tell him stories of his own cruelty and neglect, which, bitten by her teeth, must have been harsh beyond bearing.

"Come on, pick another tone, Cindy," he'd say as she started in.

But there was no talking her out of it. "You don't care anything about me. You forget that I'm alive," she'd yell over his shoulder.

"Listen," Harris would say, turning around and pointing a paintbrush at her, "you're just using me as an excuse not to grow up."

This would make her crazy.

"Please," he'd say finally, he'd beg her, "please shape up, Cindy, please."

These were tough days for her. Her only comfort in her ratty pink bathrobe was her self-righteousness and this she protected all the more because Harris injured it. She threatened to cut her throat and instead came home to me.

I welcomed my daughter. "Where's the baby? Go, get the baby. Your father's got nothing to say about it."

"The baby's fine with Harris."

"Are you crazy?" I yelled. "Against all reason you have a child and now you're leaving it with people who never asked for it?"

"The baby likes Harris better than me," Cindy said and retired to her room for several days.

Now, I was heartily sorry for whatever contribution I'd made to the fissures in my daughter's sense, so I kept my outrage down. I thought she'd get over this. "Cindy, do you want me to fly back to get the baby?"

"I'm sure the baby's taken care of," she'd say as she hung up a skirt or rinsed some dishes or weeded the lawn. She didn't say much more to me and she wouldn't talk to Harris at all. It embarrassed my soul that I'd produced this hard creature. It seemed so consciencelessly easy for her to forget everything and settle into her girlhood bedroom like anyone else's cracked-brained twenty-year-old daughter. I couldn't sleep at night so I'd kick the refrigerator or wolf a drumstick or wander outside and gouge crabgrass and say to myself, "It's too much trouble for her, her baby's not worth the plane trip back for her."

There is something about those blue eyes that focus on an object and obtain it which is very foreign to me. And when Cindy can't make out what she wants, still, no one's damn directing hand sits long on her shoulder. As we would wander through the woods heading for town, it was little Cindy who dragged me along the path and it was I in high heels who dropped straight down like an uncoordinated toddler. No one can steer a course by a baby, which offers the most variable of destinations, but Cindy never gave up the wheel. No, you have to live for the smell of a fresh-powdered bottom and for the sudden drizzly smiles against your shoulder. At the root of all that is womanly, it seems to me, is a deep appreciation for the inadvertent.

And here was Harris in front of us once again.

* * *

Cindy and I said almost nothing as she and I killed the afternoon around town. As she entered Harris's apartment at six-thirty, the last sun made her eyes painful to see. She stepped into the living room and scanned it fiercely. "Where's the baby?"

Harris laughed at her abruptness and ran his hand through his thinning hair. "Look, Cindy, I was not a one-man show of a mother. My parents help me out with her. She's with them now."

Because I didn't want to upset them, I hadn't told Harris's parents who I was when I telephoned. They'd had no reason to mention their granddaughter, and I'd just assumed that Harris would keep the little girl with him. I was disappointed in Harris, but mostly I felt sorry for his slow-talking parents. No sundown honeymoons for them. I put my hands on my hips and was grateful for my freedom.

Cindy seemed first disappointed and then relieved. She stationed herself next to Harris as if she belonged there and leaned against the sink as he chopped garlic. Really, she was twenty-five years old and still had settled into no man and no set of rooms for too long. I wandered around admiring the decor. Harris's drawings and paintings hung all over. I didn't see much in these, but there must have been twenty old clocks clacking away, happy in their rediscovered usefulness.

"You're looking pretty good, Mother," Harris boomed over his shoulder.

"It's because I'm looking for romance," I told him and winked.

"Oh, God, Ma," Cindy said. "She's divorced now, Harris."

"Well, I'm not so surprised," was his reply.

A clean break, and now I might find anything around any corner. I smiled. "I'm tagging after my heart before I get too lame."

"This is a pleasure trip for you two?" Harris asked, waving a wooden spoon.

"All pleasure for me," I said. "We drove from Connecticut and stopped where we liked." It was odd that Cindy had agreed to take this ramble with me on her summer break. I think she was worried about herself, for although she'd been in school for three years now and had the beginnings of a reasonable life, still she was often finding unreasonable frowns on her face.

"Did Cindy tell you that she's going to get a B.A. next year? You finally wore off," I smiled. Cindy gave me a cold look, so I went back to examining the furniture.

I tripped over the spoils of Harris's morning dig. A metal boat hung from the porch roof and red plastic lobsters poised for attack above the front door. I didn't like the old optician's sign above the couch—you could see that kind of thing in a lot of Connecticut living rooms—but the printed circuit boards all askew over one wall made me smile.

Cindy had surveyed the place with the kitchen counter at her back, her legs crossed in front of her.

"Harris, why do you save all this garbage?"

He wiped his forehead with his arm. "Don't you think it's happy crap?"

Cindy didn't look as though he'd answered her question.

"Look," he said, "it's a sad thing, all this stuff trashed by people who don't have the imagination to use it. It's sad."

Cindy shook her head toward the paintings. "I remember those from seven years ago. What, are you a full-time fix-it-all now? What do you do for money?"

"I build sets for the drama departments of a couple of colleges around here."

"Great," she sneered.

I felt sorry for Cindy. It looked as if she was having a hard time keeping herself from falling against him. It looked as if her every eyelash and strand of hair was straining towards Harris beside her. She was taking the snotty tack in defense, or maybe she really had forgotten that Harris was not some plowing cracker-head. If only he would have admitted a little ambition, he would have been a prince in disguise, not merely the rude force that had shaken up her life. But Harris wouldn't give an inch. He leaned over his pot, stabbed a piece of sausage, and ate it off the knife. When he looked up at her, he gave her a stony look.

She played with the salt shaker as we sat at the table waiting for him to serve the food. The shaker spun with greater anxiety each time she looked up at him moving his rude pots and stained potholders with an angry stiff back and an angry bent neck. When he sat down, she set her transparent eyes at him.

Cindy laid her hand on Harris's brown arm.

"Not going to let me take a bite, huh?" he said kindly. He really did have a sweet and forgiving side.

"Hiya, Harris," she said, and gave him a rare, feeling smile.

The food was delicious, a big tomato sauce over spaghetti, but a little much in an un-air-conditioned apartment in July. Still, even though it didn't occur to either one of them to pull out any pictures of the little girl, it was a nice dinner, a lot of wine, and they didn't leave me out of the conversation. When Harris led us to the door at the close of the evening, he tapped a lobster over his head and said, "Why don't you ladies stick around awhile?"

We got a hotel room in King City and Cindy called Harris in the morning. The three of us wandered together all afternoon. I watched them play pinball. They were pretty competitive and there was a lot of precise buzzing and ringing and many a determined spring of the pin from the hip. The points racking up and Cindy's flicking her hair off her shoulder seemed increments in some larger sweep of communication. Truly, I think they let each other know they were as alive as they'd ever been.

I was on my own the next day. They went for a picnic and I exhausted both the coffee urn at the hotel restaurant and the patience of the saleslady at Westlake's Western Wear. I suffered from the particular weary headache that hotel rooms provoke, the shine from the vinyl headboard and crushed velour bedspread probably responsible. I was watching the evening news when they returned.

Cindy stood over me. "We want to go to Mexico. I've never been there. Do you mind spending a few days by yourself?"

I was tired of King City, but I believe in love, which is why I left my husband and why at forty-nine I am still a pretty woman.

"You can't take that Frankenstein car of Harris's. Take our car," I insisted.

You never grow out of being a mother, force-feeding that mash of annoyance and helpfulness.

Their trip started off well. They drove all evening and then all night through the desert and got to look at the clear white stars at truck stops and rest stations. But the sun rose over Mexico as my car's air-conditioning broke and the temperature zoomed. By the time daybreak had turned into high morning, their nostrils hurt when they breathed. The car seat grew stickier and stickier under them and they drank almost everything they'd brought with them, two gallons of bottled water and three quarts of orange juice. Harris knew what to expect, but my tough daughter was a little shocked by the raw desert heat. When they stopped in fly-filled bars, beer was all she wanted out of life. By noon the sweat on her eyelids convinced her that something must be terribly wrong with the world.

"I don't think I can stand this much longer," she said.

"Sure you can. Look at the bright side," he said, putting his hand into her hair, "you may never have to piss again."

Harris had a destination in mind, and though he didn't usually make mistakes like this, continually had to revise his estimate of how long it was going to take them to get there. Finally, in the late afternoon, up over a sandy hill they found the Gulf of California and Harris said, "We're here."

When they got out of the car in the village, children scattered before them and thirsty dogs coughed their disapproval. Harris stepped comfortably through this ragged Sonora village, but Cindy was as embarrassed as if she'd just blundered into someone's front hall without ringing the bell. Her brow creased.

Harris pointed to the barrels in front of the shacks. "They have their water delivered by truck."

One look and it was clear that the only cool place here was a bottle of beer from the long low porch that called itself a restaurant. Cindy searched the sky, the shacks, the water, and her Harris, but there was no place for her to settle after the endless drive.

"Harris, when you said fishing village, I expected nice piazzas, you know."

He put his hand on his hip and looked around. "I didn't want to take you to some place that was just a nacho California. They don't see five tourists a year here." He wiped the hair out of her eyes. "Let's go down to the water."

They made their way along the beach. Rays crumbled and jellyfish cracked under their toes. Curious life had crawled out of the vivid blue Gulf, but the parched fish mouths said exactly what they'd found.

They took off their clothes when the village was a dot far behind them. Cindy followed Harris's back as the blue water slowly licked its way up her legs. Her eyes and hot forehead were brightened and soothed by shots of sky and sun and little laps of water. She dragged her hands over the surface and Harris turned and swatted her down in. The sweat didn't wash off in the warm salt water. The water made her forget everything that bothered her, but it didn't make her clean.

"It's like the day before you were born," Harris said, kicking back.

Cindy couldn't feel any demarcation between her skin and the sea. The things that slid out from under her heels were no menace. Their languid jelly arms and rubber bodies soothed her and made her smile.

"I guess these poor thirsty people get some kind of compensation," she said. Cindy laid her cheek down on the surface and saw the water sparkle off a smooth arm. She kissed Harris's shoulder, his chin, and his warm eyelids.

But as they walked back, Cindy touched her wet hair and frowned. The villagers would know that they'd been nestling in the lap of the Gulf, and this was exactly the kind of thing to bother Cindy. "Harris, let's camp away from town," she said.

They drove off the main street onto a dirt road, past pyres of smoking fish heads and beer bottles. They stopped every few thousand feet and Cindy ran up the dunes looking for the Gulf. After several miles, they concluded that the road went farther inland. Harris pulled off onto a lesser road that went through the dunes, impatient to find the water before sunset. The two of them thought they ought to sit by the water and have a beatific red sun shine their tired limbs. The car went a hundred feet and sank into the sand.

They calmly gathered brush and stones and primed the ground for the car to roll back on. Cindy got in on the passenger's side in all confidence. The car didn't go. She got out and they jacked up the front end of the car. Harris risked his neck to shove matted weeds under the wheel. The tires turned and went nowhere.

They'd been sweating since daybreak and were covered with sand like sculptures or aborigines. The sun ducked away behind Harris, who was absolutely monumental in his exhaustion. "Cindy, get me something to drink."

Slamming the hatch shut, Cindy said, "This car is so fucking tinny. I can't believe we can't move it." So they pushed with blood on the brain, the two of them eye-popping mad, all the insistence a willful couple could possess directed against the cheerful blue metal of the Toyota.

Harris's chest heaved as he sank onto the fender. "I'm dizzy. Excuse me." He ran off a few steps and spat up the orange juice he'd just drunk. His stomach kept lurching the frothy business. "Cindy, I need something to drink."

Harris drank heartily, staggered, and vomited again. He sat on the sand and moaned. Cindy kept her head and dug a ratty first-aid pamphlet out of the glove compartment. It said that Harris was sick with heat exhaustion. "Shit, you need salt, Harris," she said. Cindy found a shaker in their bag of groceries and Harris was able to keep down the mixture of warm bottled water and salt that she made. He hunched over his crossed legs on the sand. "Do you need a doctor, Harris? Should I walk to the village?" she asked.

"No," he said.

Wandering over that dark desert would have been a horror and the village probably didn't have a telephone, let alone such sophisticated gear as a doctor. Cindy piled the things from the back of the car into the front seat and onto the roof. She secured the pots and pans on the hood. "Battened down, Harris," she said.

She and Harris climbed in the hatch, which was not nearly big enough for the two of them. Harris moaned and twisted and Cindy's warmth only chafed him. Cindy pulled a towel from underneath her and wetted it with the slush from the cooler. Harris almost cried, it felt so good as she ran the cloth over him.

The heat didn't dissipate with the light; it was only more oppressive when no source was apparent. Like the gray clouds of the starless sky, it was a stifling blanket. Harris kicked in his sleep. Covered with sweat and sand, Cindy was miserable. She sat up and thought about how stupid they were. Taking off the way they did was crazy. Now they were beyond telephone lines and through the tender cellophane marking civilization to a spot where lifesaving was not a mechanical certainty. Cindy had camped with Harris before—back when she was always getting into trouble for just taking off with him—but her present anger spoiled the open spaces for her. As she recalled even the handsome mesas and plains she'd passed with me, the land became a nidus for crime, accident, and sickness. She longed for a sunny kitchen corner, storm doors, and a formidable cleaver.

Harris woke whenever the air had spoiled his compresses. Cindy held his head, gave him water, and then washed his skin until he could sleep. I'm sure it scared her to see that something as substantial as Harris's body could be so easily knocked over. She kissed his salty shoulder. "Cindy," puffed from him whenever he turned over in the cramped space. Cindy's feeling for Harris, which could have filled all the space between cactus and clouds, overwhelmed her in the car. I'm sure she began to suspect that it could accommodate a child too.

The rattle of a snake's tail terrified her. She slammed the hatch door shut above them. As the windows steamed and the air became scarce, Harris moaned. For the sick man, Cindy opened the side windows halfway and sat rigid guard against the exposed rectangles of desert. She expected a strike. She thought about having to cut and suck a snake wound. The puckered X's of cut flesh would grow black as they stumbled towards no help at all.

Cindy was not a skittish girl, but she knew it would be easy to die there. The desert was noisy. The sounds that came from the village made her think of rollicking banditos, of happy black mustaches spreading at the thought of robbery and rape on such easy prey. Dry rats on eerie missions made delicate noises as they tripped past. The insects chided and laughed and screamed in thirsty misery, and the bushes raged hoarsely for water all night long.

Cindy woke Harris in the overcast morning and they moved their things inside the car. They ate breakfast on the roof and it seemed downright stupid, cornflakes in the big sullen desert. Harris was weak and stopped frequently to rest as they trudged to the village. Cindy watched the pockmarks in the road. She tensed as they passed little burrows, expecting something to spring at her leg and sink its teeth into her calf with crazy rodent fury.

The dogs coughed at them and the women grew silent as they passed. Harris distracted the men from their nets and drew in the sand to describe their problem. The men laughed, but one of them pointed to a yellow jeep. Two men sat with them as the owner went inside a shack. A round little girl followed him out again and hugged his leg as he tried to step into the jeep. He swooped her into his lap and started his engine when another little girl ran out of the hut, crying because she was left behind. He called her over, caught her in his arm, and swung her high towards heaven as he'd probably done in many a bedtime story. She sat beside her sister.

I am sure Harris and Cindy watched attentively as the man's smile grew out of his daughters' and his broadened theirs. The girls' cheeks had that dry rosiness of recent awakening until they were polished by the early morning wind over the hood. The man spoke to his small daughters the entire way, pointing things out to them along the desert road.

The jeep pulled the car out. The men didn't want any money, so Cindy gave them peaches and beer. Harris leaned back with a wet cloth on his head, and Cindy drove the fifty miles to a town with an air-conditioned hotel. Her eyes occupied by the narrow road, Cindy reached absently over and patted Harris's wet cheek.

"Great, that guy with his kids, huh?" Harris said and put his hand into Cindy's yellow hair.

"You know," she said, "before I saw that I couldn't figure out how these people live. No fresh water, nowhere to go."

Harris shifted in the seat. "Lucky them. There's nothing to get in the way of their families here."

"Yeah," Cindy said and imagined, I bet, having Harris and a child, a fortress of feeling to keep out any bad experience. But after two nights without sleep, Cindy's grip on things was sporadic. When the hotel clerk told them that their room wouldn't be ready before noon and that no, he was sorry, they couldn't wait in the lobby in such a state, Cindy became a lump of sheer discomfort. She started to cry.

Harris put his arm around her and offered, "Look, we'll go buy ice. We need ice for the cooler. You should see how they sell it here."

They bought a ticket and held it up beside a chest-high platform. Children slouched against the wall and then came to clamorous life as the men stormed out and worked with the crazy speed of a clown show. A huge block was pushed out and tickets were grabbed. A smash of the pick, one, two, three, four little holes, yet somehow the ice was made to divide. After the block gave way, the men retired behind the scenes to get the next block and the kids sucked the shards left on the platform.

Harris, behind Cindy, grabbed her elbows and pulled her back into him. "You took good care of me last night."

She turned her head and kissed his neck.

"You're not such a miserable girl really. Not nearly as bad as I've been telling people."

"Yeah? Thanks," she said and bit his T-shirt.

"I could live with it. What do you say, Cindy, do you want to live with me and my daughter?"

"Yes. Okay," Cindy said, but by the time the men had shoved a block of ice their way, Cindy was smashed over the head by lack of sleep and leaned her face against the slimy cube and cried.

Nor, as they walked to the car, did she see the humor in the little kids who'd strapped the bare ice to their bicycles and were pedaling furiously away against the drip, drip behind.

Cindy thought of how beautiful Harris was even though he was sick and dried now, dried down to the elemental Harris. But she was solemn and miserable as they waited on the stoop in front of the hotel. Cindy accepted that the rub in her thoughts was caused by her not liking Harris nearly so well as she had a hour before. I'm convinced it was some brush of dishes and juvenile demands and pinched will that nettled her.

But a hot shower shook the sand from their ears and the sweat from their eyes. After a hot shower and a long sleep in clean sheets, I suppose things appeared rather different. Once she was comfortable, Cindy probably couldn't find any reason in the world not to have exactly what she wanted. By the time they brought the car back to me, they leaned against each other like a couple in love.

"Mom, I'm going to be staying with Harris for a while. I guess you'll have to finish the trip without me." Cindy's marble eyes shifted away from me to another point closer to the horizon. "I know it's expected that we get the baby, but we just met again. We'll wait and see."

"Are you crazy?" I yelled.

Harris winced.

"You don't make a baby and then forget about it," I yelled. "Harris, tell her."

He put his arm around me and kissed my cheek. "Not to worry, Mother."

The two of them looked pretty grand as they walked off into the King City sun. The sight of it made me sick.

MARGARITAS

■ Teresa Yunker

I like this story because it tells the way it is. The dialogue is so well-tuned it could be going on at a table next to yours, and the author does a splendid job at cranking it up as her characters become progressively inebriated. The protagonist—we know her only as "California" —molds herself to fit her date's conception of her as he becomes increasingly belligerent and asinine, inventing outrageous—and hilarious—lies. She plays the game, and yet, somehow, too, it is his conception of her as the quintessence of a sort of mythical, liberated, anything-goes California that most appeals to her. In her exile, she wants to recall California and all it represents to her through the margaritas, the inauthentic Mexican restaurant, the ingenuous date who is truly wowed by her "exotic" presence. But things don't turn out so well. And isn't that the way it is?

Teresa Yunker is twenty-three. She is a graduate student at USC. "Margaritas" is her first published story.

—T. CORAGHESSAN BOYLE

*T*he Margarita stands tall, beautifully iced, with salt crusted thick around its edges. This margarita is a work of art; this margarita is a gem. Its delicate tint, its proud slice of lime, its promise of tequila bite makes this particular margarita the winner of the evening. Of course it is the first margarita. That one is always the finest.

She reaches for it.

"Wait a minute," he says. "A toast to, well, to . . ."

"To us," she says, not caring that it is hardly original. They click glasses and have their first sip. She smiles at him and he smiles back. It is Thursday evening. They have met here right after work. They work in the same building, the John Hancock. She works for an advertising agency, he works for a law firm. Right now they are in a place called El Jardin, which means The Garden. El Jardin is known for its dangerous margaritas. Otherwise the food is Chicago Mexican rather than California Mexican. The waiter appears.

"Do you want anything to eat? Some guacamole?"

"No, this is fine for now."

They are sitting outside on the patio. The weather has not yet turned cold even though it is October. Of course she doesn't want anything to eat. Ruin this first margarita?

"Well," he says, putting down his margarita and inching his chair closer. "Now I can find out more about you."

"And spoil the mystery?" she says. My god, what a line.

"So how do you like Chicago so far?"

"Fine, just fine."

It seems he had seen her driving to work in a car with California plates. She hadn't learned then that it was easier to use the subways.

"You prepared for winter?"

"Hardly!" And they laugh as if she's said something hilarious. They both take deep swallows from their drinks. Her mouth feels particularly sharp from the salt. "Really, I can't imagine it," she says. "Thirty below and all that."

"Well, you'll find out. This isn't called the Windy City for nothing. Sure isn't California!"

Yes, well. She hopes to get him off the California bit.

"So you're a lawyer?"

"Working on it. Right now I'm in law school and working part-time at a law firm."

"Uh-huh."

"What do you do at the advertising agency?"

"Well, just about everything." Her margarita is nearly finished. She glances around for the waiter.

"You know, it's hard for me to have any time at all between law school and work. Law school is really something . . . the time it eats away." Ah, she sees, he wants to talk about himself but that's okay because the second margarita is placed before her, all fresh and clean.

"It must be very difficult."

"Oh, it is," he says, leaning forward. "I hardly have time for anything other than classes, studying, and work. It's been hard to meet people."

"I can imagine."

By people she supposes he means women. Here he is with her on what is probably his first date in months.

"Law students are all so uptight, you know? Including me I guess, but you can't study all the time, right?"

"Right."

He has hardly touched his margarita. She had better go slower.

"Conservatism is what you would call it. Do you call yourself conservative?" She is bemused. Exactly what does he mean, conservative? "I mean, the Midwest must be very different than California that way."

"Well, yes, in a way."

"And you're an artist, too. I noticed your way of dressing right away. I could tell you were an artist."

"I'm certainly flattered, being called an artist," she says, "but commercial art is bound by certain, uh, certain . . ." What is she saying? Is this a serious conversation?

"I mean, certainly it's more creative than law, say."

"I don't know anything about law. . . ."

"You have to come up with ideas and everything, right? I'll have to start watching TV more carefully."

"Oh, I don't do anything for television. . . ."

"The colors, the makeup, the actors . . ."

"No, I do ads for mag—"

"Did you work for CBS or something in California?"

Her head is spinning. What are they talking about? She sips her drink to clear her head.

"I know it's a typical thing to ask, you know, like have you met any of the stars. Of course you must get asked that all the time really, except you did work for TV out there and people just naturally assume, you know. . . ."

"No, I never . . ."

". . . at least see people like that, maybe in a restaurant or something, but it's a stupid thing to ask, really but maybe you did meet a model, Lauren Hutton, say . . ." He takes a gulp of margarita. Is she right? Is he asking her if she's ever met Lauren Hutton? Lauren Hutton! "It must have been really interesting to work in TV," he concludes.

"So have you ever . . . well, I was wondering . . ."

There is still margarita left, but hardly any salt. It needs salt. "Oh yes, lots. You'd be surprised how many big-time stars want to be in commercials. So lucrative, really." She'd had a little trouble over the word *lucrative*. But he doesn't notice. He is glowing.

"I bet! I bet it's lucrative! Yessir!"

Really, the last bit in the glass just isn't any good without the salt. It's all ice, anyway. Just melted ice. Anyone could see that.

"Imagine all that money!" he says. He looks a bit damp in his suit.

"You should take off your tie," she tells him.

"Damn right it's lucrative!" he says. "Hey, time for another, wouldn't you say? Hey, waiter!"

"You really should take off that tie."

"My tie?"

"You look really hot." He seems confused. He looks as if he's forgotten where he is. Maybe he has.

"Well, sure, if you say so. Why the hell not? I'm not at work now, am I? So why the hell am I wearing this tie? I'll take it off right now!" He grabs it and yanks it so violently that the table shakes. "So how about those margaritas, huh?" She sees the waiter bearing down on them with his tray of drinks.

"Here they come," she says, but he doesn't seem to hear.

"Didn't we order them awhile ago?" he asks. "So where are they?" He snaps his fingers, his elbow nearly smashing into the tray. The waiter backs off. "Ah, here they are!" he says. "Here's our margaritas! Say, you want something to eat? Some nachos or something?"

The waiter sets down her third margarita, all shining with salt.

"I'm not hungry."

"Fine! Later, we'll eat later," and he gestures hugely with one hand.

Hmmm. It just tastes better and better. She'll have to come here again. What's the name? El, El, well of course they all begin with El. Or La. She starts to giggle.

"What's so funny? Huh? What are you laughing at? You laughing at me?" He is grinning wildly at her. Around his forehead bits of damp hair are sticking up like porcupine quills. He keeps raking his head.

"I was just thinking of the time I saw Johnny Carson fall on his ass," she says.

"You are kidding me! Carson on his ass? That's terrific!"

"He, he," she gasps for breath between snorts, "he tripped right over my foot and fell backwards on his ass!"

"Tripped over your foot?"

"That's right, and then he leaped up like nothing happened and apologized for stepping on my shoe!"

"That is wild! Did this happen at work? At CBS?" He just seems enormous to her suddenly, all sweaty with huge, glazed eyes.

"Oh no, this was at the Christmas party."

This is amazing. Carson and the Christmas party? Well, why not? Why not put some glamour into this poor guy's life? "Every year at Christmas there's this big party and all the stars come and kiss ass because they want to do commercials for us."

His mouth drops open. "Like who?"

"Well, like, like, uh, Ali McGraw, say." How in God's name did she come up with Ali McGraw? "If the truth were to be told I don't give a damn about Ali McGraw." He just gapes at her. "That's right. Who the hell is she? Just some actress, right?"

"Do they have sex at these parties?"

"You know," she says to him, "you shouldn't care so much about these people." This statement moves her deeply. He should listen to her. She is telling him something important. Something that could change his life. She takes a long drink. He is staring at her blindly.

"Do they?"

"Huh?" She hasn't followed, that much is clear. He wants something.

She turns her head away and the potted plants sway sickeningly. The tinny, Mexican music seems very loud. "Did you just ask . . ." she begins. It is so loud out here. They are outside, aren't they? "Are we still here?" she asks. "Are we outside still?"

He is getting impatient. He is tapping the tabletop with emphasis on each beat. He has long thin fingers and she is suddenly convinced he'll make a fantastic lawyer.

"So, what, are you trying to tell me they don't? 'Cause I know for a fact that they do. Everybody knows that. Those people are so rich, they'd do anything for excitement. Life must get bloody dull when you're so rich you can go anywhere. Imagine that! I hear a lot of them are gay. Lots of actors are, you know. Right? So what happens? Tell me!" He looks right at her. She is scared of him.

"Well, I don't really know. . . ."

"But you were there! You just said Carson fell over your foot! Was he on something? Was that it?"

Is this really happening?

"It was just a joke," she says, "I was kidding you."

"I bet he was high. I bet it was coke. You do coke? But what am I saying, of course you do, you're in TV. I've done it now and then, but it's so expensive. But that's not *their* problem, right? You want another?"

"Oh no, thanks."

"And you too, huh? Of course you must join in on all of this. Maybe in a way so as not to lose your job or anything, right?"

She chokes on her drink.

"Being a commercial artist and a Hollywood starlet are two different things. Besides, it's the 1980s, not the 1950s." She isn't sure what she means by this, but it stops him temporarily.

"Now come on," he says after a minute. "You mean to say that you don't sleep around at those things? You mean to tell me that?"

"I don't have to tell you anything!"

He looks at her like he can't believe his ears. "Hey now, you listen to me. You started this, you know. You brought up all this crap about Carson. So now I want to hear it."

She is sick with anger. She downs the last of her margarita.

"Will you order me another, honey?" she says, standing up. She can't believe her own voice. It's as sweet as chocolate.

"Where are you going?" His expression is still sullen, but a smile is beginning. He has taken in the *honey*.

"Just to the bathroom. Be right back." And she waggles her fingers at him. She has to concentrate hard not to list from side to side. It takes a bit to find the door but once out onto the street, the walk to the subway doesn't seem too long.

*   *   *

The next day at work she is in the elevator before she sees him standing in the back. She curses to herself as the doors close.

"Hi there!" he says, his cheerful voice rising from the rear. Her head cracks.

"Hello," she calls, without turning around. The people in the elevator shuffle with irritation.

"Cold enough for you?"

"Certainly is."

This morning, abruptly, it has turned cold. She is in Chicago—angry, capricious Chicago.

"Might snow soon, you know. What do you think of that?" he continues.

"Wow," she says and like a blessing the door opens at her floor. She walks out.

"See you, California." There is special emphasis on the word *California*. She whips around with a wide, dazzling smile.

LORE

■ Douglas Bauer

Douglas Bauer was an editor at Playboy *magazine when he quit journalism to go back to school and write. What you are about to read of his work is a chapter from a novel soon to be published by Simon and Schuster. It is called* Dexterity, *just as it was when it existed only as a short story submitted to a writing workshop I used to teach at the State University at Albany. That short story was a revelation—that here was an extraordinary writer. The story of Ed and Ramona, one of the oddest couples in modern literature, is endlessly surprising. Doug Bauer is a champion of the language, as any reader will quickly discover, has a great ear for the vernacular, but most important of all, has an extraordinary talent for penetrating into the souls of his characters. He is masterful with the nuance. In an age when minimalism is in vogue, he tells his story with a density that we associate with Henry James. I have not read the final version of* Dexterity, *but I have seen it in assorted stages of its progress and I am convinced that it will be a great and original book.*

—WILLIAM KENNEDY

*E*d eased himself off the truck and watched Adams push a roll of snow fence from the front of the flatbed toward him. The fence sagged as it was rolled, its wooden pickets creaking agedly.

"Okay, drop it," Ed said. Adams kicked the fence off the truck and went to get another roll.

Ed turned to the field beside the highway and squinted into it, his gaze traveling back toward the town. Especially, he tried to make his eyes detail the back of his own house, to see if he could trace its features from where he stood, the field's full length away. He was not surprised to see it as merely a squat white cube at the bottom edge of Myles, but a sense of disappointment passed through him nevertheless. When Bill March had told the crew they'd be spending the day running snow fence along the edge of this field, a span notoriously prone to drifts that spilled onto the highway, Ed had felt a lifting hope, in spite of himself, that he'd be able as he worked to keep his house in view, to see it well enough to spot Ramona at the moment if she returned today.

Adams dropped another roll of fence off the truck, watching Ed furtively all the while. Ed had seemed to him this morning even more preoccupied than usual and Adams had thought that hardly possible. Except for his recent outbursts of accusation, Ed's attention, Adams sensed, had been turning ever further inward to concerns which Adams couldn't possibly guess. Despite his conscious efforts, his private rehearsals of disavowal, Adams had been unable to be free of Ed. If anything, his interest had been drawn in even more by Ed's withdrawal.

Not until the truck had pulled to a stop was Ed's mood this morning made suddenly clear to Adams. Only then did he realize, as he told himself he should have immediately, that they'd be working along the edge of the field which Ramona had walked to reach this highway.

Mitchell and Day began to set out orange warning cones behind the truck. Ed heard from the cab the ceaseless voice of Waycross as he and March climbed out, March slamming his door with an air of gravity. "Most amazing damn thing I ever seen," Waycross was saying. He moved with his bent-backed step, surprisingly quick for a man who tried hard to be old in every other way, as though his nimbleness were a habit he'd not been able to break.

"This was when Everett Van Zandt owned the Hill Top, years before Moon bought it," Waycross said. He was supposedly speaking to March, who received the flow of his talk as he sat beside him in the truck through the day, but for all Waycross cared he was speaking to the air, to the fields. Waycross needed to talk as one needs to exhale and it was possible to imagine that, deprived of the ability, he would simply, quickly die.

Dead leaves covered the roadside, hiding the lay of the ditch, but Ed shuffled through them without looking down, knowing, as he knew the features of the road land everywhere in Columbia County, that the leaves hid no tricky fall of landscape here, nothing but a smooth and shallow dip. He knew that a hundred yards north the ditch grew steep. As he walked, he kept his eyes on the speck of his house. He carried pointed steel stakes in the crook of one arm. They looked like a collection of hideous spears. He held the sledgehammer he'd refused to let anyone else use. It swung pendulously with his step.

"When Van Zandt seen this guy—guy's name was Chesley—coming down the street he'd draw three beers and set them on the bar, in a row like." Waycross and March helped Adams empty the truck. Mitchell and Day rolled fence through the ditch leaves toward Ed, who had dropped all but one stake and stood, his back to Waycross.

As he often had, Ed tried to imagine her as she'd walked through this field. He wondered again how she'd looked that morning. Had she taken slow, even steps, so as not to draw suspicion from anyone who might see her? Had she raced through the weeds, thrilled in her escape? Had she lurked between those extremes, checking her impatience for a few slow steps, then bursting forward, unable to hold herself in?

"So when this Chesley come in the door, there'd be the row of beers waitin' for him and he'd drink one in about a second and a half and give it to Van Zandt and Van Zandt'd draw another glass and set it down at the end of the row and by that time Chesley would'a almost drank the other two and that's the way it'd go, Chesley drinkin', Van Zandt fillin'."

Ed decided, as he always did, that she'd moved haltingly, stumbling, often pausing, looking back.

"Chesley drinkin', Van Zandt fillin'. Neither of 'em sayin' a word, like this was serious business they had to *con*centrate on. And I one night watched him drink *eight-teen* glasses of beer like that, never stoppin', drinkin' beers like he was a goddamn machine somebody had invented to drink beer, before he stopped to blink an eye. Eighteen draws. Now I ask you, is that a-fucking-mazing or not?"

"Not," Mitchell said, scowling. "That is bull fucking shit. That is what it is." When Waycross told these stories of the past, Mitchell and Day, for different reasons, were always drawn in. Mitchell ran his fingers through dirty blond hair that hung to the top of his back. He shook his head disgustedly. "Eighteen draws my ass."

"By god, I saw it," Waycross said. "I'll bet you a dollar to a dog turd and hold the stakes in my mouth he did."

Ed set the point of a stake in the ground and gave it three strong blows. It sank into earth not yet too firmly frozen. He sited down the field's edge, anticipating the line of evenly spaced stakes he would set to hold the fence, and then a new thought came to him: that if such a fence had been up last summer, it might have been obstacle enough to have kept her in the field. In his mind's eye, he saw Ramona trying to climb over a snow fence, one that didn't stop, as this one would, but ran the field's entire width. He saw her working futilely to push herself over and clear, then surrendering, glancing around to see if anyone had observed her struggling so absurdly, and heading back toward the baby carriage.

"What'd he do then?" Day asked Waycross, his eyes magnified through thick glasses which were held in place with an elastic band behind his head. All but the foreman, March, had reached the ditch. They gathered near Ed, whose driven stake was as a flag that claimed the spot where work would start. March was walking the roadside to remind himself where the ditch became deep enough to hold the drifts and snow fence would no longer be needed. Reaching that spot, he sank an orange-flagged stake into the ground.

"Whaddaya mean, what'd he do?" Waycross asked Day.

Day was Mitchell's temperamental opposite. He believed everything anyone said. He read the newsstand tabloids devotedly, relaying their contents in a tone of airy Scripture-citing awe. "You said he stopped after eighteen. What'd he do then?"

"Well . . . he just stood up, let go a belch that, if it'd been a rope it woulda' wrapped twice around the room, and said, 'Hot out. I was thirsty.' Paid Van Zandt for his beers and walked out the door."

"Oh, god, go fuck yourself, old man," Mitchell groaned.

Adams laughed and shook his head and flittingly glanced at Ed, whose gaze into the field with his back still to the crew had been making him nervous, even a little angry. That part of Adams still deeply invested in Ed's behavior felt oddly responsible for him at moments such as this, almost embarrassed by him, as though Ed's actions reflected on him.

Now Ed moved to face them and his turning around, like a healer's sweep of hand, eased Adams's tension.

"And I'll tell you somethin' else," Waycross said. "From the time he walked through the door till he stood up to leave, there was exactly *fifteen* minutes passed."

"Oh, my god!" Mitchell said, sounding deeply offended.

"I was sittin' next to the clock," Waycross said.

"Fuck you!" Mitchell cried, his voice high as a child's.

"Jee-zuz," whispered Day, "that *is* amazing."

Adams laughed again and then, out of habit, they all paused to hear from Ed. As remote and unpredictable as he'd become, as wary of him as they'd all grown, there was a pattern working now which was so well established that no one except Adams gave a thought that Ed might not respond as he always had, after waiting in silence until Waycross had finished. Sometimes he gave another version of Waycross's story, one he'd heard and stored among the Myles lore he loved. Sometimes he told a contrasting anecdote which instructed them parabolically; and sometimes, when he was tired or hung over or just fed up with Waycross's bullshit, he'd simply ask three or four questions, a kind of cross-examination that immediately showed whether Waycross was building on memories or lies. Ed approved of an improved fact, so long as it could be traced, but a moment of the past that turned out to be pure fantasy threatened something he simply sensed as elementally important: the history of Myles, which gave the place its very language and required the root of truth.

The others had always heard Ed's words as a verdict on Waycross's tale while the old man himself bristled and cursed but never appealed and soon afterwards launched another story, so plain was his need.

Now they all waited. Ed stared into their faces and Adams could see, from Ed's eyes, that he'd been watching more than the fields while his back was turned. Their cast seemed to Adams to be aberrantly angled, like headlights out of line, high and to the side on a fully private world.

Ed had paid no attention to what Waycross was saying, his voice mere pulsing noise, locusts' droning. And now he saw that they were waiting for him. He blinked and cleared his throat, as though stalling until a flicker of senility had passed, and said at last, "I got work to do." Then he reached down to pick up the pile of stakes and called to March, "How far apart you want 'em?"

* * *

He drove a stake with his sledgehammer, walked a line of carefully measured steps, boot heel against toe, then drove another, progressing toward the orange flag that Bill March had set. It was the sort of chore Ed loved, could normally lose himself in, the precise recurrence of the work enfolding him as he saw in each repetition the chance to duplicate exactly the sequence just completed. Adams did the same work across the road in the opposite ditch; the rest of the crew mended cut and crumbled roadside. When enough stakes had been set, they'd all unroll fence and attach it with wire.

But today Ed's concentration wasn't on his work. He stopped, picked up a stake, looking not ahead toward March's orange flag, but through the field toward the tiny square of his house. His eyes left it only as he drove a stake; otherwise he held them on the house so strongly that he caught himself walking a crooked line, drawn into the field by the pull of his focus. And the harder he looked, the larger the house seemed to him to grow, the more finely its lines showed.

He thought he could make out a smaller pale shape next to the house—the low sweep of the Dodge. The thought of the car made him smile and then wince. He smiled at being reminded that he no longer felt the sense of Ramona inside it. Inexplicably, like a fading odor, it had gradually disappeared and now lived only in the house.

He winced because the Dodge reminded him of last night, when he'd fucked Wilma Jean in its tight back seat. Instead of lifting him free, she'd become still another source of trouble, constantly telling him things he had no wish to know. Every time he fucked her she talked of high school days, her memory and impressions incredibly fresh, scenes involving her and him and Ramona in which Ramona hadn't been as good to him as she would have been. He could hardly get her to be quiet long enough to fuck and as soon as they'd finished she'd resume her memory where he'd stopped it, her anger at Ramona in his behalf at exactly the pitch she'd left it when he'd peeled her jeans down her legs.

Behind him, Day and Mitchell shoveled loose chunks of highway onto the back of the truck and spoke of a waitress at the Legion Hall in Mellenville. Mitchell said, "I think she wants to fuck me."

"How do you know?" Day asked, pausing with his shovel.

" 'Cause Tuesday night, I was in there, she come over and whispered in my ear, 'I wanna fuck you.' "

"Really?" asked Day.

"No," Mitchell said.

They hooted in unison and their laughter seemed to Ed to be purposely interrupting him. He concentrated even more on his house, trying to bring it closer so he'd be able to see her if she came around to the back. He narrowed his eyes to sun-squinting slits and the view seemed to tighten and he stopped, holding for several moments the conviction that he *had*, by the force of his will, drawn his house toward him.

"Anyway, she ain't the only one," Mitchell said. "There's so much ass in that town, all you gotta do is show up."

He tried to fight off Mitchell's voice. Wouldn't it be something, he thought, if she picked right now? His eyes burned fiercely from his effort to hold them on the house, but the thought sent a sense of triumph through him and he risked a cautious pan, first left, then to the right.

"That is true about Mellenville," Waycross interrupted. "It's always been that way. I remember once—"

"No, old man!" Mitchell shouted. "Don't remember nothing. Don't remember another fucking thing!"

And then Ed saw . . . that, of course, the enormous maple which towered above his house was a featureless twig from this far away and that the length of his backyard was no more than a faint brown thread.

He let the sledgehammer slide from his grip and placed his hands over his eyes. He began to laugh silently, his back still to the others. Jesus Christ, he thought, what'd I *think* I could see? His laughter was growing but he kept it soundless, letting it escape through the side of his mouth, his body quivering like a dog's passing dreams. How'm I gonna know? he asked himself as a vision of Ramona's return appeared to him with the clarity he'd been trying to give to his house. How'm I gonna know if I'm not there? She's gonna sneak back and I'm not gonna fucking know. He felt his body shaking and fought to still it with the strength he would use to subdue another man. Christ, yes, *that's* what's gonna happen. She knows when I'm workin', and that's when she'll come back.

As he'd imagined her return, all his thoughts had been of the instant itself, of the sight and especially the shoe-scuffing sounds of Ramona making her way up their walk, while he stood motionless at the door watching her approach. He'd glimpsed in his mind countless versions of his response, a range of behavior showing him how soon he would be violent, how violent he would be. Ramona, on the other hand, was unvaryingly the slumped defeated figure pleading forgiveness on any terms he chose.

Every impulse of revenge depended entirely on the scene. Ed had no imagination for the day afterwards, for any kind of life they might resume. Nothing had mattered in his mind but this satisfying moment, and now he was struck with the certainty that she would easily avoid it. A sourness rose in him. He couldn't believe he hadn't seen something so obvious until now and the fact of it ran through him, leaving him weak inside a silent fit of acid-tasting laughter.

Day, who habitually did even less work than Waycross, ate enormous lunches. He sat on the floor of the truck with his legs extended, a banquet of sandwiches and packaged desserts fanned out in front of him. The others were scattered near the truck, taking strong autumn sun that kept the chill in the air at their perimeter.

From the edge of the ditch, where he sat, Ed watched Day, whom he'd always disliked, for his careless work, for his gullibility, and because he ate so much, a kind of unearned excess to Ed's way of thinking. He'd mostly ignored him in the past, but watching him now, his anger moving immanently after the revelations of the morning, he wanted to hurt Day badly.

"I was readin' about this woman?" Day said as he chewed. "She was runnin' in one of those marathons? And she gave birth to a baby about halfway through the race and still finished second."

"Jesus," Mitchell said wearily, gnawing a chicken bone. Day did not irritate Mitchell as Waycross did. He knew Day made nothing up, telling only what he'd heard or read. "Why do you be*lieve* that shit, anyway?"

Day asked, defensively, "So why do they print it, then, if all it is is bullshit?"

"So dumb fucks like you will buy it," Ed said. His words were quick and in pursuit, as though his anger had caught the scent of Day's ignorance. The others raised their eyes uneasily, recognizing the new sound they'd been hearing in Ed's voice. Adams felt his stomach tighten.

"What else'd you read, Day?" Ed said. He lay on his side against the ditch, propped up on one arm. "Tell me some more *news*."

"Jesus, Ed, forget it," Day said.

He seemed to Ed a pouting child, and when he said nothing more and reached in front of him for a fruit-filled turnover, Ed's anger cohered as many whorls inside his head.

"Forget it? I don't wanna forget it, Day. I want you to tell me about that woman havin' a kid while she run in the race. That musta been something to see, huh, Day? How'd she do it, anyway? She run kinda spread-eagle, so the kid could just pop right out while she's waddlin' along?" Day no longer seemed to Ed too worthless for his fury. Nothing did. "Did she carry the kid, Day, or what? Or did she bring a knife along to cut the cord?"

Bill March put down his mug of coffee and stood up. "Okay, Ed. Okay."

Ed stood too. The whorls were making a quick-beating hum and a luminous red tint like the chroma of a lens was on everything. "Shit, March. Don't you wanna know the news? Ain't you interested in this amazing goddamn woman Day's tellin' us about?"

Adams watched, unable to speak, wanting more than anything to stop him. But though he sensed Ed losing control, and was hearing again the witless rage of Ed's new abuse, Adams could not step into its way. He'd always been the one who'd taken what Ed gave and it was all he knew how to do.

Waycross sat on the ground, hunched and cross-legged like a shrunken Indian, sprinkling tobacco into his cigarette paper. "Come on, King," he said. "Sit down, why don't ya?"

Ed spun toward Waycross. "I don't need your shit, old man." The red tint was deepening. "I do *not* need your shit." He looked into Waycross's wrinkled face. "If I want any shit outa you, I'll squeeze your fuckin' head, Waycross."

Waycross looked at March, then shook his head and licked the cigarette paper.

"Come on, Ed," March said. He glanced at his watch. "It's almost one. Let's all get back to work."

Ed pointed at Day. "Day can't go back to work. He ain't finished with his lunch. Lookit! You got three, four, pieces of pie still, right, Day?"

"Jesus Christ, Ed," Day said softly. "What'd I do to you? Just leave me alone, okay?"

Ed started toward him. "You're right," he said, speaking with an abruptly turned softness. The red-tinted world was pulsing. "You're absolutely right, Day, and I'm gonna apologize by giving you a hand." He walked calmly past March and reached Day, on the truck. "I'm gonna help you eat your lunch so nobody's waitin' on you and we can all get back to work."

Day looked dubiously at Ed.

"Gimme one of them pies," Ed said, pointing to a turnover wrapped in waxed paper. "Come on. I wanna help you out. I'm apologizin', see?" He continued to point. "Gimme that one there."

Day tried to look for help, for some signal of advice, but Ed stood directly in front of him, blocking his view of the others. Ed's face was solemn charity.

"You heard March," Ed said. "He wants us back to work."

Day reached slowly for the turnover and handed it to Ed. "I'm helpin' you, Day," Ed said again. "You ain't got *time* to eat all you got there."

As he walked away his fingers closed on the turnover. He looked down at it in his hand, feeling some of the rage move out of his head and down his shoulder as he squeezed. Bright-red fruit filling burst through its package and ran between his fingers. He watched it eddy thickly, coagulative with sugar, at the base of his palm. He thought of blood.

When he turned back to Day his arm felt separate and bloated with strength. He aimed at nothing in particular, wanting to be rid of everything inside him, and flung the pie past Day; it splattered against the end slats of the flatbed.

Ed breathed deeply three times; he had nothing in his chest. Nobody moved or said anything, so the sound of his breathing was an exhalant breeze. He walked toward the ditch and along the edge of the field to the last stake he'd driven before stopping for lunch.

Adams watched him, feeling in a way he couldn't name a sickening sense of loss.

Everyone worked quietly for an hour or so, moving about with a quick constricted step. Low murmurs drifted among them. Adams continued to set stakes, nervously conscious of Ed across the road.

Ed was furious now at several things, at Day for provoking him, but chiefly at the certainty his morning's thoughts had brought. What returned as he worked was the picture of her leaving and he began to imagine it with a gift for details he'd never had. It was nothing he was trying for, they came on their own, but he had no trouble whatsoever feeling the sun of that morning. Suddenly, he was breathing August heat, inspiring him to sweat, and he saw Ramona's face, beads of sweat on her forehead, sweat-blisters above her lip, her neck slick and glistening. He unzipped his hooded sweatshirt and tossed it on the ground.

Gradually, the mood among the rest of the crew loosened. March told Waycross, Mitchell, and Day to get in the back of the truck while he drove it forward several yards to the next bad patch of highway. Day climbed up onto the flatbed and Mitchell goosed him with the handle of his rake. "Oooh," Day cried, "that felt good. That all you got?" Seeing Mitchell goose Day inspired Waycross to memories of the Army, barracks life in Oklahoma, where a PFC from Georgia used to regularly jack off the camp's pet dog, a skinny mutt who stood on his hind legs in obedient ecstasy while the private held his front paws in his left hand and worked him rhythmically with his right, as though coaxing an udder.

Hearing the story, Mitchell shrieked and threw a glove at Waycross, but not with any anger, as the truck pulled to a stop twenty feet from Ed and Adams.

Ed again heard their voices distinctly. They'd been talking about him since lunch, he was sure. He'd heard their laughter, and even though they spoke softly he'd caught a few words now and then that he was convinced had his name in them.

But now that they were close he was sure that they'd be quiet.

The Ramona he was picturing could barely lift her legs through the field's high grass. The heat and the weight of the air were stopping her. He imagined the voluminous sigh of the weeds as she shuffled through. He heard her panting.

Waycross leaned on his shovel, moving his toothless gums back and forth across each other. Waycross didn't know what Ed's mood had become since lunch but he had no interest in testing it, so he spoke in a very low voice.

"You guys heard about Bob Petrie, didn't ya?" he asked, almost whispering.

Day raised his eyebrows in cordial invitation.

"You ain't? I thought everybody's heard about it." A sibilance drifted. "Well, you know Petrie took in the Tabler kid after Tabler's old man kicked him out."

Day said, "He's livin' in Petrie's basement, right?"

Waycross nodded.

Ed pictured Ramona walking directly toward him. She was near enough to show him the expression on her face, a grimace of exhaustion. He listened again for the labor of her breath but heard instead Waycross's whisper carrying his name.

"Everybody's just a happy little family at the Petries' house. Petrie and his old lady, Connie, and the Tabler kid, snug as fucking bugs." Waycross's sarcasm was perfectly pitched, enticing even Mitchell.

Ed heard *happy little family* and *his old lady*. He tried to act as if he didn't know Waycross was talking about him. He started to measure his steps to the next stake, but lost the count and had to start again. He felt suddenly surrounded: Ramona inching toward him through the field, showing him how much she was willing to hurt to get away, while Waycross and the others were having open fun with him.

He tried a third time to walk thirty steps but stopped, mindless of the count.

"So one day," Waycross said, "Petrie comes home from work and calls to Connie. Yells, toodle fucking loo, but he gets no answer. He figures his old lady is gone, which is strange since she don't leave no note like she always does."

The others snorted delightedly, knowing now what was coming. Adams stopped his work, too, and walked up to the truck to listen.

Ed heard *lady . . . gone . . . leave no note*, and the smothered snickering of the others. The anger was sounding again, the same hum as before but softening beneath Waycross's whispers, as though its deft accompaniment.

He looked into the field and imagined Ramona coming to a stop as she saw a span of snow fence at the end of her path. He saw her bend over, her hand on her knee, to get her breath. He felt a pulse of hope.

Waycross began to make a cigarette. "So Petrie calls again, and still don't get nothing back, except he hears some funny rustling from the basement." March and Day were already laughing. "You ain't heard about this?" Waycross said. "So he thinks, 'What the fuck is goin' on?' and tiptoes down and it's just a damn shame, really, for all of 'em, that there ain't no way to get outa the house from the basement except the stairs Petrie's standin' on."

Ed picked up a stake and drove it, not caring where.

No way to get outa the house . . . a damn shame, really.

He imagined Ramona rising up and looking directly into his eyes. He picked up his stakes and hurried to set another. Then he saw her look to her right and immediately head off again, angling through the grass toward March's orange flag, where the ditch became steep past the end of the fence.

His panic bloomed as he saw her moving toward the end of the field where there was no fence. He managed to choke his scream; it came out as a thin, high sound only Adams picked up, and when he heard it he turned from Waycross to watch Ed.

Ed kept himself from running through the ditch. He imagined cutting her off, driving stakes as he ran, all the way to the field's end. Somehow he'd move quickly enough to get the fence set in time. But he stayed where he was, closing his eyes against the vision of anything more, and it worked. He saw only soft bleached light with his eyes closed.

"And there they was, Connie and the Tabler kid, naked as jays in the Tabler kid's bed. And you know what she says? She stammers around and kinda whines, 'Oh, Bob. I thought you was goin' to Chatham today.' Like the whole thing's really Petrie's fault for not goin' to Chatham!"

Ed felt their laughter engulf him. He picked up the sledgehammer, aimed it at the stake he'd just set, and brought it down with all his strength. A resonant clang filled the air. He raised the hammer higher and brought it down again. The stake appeared to be descending on its own in deep eager jerks, seeking refuge beneath the ground from yet another of his blows.

He beat the stake again and again, the clanging regular, the ring of a vicious bell, and it stopped the others' laughter. They turned toward Ed and saw the hammer lifting above Ed's head, rising with the ease of a limb. It flew through its arc, struck the stake once more and drove it almost flush with the ground.

Ed dropped to his knees to give it still another blow.

"Ed!" Adams shouted. "Stop it!" He broke away from the others and started down the ditch.

Ed heard enough of Adams's cry to make him pause as he started to swing down. He struck the stake with the neck of the hammer just below its head and a dull splintering sound reached the crew as it watched him. Ed felt the pain of his miss, slivered steel flying up through his forearms, before he looked down to see the hammer's shattered handle. It seemed to him wounded, a horribly fractured bone. He felt a sudden deep grief.

Still on his knees, he shifted around to see Adams coming toward him and he knew that Adams, in calling to him, had wanted this to happen. He'd tried to guard the hammer from the others with just this fear in mind.

He got to his feet as Adams approached. He looked up at the others and saw their faces, the pleasure of Waycross's story still held in their loose smiles, and knew that they were no longer even trying to hide their laughter from him. He picked up the sledgehammer as an impulse went through him which made him smile.

Ed's crooked grin stopped Adams, made him stumble, but it filled him with a warmth, the sensation of a longing being touched. He saw Ed's grin as something once again affectionate, a sly show of their conspiracy restored, and Adams instinctively smiled in return and walked to Ed, feeling eager and secure, ready for whatever Ed had in mind. He'd missed Ed's old strength so much he thought he recognized it.

Ed saw Adams walking toward him through the pulsing red screen. He said, "Laugh at me, you motherfuck," and Adams knew he'd been mistaken, knew it quickly enough to see the sledgehammer moving. He lunged and grabbed it at the top of its swing and the two of them held its handle, held each other through the wood, struggling through a violent dance, spitting wet hissing noises through their teeth, the hammer high above their heads in brutal equipoise.

FROGCHILD ON THE DAY OF CORPUS CHRISTI

■ Robert Antoni

Good Lord, the Eighties. The tyrannies of the anorectic. The horror of safe sex, the voodoo of economics and the microchip. And that fun-loving cadre of bloated politicians, harping from the bridge of the ship of state. What swell guys to sail with through a decade. Oh ho, the Eighties, the stress fractures in the national soul, the fatigue of the cultural imagination. The ascendancy of Diet Fiction, Lite Prose, no-cal Lishy treats, astronomical surges of hype cranked from the Noise Machine. Shake me when it's over.

But turn past Page One, Section A, undercut the explosive surface of any decade and—be reassured—you'll find sane good news, the timeless and undaunted crusade for creativity. The vital work is shared by many; the collective traits of their labor as valuable today as in the past . . . as in the future. Take, for instance, the fiction of Robert Antoni, an American whose heritage is hemispheric (lucky man), a synthesis of north and south. Here, by his hand, you will find maintained the courage of the multiple clause. Not an anachronism nor an indulgence, but a painstakingly developed strength. You will find impetuosity of language and story. Language—Antoni adores language; its energy, its complexity, its fertility. And he narrates—not like a self-starved teenager of glutted affectation, but rather like a penniless grandfather who in his day has feasted on a world of wonder. Nor is Antoni compelled to smash the atom of meaning in his prose. There is meaning enough in the equilibrium of his humor, the grace of his wit, the integrity of intelligence brought to bear on the imagination. What more is it that we want—need?— when we sit down with a book to suck the dream from the words? At today's market rates, measure your money's worth in paragraphs of this writer's work. Taste the delicious opening of "Frogchild on the Day of Corpus Christi" and you'll know immediately you've spent well. If you get addicted, blame it on the fundamentals.

—BOB SHACOCHIS

*T*he bottle was big and obzockee. I was having a hard time toting it. It was the day before my thirteenth birthday, seventy-seven years ago: tomorrow I will be ninety years of age. I am still a practicing physician, and as I sit here in this library, at this desk of my father's, of my father's father—dug as a chunk of purpleheart wood by six Warrahoon Indians out of the misty jungles of Venezuela, floated down the Orinoco and towed across the Caribbean behind three rowing pirogues, my grandfather calling the cadence stroke by stroke in a language nearly forgotten—I feel I should be smaller, sitting behind this desk, looking out of this window at this moon above the same black sea. I should be smaller. I am too big for this chair, its arms pressing uncomfortably into my sides, but I was so skinny then my navel stuck out in a tight knot. I held the bottle against my chest. I was bareback—wearing only my baggy school shortpants and some sandals—with my arms hugging the bottle, my fingers cupped into the hollow of the bottom, the top butting my chin with every step. I couldn't look down, so I didn't have to see what I knew was inside. It was a very old bottle, the kind used to preserve fruit, made of thick glass with wire clamps to hold-down its glass lid. I was sweating. My stomach kept sticking to the bottle. My bung navel rubbed against the glass, sometimes pinching and sending a shock down my legs to my toes. I sucked in my belly as I walked.

The sun was already rising behind me, rising with the dust stirred up by my hurrying feet. I was thinking: Maraval must be ten mile from Domingo Cemetery at least. How you could foot it there and back in time? Thinking: Ten mile from Domingo Cemetery to Maraval Swamp fa the least. Daddy ga box you ears fa true if you don't get back in time. This bottle heavy like it fill with rockstones. And these arms only crying to drop-off. But how you could stop to put it down?

There were no people on the road yet, only some potcakes curled up among the weeds pushing out in the middle, and a few boldface billies on their way to pasture, lengths of twisted rotten cord dragging behind them. They were tall as I was, and they came at me snuffling, pressing their bearded faces into mine, staring at me through silver eyes from another world. I kicked them away, thinking: How she could be dead if she eyes aren't closed? But if she isn't dead, and you are home in you bed dreaming all this, then how you could be tired toting this bottle? Thinking: You know they ga start with the funeral first thing as she was so hurry hurry. So you best just keep on walking, and don't even bother templating bout stopping to put it down to baste no time, and anyway you don't want to have to look at his face neither.

There were small villages along Divina Trace, the dirt road which began behind the convent, weaving its way through the tenements in the outskirts of St. Maggy. Then it stretched-out through cocoa and coconut estates in the country, canefields, finally ending with the Church of Magdalena Divina at the edge of Maraval Swamp. The trace curved through bush—with the shanties and roukou-scrubbed mudhuts hidden behind tufts of bamboo, schools of yardfowl scurrying in dustwaves across the road, the odors of cookfires, stench of garbage—unless the trace passed through one of the estates. Then it ran straight, mossy gray cocoa trees on either side, with nutmeg or brilliant orange immortelle between to shade them from the sun. Otherwise Divina passed among thick groves of coconut palms, their fronds rustling in the breeze high above, or it would be closed in by impenetrable walls of cane, the air sweetsmelling, charred if the field had been scorched to scare out the scorpions for harvest. There were hills from which the mountains could be seen at one horizon, hot black sea at the other.

I'd been to Maraval Swamp many times before, but I didn't want to believe it was ten miles away. I kept thinking: Maybe it's not so far as that? You know it is ten mile at least. How many times you been to the church with Mother Maurina and the whole of St. Maggy Provisional to see the walking statue and hear about the Black Virgin? How many times you been to the swamp with Monsignor and the whole of form-three-science to collect specimens fa dissections? With daddy and all four troups of seascouts to catch jumpingfrogs fa the summer jamboree? Thinking: You know it is ten mile fa the least. How many times you been with you jacks to catch guanas to pope them off on the Indians by Suparee fa fifty cent fa each? Running and grabbing them up quick by they tails and swinging them round and round until they heads kaponkle, and they drop boo-doops sweet in the crocassack! And the time you get a dollar fa that big big one, and you eat so many icyhots fa that dollar you belly wanted to bust frop-poops! How them coolies and Warrahoons could eat them things? But Granny Myna say Barto use to eat guana all the time in Venezuela when they was first married, and they had the cattleranch in Estado Monagas where daddy was born. And the time Barto try to bring one inside and she chase him out with he own cutlass—because one thing Granny Myna wouldn't stand in the house is lizard or nothing so—and it is from eating that nastiness that kill Barto young like that. But daddy say a Warrahoon bring him a stew one to the hospital once, and he couldn't tell the difference from fricassee chicken.

I didn't want to think about the contents of the bottle, about the ten miles ahead, and I didn't want to think about getting back too late for the funeral. I'd been up the whole night, and I was already tired carrying the bottle: I'd only just left the cemetery. I hadn't been able to fall asleep that night, turning in my bed thinking about old Granny Myna. She'd told me a story once about a frog she'd seen suck out the eye of a woman in Wallafield, and I could not dissolve from my mind the image of this woman struggling with the huge white frog. The woman had been sitting good as ever beneath a tamarind tree, and when she looked up the frog jumped out and stuck to her face. Granny Myna told me it took two big men to pull off this frog, and when he came off the eye came out too. She said that if Barto had not been there to pick-up the eye from out the mud, to spit on it and rub off the mud and push it back in, the woman would have walked away from that frog without an eye.

It was not unusual for me to awaken in the middle of the night and begin thinking about Granny Myna and one of her stories—I'm sure I wasn't worried about her—but I remember I could not put her and the frog out of my mind. My grandmother was ninety-six, always talking about dying, yet Granny Myna had never known a sick day in her life, and we were convinced she'd live forever. I couldn't fall asleep, so I woke up my younger brother to ask him about the woman from Wallafield. He cussed me and rolled over again. I remember I lay there listening to the oscillating fan, its noise growing louder with each pass, until it seemed to be screaming in my ears. I threw off the sheet and jumped out of bed. I pulled on my shorts and sandals and walked quietly down the hall. Papee Vince, my grandfather on my mother's side, had his room at the end. I hurried past and on down the stairs. Granny Myna's door was open, so I stuck my head in: she was sitting up in her bed waiting. I went and sat next to her. She looked at me for a long time, reached across me to put her beads down on the bedstand, and she began to talk.

He was born a man, but above he cojones he was a frog. It happen so, because Magdalena Domingo was a whore, and a black bitch, and on top of that she was a bad woman. Magdalena make this practice of going every Sunday to Maraval Swamp— because I use to follow her and sometimes she would meet there with Barto beneath the saman tree—she go to Maraval Swamp because she like to watch the crapos singando. Magdalena just love to see the frogs fucking, and is that she must have been looking the moment she conceive the child, because Barto use the same principle to create a zebra from two donkeys by putting them to do they business in a room he have paint with stripes. So too again everybody take you daddy for another St. John, because above my bed I have the picture hanging there with him still smiling happy on the dishplate that I use to look up at it in all my moments of passion, and that is why you daddy have those same curlycurls, and the same crease right here in the forehead, and how else could it be you daddy is the only Domingo of all of us with those eyes always watching you just like St. John? You see how Papa God does do He work? In the same way Magdalena make that child with the face of a frog to mimic she own, and with the cojones of every man on this island of Corpus Christi!

When Dr. Brito Salizar see this child coming out, he only want to push it back inside Magdalena pussy and hide it from the rest of the world. Dr. Brito know nothing good could come from this child that is the living sin of all the earth. Because it take Magdalena only one look in the face of this frogchild to kill sheself dead: she press the pillow and hold up she breath until she suffocate. By the time Dr. Brito have realize and cut the pillow from out she lock-up jaws she was already dead. Feathers was gusting back-and forth in that little hospital room like a blizzard. Dr. Brito blow into the air before him to clear way the floating feathers, he cross heself, and Dr. Brito open he mouth wide to bend-over to bite-off the cordstring from the belly of this crapochild to join the world of the living with the world of the dead for the whole of eternity!

That night there was such a great rain that the Caronee have overflow sheself, and the next morning there was cocodrilles in the streets and the basements of all the houses. So when Barto arrive now dress in mud up to he cojones, and holding this shoebox in he hands, I grab on to he mustache and I put one cursing on him to say he is never coming inside the house with that crapochild! But Barto is a man that nobody couldn't tell him nothing once he have make up he head, and he don't pay me no attention a-tall never mind my bawling to break down the roof. I tell him Papa God will kill him and all of us too if he try to bring that crapochild inside, but Barto can't even hear, because he walk straight through the livingroom and he put this shoebox down in the middle of the diningroom table. And if I would have give

Barto only half a chance, he would have lay this frogchild right down next to Amadao who is the last of the nine sleeping in my bedroom in the crib, born no even six months before.

Well Evelina—she is the servant living with me even in those days, just a little negrita running about the estate when she mummy dead and I take she up—Evelina only have to hear about this crapochild coming inside the house, and she start to beat she breast and shout one set of Creole-obeah bubball on the child, and she run quick to she room to bury sheself beneath the bed. Reinaldo and Paco—they is the only two young ones left in the house then besides Amadao—Reinaldo and Paco come running to Barto to question him where do he find this chuff-chuff frog, and could they please take him in the yard to find out how good can he jump. But Barto only have to make one cut eye on these boys for them to know he is no skylarking, and little Reinaldo and Paco take off running and we don't see them again until late in the night. As for me now, after a time I have quiet down little bit, and Barto turn to me—because of course at this time I am still nursing Amadao—and he want to know now if I am ready to feed he Manuelito, which is the name Barto name the child. Sweet heart of Jesus! I look Barto straight in the eyes, and I tell him if he only bring that crapochild anywhere near by me, I will squeeze he cojones so hard they will give off milk like two balls of cheese, and he could feed that to he pendejo frogchild!

But nothing couldn't stop Barto. Like he want to take on Papa God-self. Because next thing I see he have pick up he revolver again to protect against the cocodrilles, and he go outside to the shed for the big cow that we have there by the name of Mariquilla. And this Mariquilla have been with us so many years that she have come tame tame, that the boys use to ride her all about the place like a horserace, and we have to be very careful no to leave a plantain or anything so on the table, because soon as you turn round she would push she head in through the window and carry it way. So here is me now only standing up like a mokojumbie watching at Barto leading this cow through the mud that is high as Mariquilla belly, and Barto carry her straight through the door right past the entrancehall into the diningroom up on top the table! Oui Papayo! Well now I know I am soon to go vie-kee-vie!

Barto leave Mariquilla there just so, and he gone to the sea for a bucket of water to wipe off the mud from Mariquilla pechugas. But when Barto pick up this frogchild out the shoebox—and I have a good look at this frogchild face for the first time—I take-off with one set of bawling again because you never see no creature on the skin of Papa God earth so ugly as that! Even Mariquilla have to jump when she see this crapochild, and Barto have to hold her down to keep her from bolting out the door. But nothing couldn't stop Barto once he have make up he head, because next thing I see he is untying the bandanna kerchief from round he neck, and he fix it to blind poor Mariquilla eyes. In no time a-tall she have calm down again, and Barto pick Mariquilla up on-top the table again holding this crapochild below her with the tot-tot in the big frogmouth, and he is sucking down milk that is spilling all over the ugly frogface, and he is talking one set of froglanguage like oy-juga oy-juga oy-juga!

That night I am in my bed trying my best to sleep with all this confusion going on in the house, and Barto come inside the room—because Barto use to keep he own bedroom upstairs, in the one you mummy and daddy use now—he come inside the room just here at the end of this bed pointing he revolver at me with he eyes only spitting fire, demanding to know what have I do with he Manuelito! Sweet heart of Jesus! I answer him that this frogchild have make he brain vie-kee-vie now for true—because is no me a-tall to touch that crapochild no even until the ends of the earth—and if he have disappear I don't know nothing as the last I see him he is still sleeping happy in the shoebox cradle in the middle of the diningroom table. But Barto have reach into a state now over this crapochild, so I decide to go and wake-up Evelina and the two of us begin to ransack the house—looking in all the drawers and beneath the beds and all about for this child—that we can't find him nowhere a-tall and we don't know what we will do. Just then I hear Evelina scream someplace outside, and I take off running to find her there by the pond for all the ducks to come and bathe theyself, there standing-up with she eyes open wide wide like she have just see a jab-jab, only watching at Reinaldo and Paco and this frogchild swimming!

Next morning the whole of St. Maggy have reach at my doorstep to see this crapochild. The Caranee have no even begin to go down yet, and the mud in the streets is still high as you knees, but nothing couldn't slow down these people. In all they windows they is jam-up standing one on top the other waiting half the day for only a glimpse of this frogchild, and some little baboo-boy see the crowd and come running pushing he bicyclecar through the mud with all the bottles of canesyrup spilling-out, and he begin to shave ice like he catch a vaps, selling one set of snowball to these people only looking through the glass licking licking licking with all they tongues green and purple and yellow like this is one pappyshow going on now with this cow and this crapochild inside the house! Everybody is bawling and laughing and making one set of frogfaces to imitate this child, and soon I begin to hear someone mamaguying me about how I is the mother of this crapochild—when they know good enough the child belong to Barto and that black jamet Magdalena and I don't have nothing to do with him a-tall—and how they use to see me with Barto all the time by Maraval watching the frogs fucking! Sweet heart of Jesus! I run quick to that shoeboxcradle and I grab up this crapochild, and I go to Barto on my knees to beg him please for the mercy of Papa God please to take him way!

Barto look down on me a moment, and I see that I have finally touch him. Because he reach down and he take way this crapochild that is wrap up now in a white coverlet that you can no even see the half belonging to a man. Barto carry the child to the big closet of glass that we have there in the parlor to keep all the guns. He take out the biggest one—this is the rifle all bathe in silver and mother-of-pearl that we have there since the days of General Monagas—and Barto carry the child and the gun both up to the garret. He climb-out on-top the roof and he walk straight to the very edge. Barto did no even open he mouth to speak a word. He stand up there just so in he leather clothes that I have rub all over with sweetoil until they are glowing, and he is holding this frogchild with he legs spread wide and the spurs on the boots and the eyes only flaming, and he reach out slow with he arm straight and General Monagas big rifle pointing up at heaven to fire so—boo-doom!—and these people take off running swimming in the mud like each one get jook with a big jooker up they backside!

People had begun to appear on the road, most going in the direction of town. They were dressed in their best clothes for church, or they were already costumed as some saint or Bible character. That day was a big one for Corpus Christi: it was the religious feastday after which the island had been named. We all went to Mass in the morning. In the afternoon there were parades through the streets of St. Maggy, the fetes continuing until midnight. Because at the stroke of twelve all the music stopped, and we returned to church to begin the Easter Vigil. There were never any motor vehicles on Divina other than the occasional truck or jitney belonging to one of the estates. Bicycles and donkeycarts went by, all decorated with crepepaper and papier-mâché.

Everyone who passed looked at me toting the big bottle. I was sweating, covered in dust, thinking: Supposing somebody see this frogbaby now and push out a scream? Supposing somebody question you where you get him from? What you ga say? You dig him up in Domingo Cemetery? You catch him in Maraval Swamp? Then I began to think: But nobody seeing this frogbaby a-tall! You sure you have anything in this glassbottle? Maybe it's only fill with seawater? Maybe this frogbaby is only something you dream-up? Some jujubee granny Myna push inside you head?

Just then a boy about my own age—costumed as Moses in a white turban, and dragging a big tablet of pasteboard commandments behind him—grabbed his father's sleeve and pointed at me:

"See that, Daddy? Look the frog that boy hold up inside he glassbottle! He big as a mon-key! He live you know, Daddy! He swimming!"

Magdalena just love to go to Maraval to see the crapos singando, because she use to walk all the way from St. Maggy Convent every Sunday parading through the streets dress-up in she clothes of a nun before the Face of Papa God, when beneath she is nothing but a black whore. And it is those frogs fucking Magdalena must have been looking to make the imprint of that frogface the moment she conceive the child, because a crapo is the only creature on the skin of Papa God earth that can hold on and singando passionate for three days and three nights without even a pause, and how else could he come out a perfect man from here to here with the big business hanging, and the rest a frog? Of course Dr. Brito realize right away this child is a crapo above the cojones, and he say that he have hear of more frogchildren even though he have never have the priviledge to see one before heself, but I know that is impossible because this world could never be big enough for two. The other schoolboy doctor in the hospital then—he is the first to come from England with a big degree stamp by the Queen that was Elizabeth the segunda one, but how can anybody with sense listen to a doctor who learn everything from a book without ever seeing a sick person?—this bobo little schoolboy doctor say the child isn't no frog a-tall, but he have a kind of a thing in the gents or the blood or something so. He bring out the big black book that is so big he can hardly tote it, and he point to the picture of this thing now, and he mark it down on a piece of paper for me to see it: ANNA-AND-CECILY. The little schoolboy doctor say this thing means to be born without a brain, and that is what cause the child to look like a frog. But it is you Uncle Bobby—he is the scientist of bones and rocks and a very brilliant old man—Uncle Bobby prove without any questions that the child is a frog, and he do have a brain, even though it is no bigger than the size of a saltprune.

The frogchild didn't have no skull a-tall, but only the soft soft covering on the head like the skin of a zabuca. So all Uncle Bobby have to do is cut a little cut with the scissors, and squeeze on the both sides, and the little brain pop-out like a chenet out the shell. Of course the first thing Uncle Bobby do is run quick to Maraval for a big crapo-grande, and he take out the brain of this frogbull to compare it with that of the child. Well the two was so much the same in size and shape and weight and everything so, that soon as Uncle Bobby go outside for a quick weewee and come back, he forget who belong to who.

I only wish to Papa God Uncle Bobby could have satisfy heself with the brain. But when it come to he science nothing couldn't satisfy you Uncle Bobby. By the time we have finish with the brain he was all excited, and he decide now he want to preserve this crapochild for more dissections. It is Uncle Bobby then who put the child in the bottle of seawater, but that same night Barto discover him floating downstairs on the shelf in Bobby laboratory, and that, is the beginning of the end!

"Eh-eh, white-boy! What you say?"

A man in an oxcart going in my direction stopped beside me. I stood staring up at this old East Indian dougla who'd wrapped himself and his entire oxcart in aluminum foil. He nodded his nose at the bottle:

"Where you going toting that thing fa health? That glassbottle big as you own self! Why you don't climb-up here rest you load, let me carry you little bit down the road?"

"Who you is?" I asked. "Ro-bot?"

"Robot fa fut!" The old man chupsed: he sucked his teeth in exasperation. "I is the archangel St. Michael, this my chariot going to battle! And you best get you little backside up here fa sin, you ga kill-up youself toting that big glasstin! Ro-bot!" He chupsed again.

I gave the bottle a heave and put it on the shelf next to the old man's feet. He leaned over and studied it for several long seconds. He sat up again, his costume crinkling, and we looked at each other.

"Come, boy!" he said, and I climbed-up onto the bench next to him. "Plenty more tin-paper back there fa you you know. Why you don't costume youself proper, we to play mas' fa so!"

"You don't think one robot is enough?"

He chupsed, and he gave the worn rope he had for reins a tug. We left slowly, pitching from side to side as we went, the solution sloshing in the bottle at our feet. The ox was a huge coolie-buffalo, with widespread s-shaped horns and a sticky mist rising from its bluegray hump. After a while the old man looked at me again, his face beaded with perspiration. His white stubble of beard, gray eyes and lashes looked silver against his black sienna skin. It all seemed to match his aluminum outfit.

"Where you going toting this bottle on Corpus Christi Day?" he asked. "Corpus Christi is the day fa play is play!"

I was looking up at his cone-shaped hat, the cuffed brim riding on the bridge of his nose like an oversized sailorboy cap.

"What wrong with you, boy? You don't talk?"

"You not hot inside all that costume?"

He chupsed. "Where you going with this glassbottle, boy?"

"You ever see a frogbaby before?"

He sucked his teeth again. "Ninety-some years I been walking this earth, my mummy tell me. Still plenty things I never see."

A breeze came up and the old man held onto his hat. I shielded my eyes against the dust raised from the road.

"You think somebody could die with their eyes open?"

He turned to look at me. "Everybody born with they eyes close-down, and everybody die with they eyes open-up round. Papa God mistake is He do the thing back-to-front. And that boy, is the beginning of all this confusion and quarrelment. Now tell me where you going toting this glassbottle!"

"Maraval."

"Quite so to Maraval footing? Good thing I stop, boy. You would have dead up youself polapee-zoy, time as you arrive by the swamp with this big glasstin!"

He reached behind and handed me the roll of aluminum foil. "Corpus Christi not the day to tote no heavy load. Dress-up youself proper let we play! We ga meet up the band down the road, do one set of monkeybusiness before we pray!"

I told him I had to go to Maraval Swamp.

He chupsed. "Suit youself then, white son. Time as we bounce-up with the flock of seraphim, you would almost reach you destination."

I put the roll of foil down as we continued, the ox walking at its slow steady pace, the cart pitching on its unsteady wheels.

* * *

I never hold nothing against Magdalena. Papa God is she judge, and if she is a whore she must answer to Him. Who am I to say she is wrong to be Barto mistress, and how can I hold that crapochild against her, or Barto, or anybody else when he is a creature of Papa God, touch by He own hand, make of He own flesh, breathing of He own air? And so I pick him up. Even though he is the most hateful thing to me in the world, he is still the son of my husband and I must go to this child. I am with Evelina in the kitchen in the middle of preparing dinner when I feel something touch my heart. I don't even finish putting the remainder of the banana leaves in the pot of boiling water to make the pastelles, but I leave it there just so and I go to this frogchild. I pick him up with so much tears in my eyes I can hardly see, with so much trembling in my hand I can hardly hold it steady enough to push my tot-tot in he mouth, but I do it! For the love of Papa God I do it! I feed that frogchild with the milk of my own breast!

I never hold nothing against Magdalena. I try my best never to listen to what people say, and let me tell you people can say some words to push like a knive in you chest. But I never hold nothing against Magdalena. I am kind to her, and when I meet her in the Cathedral with all the other nuns I make a special point to wish her a pleasant todobem, because who am I to say Barto must give he affections to me alone when he have enough love in he heart for all the world? No husband have ever honor he wife more, and offer her more love and devotion then that man give to me. Barto raise me up on a pedestal, you hear! On a pedestal!

But something happen when that child begin to suck at my breast. Something happen, and I don't know what it is. Like some poison pass from out he mouth to go inside my blood, because next thing I know I am running back to the kitchen for that big basin of water boiling that is waiting for me to finish the pastelles, and I push him in! Evelina scream but I can no even hear her, because before I can know what my hands are doing they are bury up to they elbows in this boiling water—and how it is I can't even feel it I couldn't tell you not to this day, but when you go crazy like that nothing can pain you—and here am I drowning this child in the basin of boiling water with the banana leaves swirling swirling like the green flames of hell! Soon as I can realize myself I pull him from out the water, but by now he is already dead. I can no think what to do. I can only plead with Evelina for the mercy of Papa God please to take him way. I beg her to carry him back to Maraval where he belong, but Evelina refuse to come anywhere near this crapochild no matter if he is living or if he is dead. After a time though she have accept to carry him way for me—and I swear her to go straight to Maraval and pitch him in—and I go outside in the street to look behind Evelina walking with this crapochild hold upside down by the legs like a cockfowl going to sell at Victoria Market. I watch behind Evelina until I can no see her anymore, and I go back in the house to try to finish seeing about the pastelles. I only wish to Papa God I could have remain in that street! Because I put loud goatmouth on myself saying about that crapofowl, as no sooner have I go back inside the house when Evelina turn-round to come all the way back only to sell this crapochild to Uncle Bobby for a scrunting five coconutdollars! Uncle Bobby have decide now he want to make some of he science on the child, and that night Barto find him floating on the shelf down-stairs in Bobby laboratory. Sweet heart of Jesus! I thought Barto would kill me! I have never see him so upset as when he come to me with this bottle, and he command me to tell him what happen to the child. When I have finish—and I am kneeling down on the ground pleading with him standing above me with he eyes only flaming—he tell me that I will suffer for this the whole of my life and death, because I can never even look forward to lying in the ground in peace next to my husband, as between us will be this crapochild to remind me on myself and torment me until the ends of eternity! And with that Barto leave toting the bottle into the night.

But I can never suffer anymore. After ninety-six years I have no more strength left to go on. My eyes have dry up, and there is no more tears left to pass, and Papa God have forgive me. He have forgive me, and tomorrow I will be with Him in heaven! Papa

God have forgive me—and Barto must forgive me now after all these years of crying in the dark—and I am ready. I am ready to lie down my bones in peace—peace that I have earn with sweating blood cold in the hot night—but I will never know peace so long as I have to be bury next to that crapochild! Never! But you will take him way, Johnny. You will go for me tonight to Domingo Cemetery, and you will dig him up, and you will carry him way. Now I am ready to die. Go and call you mummy and daddy.

We could hear the Divina churchband singing and beating steeldrums in the distance long before we met them. The sun remained hidden behind the dark clouds, but the old-man continued to sweat in his aluminum outfit. A breeze came up and blew away his hat, so I took-up the roll of foil and stood on the bench to make him another, a tall spike at the top, the helmet fit for an archangel. There must have been fifty people in the band, and twice as many children, all costumed as angels. The old-man steered his oxcart to the side of the road, and we watched the parade go by, the angels waving to us as they passed. Most of them were on foot, but there were bicycles and three or four donkeycarts. The children were running back-and-forth, screaming, flapping their wings. Each of the angels carried some musical instrument or the other—steeldrums, some horns, mandolins—but most of the instruments consisted of a cowbell, a whistle, a rumbottle-and-spoon, or a calabash with a handful of dried poincianaseeds inside. The old man began to sing, his lips flapping over his nearly toothless gums, spittle flying. He took hold of my hands and shook them up and down to the music, his aluminum arms crackling, and I looked into his eyes.

"Time to jubilate, white-son! Open you mouthgate!"

I began to sing too:

> *"Sal-ve Re-gina,*
> *Regina Magda-lena!*
> *Be-ne-dicimus te.*

Glo-ri-i-camus te.
A-do-ramus te.
Regina Magda-lena!"

When the parade had passed I got down from the cart and the old man handed me the bottle. He turned the oxcart around and waved, his costume flashing molten metal for an instant as it caught the light. I watched the old man disappear into the cloud of dust which followed his band of angels. I looked after him for a long time, until the dust had settled, and the singing had been reduced to a rumble in the distance. I looked around and realized I was suddenly alone: there was no one left on the road. It was quiet. I turned and continued walking, calm now, unhurried.

Granny Myna stared at me in silence. I couldn't move, couldn't get up from the bed. She reached and took both my hands in hers. "Go, Johnny," she said again. "Tell you mummy and daddy I am ready."

I ran upstairs and called them, my brother, Evelina, and Papee Vince waking with the commotion. We crowded around Granny Myna sitting up in the small bed, her back against the pillow against the headboard: my father in his drawers sitting next to her listening to her heart through his stethoscope, my mother holding my little sister with one hand, my younger brother's hand in the other, Papee Vince in the chair leaning forward over his big belly, old Evelina mumbling some obeah incantation, and me thinking: This is not you standing here seeing this because you are upstairs in you bed sleeping. Why you don't go see if you find yourself and then you would know it is only you dreaming?

My father pulled the stethoscope from his ears and left it hanging from his neck. He looked around, got up and went to the small table covered with Granny Myna's religious objects: a statue of St. Michael, of St. Christopher, a photograph of the Pope, of Barto, a plastic bottle shaped like the Virgin filled with holywater from Lourdes, some artificial roses, multicolored beads, all decorated on a doily she had crocheted in pink, white, and babyblue. My father took up a candle and put it in Granny Myna's hand, closing her fingers around it. He lit a match, but before he could touch it to the candle Mother Superior Maurina, Granny Myna's sister, entered the room. We all turned to look at her. No one had called her, and as far as we knew she and Granny Myna had not talked in more than fifty years, since before Mother Maurina had entered the convent. She had never set foot in our house.

My father lit another match and touched it to the candle. He told us quietly to kneel down. My grandmother studied the flame for a few seconds, took a deep breath, blew it out:

"Stand up! Pray for me to die if you have to pray!"

My father chupsed. "Mum-my—"

"Tomorrow is the sixteen of April, Holy Thursday: Corpus Christi Day. It is the happiest day in heaven, and I am going to be there. I don't want no funeral confusion. Barto have the stone and everything there ready waiting for me. Just dig the hole and push me in the ground first thing in the morning."

We didn't know what to do. My father sucked his teeth. He looked at my mother, got up again and sat next to my grandmother, listening to her heart through his stethoscope. Granny Myna's hands lay on her lap, her fists clenched. Her lips were pressed firmly together over her gums, her pointed chin protruding, trembling slightly. Her eyes were wide, unblinking—fixed on me. I watched her jaw drop slowly, her lips go purple and open a little, her skin turn to soft wax. I kept thinking: Her eyes aren't closed so she isn't dead. Her eyes aren't closed so she isn't dead. My father turned. Before he could look up I was already running.

I ran halfway to Domingo Cemetery before I turned around and went back for the shovel, thinking: If the bottle isn't there she isn't dead. Just make up you mind not to dream up the bottle too. The graveyard smelled of wet earth, rotting leaves, edged by the oversweet smell of eucalyptus. A small coral wall ran all around. The huge trees rustled in the breeze, the undersides of their leaves flashing silver in the moonlight. I went straight to Granny Myna's intended grave, everything but her deathdate chiseled into the headstone. I dropped the shovel and squinted to see the line of graves. On one side of the plot where my grandmother would be buried was Uncle Bobby's grave, Manuelito's on the other. Beside Manuelito was Barto's grave, and beside him, Magdalena Maria Domingo. I moved closer: MANUELITO DOMINGO, NACI 16 ET MORI 19 ARILIS, ANNO DOMINI NOSTRI.

I picked up the shovel again, thinking: If it isn't there she isn't dead because you refuse to dream up the bottle. You can go home and laugh at youself sleeping. But I hadn't sent the shovel into the ground three times when I hit something solid. I threw the shovel aside and got down on my knees to dig with both hands. After a moment I realized I'd found the bottle.

I tried to pull it out but my hands slipped. I fell backward as though I'd been shoved, my head thudding against a gravestone, and someone threw a clump of wet dirt in my face—like I'd been slapped. I spit out the dirt and tried to wipe my eyes. There was no one there.

I got up slowly, brushed myself off. I knelt, digging carefully, all the way around the bottle. I placed a foot on either side of the hole and lifted it out. I rolled the bottle into a clear space and got down on my knees again, rubbing my hands over the glass, spitting, removing the dirt. I bent closer—still couldn't see. I stood. Straining, I lifted the bottle over my head, the moon lighting it up.

By the time I neared the end of Divina Trace the breeze had come up. Several dark clouds eclipsed the sun. The eight or ten houses of Suparee village were deserted, not even a fowl or a potcake in the street. At the end of the road the Divina Church was small, gray against a gray sky. The thick wooden doors were wide open. It was empty, cold inside. I walked slowly up the center aisle, my sandals squeaking on the polished stone, each step echoing through the church. There was a gold baptismal font off to one side of the altar. On the other side was a small chapel, devotion candles flickering in their red glass holders, the smells of Creole incense and sweet oliveoil growing stronger as I approached.

I stood in front of the chapel, but I could see nothing in the darkness within except the bright red flames. I put the bottle down on one of the pews and climbed the steps, a line of calabash shells filled with sweetoil on either side. I knelt at the chapel railing. She began to take shape slowly out of the darkness, reflections of the red flames rising on her face, flashing through the clouds of rising incense: her gentle eyes, comforting lips, the crimson mark on her forehead, her burnt umber skin, long wig of black hair. Her faded gown was covered with jeweled pendants, her outstretched arms thick with silver bangles and solid gold rosaries—offerings for prayers answered—Magdalena Divina, Mother of Miracles, Black Virgin of Maraval! I closed my eyes: *Hail Mary full of grace the lord is with thee blessed are thou amongst women and blessed is the fruit of you womb. Holy Mary mother of God pray fa we sinners now and at the hour of we death amen.* I dipped my finger into the basin of holywater, crossed myself. I picked up the bottle again, walked quickly across the altar, left through the sanctuary.

Behind the church was an immense saman tree, spread symmetrically over a plot of green grass. Beyond it Maraval Swamp was greenish-black, mangrove growing along the edge and in the shallow areas, their thick moss-covered banyans arching out of the water like charmed snakes. I walked along the line of mangrove—picking my way through the tall reeds, the mud sucking at my sandals—until I found a gap where I could walk out into the water. I put the bottle down and it sank an inch into the mud. I flipped open the wire clamps at the top and lifted off the lid. I'd expected some pungent odor: there was none, only the stagnant smell of the morass. I tried my best not to look into the bottle, but I couldn't avoid seeing two bulging eyes at the top of a flat head: the lid slipped from my hands landing with a clap in the mud.

I took a deep breath and picked up the bottle again, slippery now with the mud on the glass and on my hands. I walked slowly, the cold liquid in the bottle spilling down my chest, and at the same moment I put my foot in the water several things happened almost simultaneously: the frogs which were making a big noise ceased their croaking, and there was absolute silence;

the light became immediately dimmer; and a gust blew, stripping blueblack tonguelike leaves from the mangrove limbs, their banyans quivering in the wind. I continued carefully into the water until it reached my waist, the bottle half-submerged, and stopped—shin deep in the mud. Slowly, I tilted the bottle, feeling its weight slip away and the solid splash before me in the water. I wanted nothing more now than to turn quickly and run: I couldn't budge my feet. Standing there, holding the finally empty bottle, seeing myself again with my baggy navyblue school shortpants billowing around my hips, feeling my feet again in the sandals beneath the mud, looking down again through the dark water again, thinking, not understanding, believing: he is alive. Swimming. I watched his long angular legs fold, snap taut, and propel him smoothly through the water; snap, glide; snap, glide; and the frogchild disappeared into a clump of quiet mangrove banyans.

EVERLAST

■ Michael Stephens

It strikes me as downright peculiar that Michael Stephens isn't better known than he is. Though barely forty, he seems to some of us to have been around for decades, and of course it turns out he has, since 1972, at least, when he published his first novel, Season at Coole. *A bawdy, lyrical howl of a book, it instantly became one of those books novelists pass on to other novelists, saying, "Read this! This guy can* write!"

The years have passed, and Stephens, with a spell at Yale Drama School, travels in the Orient, teaching stints, tours with theater companies, domestic life, and fatherhood in New York's Upper West Side, has gone on writing and publishing (mostly in small press editions) poems, criticism, plays, novels, essays, and memoirs, as prolific as an Updike and as various. And still, people pass his stories and books around and say, "Read this! This guy can write!" *as if he were freshly minted, some smart new coin of the realm who just turned up at a Books & Co. signing. Not so. Michael Stephens was drinking in the Lion's Head and The Cedars back in the mid-Sixties with Gil Sorrentino and Hubert Selby—underage, but even so, hanging out with his peers.*

The problem is that from the beginning Stephens has produced work and created literary personae that refuse to be easily tagged or categorized. In the beginning, he might have been everyone's favorite enfant terrible, *a dropout kid off the streets with a lyrical brilliance that dazzled his elders, except that he was a Brooklyn Irish tough guy, too, with an old-time naturalist's pity and ear. Which might have been okay, especially in the Sixties, with Kerouac still around, but he somehow got himself to Yale, and before long he was lumped in with all kinds of "experimental" writers, and that made sense, because his fiction and plays did use formats and artifices one normally associates with the avant-garde, European absurdist as much as homegrown self-reflexive. But then it got hard not to notice that his seat-of-the-pants, commonsensical brand of criticism made him an especially sympathetic reader of social realism, and his own fiction, such as the story printed here, was clearly contaminated by a stubbornly straightforward affection for the "irretrievables"—which kept him well outside the circle of deconstructionist Conestogas at Yale and without so much as a cot in Klinkowitz's metafictionists' camp. Not enough irony. No compulsion to parody. Too many characters intent on evoking one's . . .* passions.

By this time, the "new thing" in fiction was being called minimalism, anorexic stories wearing reflector sunglasses, and Stephens's stories look too earnestly ambitious, too "literary," to get invited to the dance, and consequently it's still other writers who keep passing his work around, usually found in a small magazine like Fiction *or* Ontario Review, *still saying, "Read this! This guy can* write!" *Which is what I'm doing here, of course. All I hope is that a year from now, or maybe two, the response is, "Michael Stephens? Oh, yeah, he's that guy who writes so brilliantly and powerfully about violence and family and alcohol, whose work has that odd mixture of detachment and sympathy we associate only with the best storywriters, the classics, Chekhov and O'Connor and Carver, he's that guy who does strange things with form and familiar, charming things with voice and tone, he's the writer who loves what he calls in his story 'Everlast,' 'the irretrievables.' " Yes, that's the guy.*

—*RUSSELL BANKS*

Gertie Hopkins spoke:

"First it was the glass of wine for comfort. Then it was the bottle at the dining-room table, alone, the grandchildren at school, my daughters out working. Next I took to drinking gin, two bottles a day, delivered to the back door of the house. I was surprised how long it took any of them to figure that one out." It was her first year's celebration, a year of sobriety, drying out, and coming to these meetings with the other old gals. Twice a week, the women had these sessions, recalling, recovering, talking it over among themselves. Father Billy Joe Williams, a black Franciscan priest, was the moderator, and they met in the basement of his church, St. Anthony's. "Two bottles of gin a day," Gertie Hopkins said, smiling. "Two bottles." Over the past year, the ladies had made both headway and what they called "slips." Staying dry wasn't easy for any of them. One day at a time. Gertie had been a nurse, and she was working again, only no longer as a nurse, but as a helper in St. Anthony's parochial school kitchen. Father Williams got her a room at the convent, and she also helped the Franciscan nuns out there, and she tried to make his seven o'clock Mass every morning. Through the years of forgetfulness, Gertie began to remember at these sessions, though certainly not everything. Names returned, places. She was originally from Brooklyn, Flatbush, in fact, and Father Williams told her that he was once stationed at the Franciscan church off Eighth Avenue near Madison Square Garden. Gertie told him that she had only been to Manhattan a few times in her life, that she wasn't familiar with the Franciscan church there. Since coming into his parish, Father Williams had tried to locate her children. He even placed a call to the church in Brooklyn where all of them had been baptized. Katherine, Robert, Joseph, Noel, Siobhann, Margaret, and Sean. Apparently there was one other child, but since he was not baptized in that church, there had been no listing for him. Her husband's name was Colum, a New York City police officer who was killed in action on the Lower East Side during a robbery at a bodega. But it wasn't her husband's death, she told him, that made her fall to pieces. Her husband had prepared her and her children for that eventuality long before. When the priest called a Police Benevolent Association in New York, they informed him that the Hopkins family fell apart after the father was killed, and that they had helped Gertie and the children for a number of years, but that she had disappeared more than two decades ago. What could they do? When he reached one of her daughters in New Mexico, she hung up. He called her back, but she only hung up again. He wrote several letters, but none were answered. Gertie claimed that one of her daughters was a Carmelite nun at a convent in New Jersey, but when he investigated this, he discovered that it was another one of Gertie's stories. There was no convent; no daughter. One of her sons, Noel, died in Vietnam. When Gertie first came to the meetings she told everyone that she had been a nurse in Thailand and later that she was a lay nun in El Salvador. Of course, he learned that she had never been outside of the United States. "The booze talking," he told her. "Yes, I'm certain of that," she confessed.

He was impressed by how quickly she admitted this, but then a little afterward she explained why: "There isn't a word for 'no' in Irish." She winked, and walked out of the basement. Sometimes he knew she went back to drinking; he smelled it on her breath when she walked in. But he believed that she hadn't had anything in over a year, and he was probably right. Even then, Gertie told her stories to them. "One of my boys was an Irish gangster," she said. "His name was Joe." The next day, having forgotten she said that, she told the group that her son Joe was a cop, just like his father was. Father Williams explained to her that making up these stories was a way for her to keep forgetting the past. "It's not that I want to forget," Gertie answered, "it's just that I can't remember." "If you could just remember the last names of some of your daughters," the priest told her, "I could maybe try to find out where they live." "They're all Hopkins," she said, "just like me." "Their married names," Father Williams interrupted her. "Ah." Gertie thought and thought, but came up with nothing. Like she said, it wasn't so much forgetting as it was that she couldn't remember anything. Katherine, he discovered, married an Italian, but Gertie told him that she wasn't good with foreign names. Siobhann married a fellow name of O'Brien, no, no, she corrected herself, it was probably O'Ryan. One session, Isabelle, a proper old Italian woman, was talking about her husband's death when they lived across the state in Miami, and Gertie interrupted her in the middle of her talk. "Their father," Gertie blurted out, "my children's father, my husband, Colum was his name, he was a cop, but he also was—a fighter." "A boxer?" Father Williams asked. "Everlast," Gertie said, then shrank back into her gray self, excusing the outburst to Isabelle. After the session, Gertie went over to the rectory and cleaned up the kitchen after the priests' lunch; she swept their backyard, then went to her room. It was like a monk's cell, only the bed, a crucifix on the wall, a writing table and a chair. There was no closet, but she had no possessions to speak of, and when she was not wearing one housedress, the other one hung on the back of the door. Her one material possession was her running shoes, blue Nikes, which Father Williams gave her for Christmas. In the box in which the shoes came, she kept three pairs of socks and three pairs of underwear, using it like a dresser. Down here on the Gulf Coast of Florida, she didn't need an overcoat, and when it got chilly some nights in the middle of the winter, Father Williams lent her a sweater. If it really got cold, he lent her his big down coat, which was a little tattered but very warm. Gertie sat at the writing table and wondered why that word Everlast came into her mind and she tried to think about Brooklyn and where the two might connect.

Everyone in her family had been born there, and on her mother's side, it went back centuries. But Gertie was the only one in the family not born in Brooklyn, World War I going on, her father was in the military in Washington, D.C. When she was born, six months after the war ended, she made the local papers, being the longest baby—twenty-seven inches—born in the District of Columbia. Her two older brothers were born in Brooklyn, as were the sisters and brothers who followed her, Kathleen Ann, Joseph Patrick, Rosemary, Andrew, Thomas Edward, Margaret Julie, Brendan. Even Gertie's imaginary friends were born in Brooklyn, Woo-Woo, Choo-Choo, and Nora Mae. Gertie had lived in the same house on Madison Street that her father had been born in and his father, too, but it was torn down during the Depression after they moved out and fire gutted it. Her mother had been a nurse. Like her own husband, her father was once a city cop. Her father left the police force and studied law and he had a good practice and that was how they managed to keep the family house, but then her father lost all of his money in the Crash, and they moved into a cold-water flat after that. Gertie was a Moody before becoming a Hopkins: like her mother, she became a nurse. Her dog Midgie, a Dalmatian bitch, was born in Brooklyn around the corner from where they lived on Madison Street. All of her childhood friends were not only from Brooklyn, but had been born there, too, as were all her cousins, her aunts and uncles, East New York to the Rockaways, Flatbush to Ridgewood, as if she were related to someone on every block of this city within a city, from one parish to the next, St. Gregory's, Our Lady of

Lourdes, St. Thomas of Aquinas. Except Gertie. Born to spite the blood, she was delivered in Washington, D.C., even if she moved back to Brooklyn not six months later. The birth carried over into her speech, and she was the only person in her family and the only one on the block who did not speak with a Brooklyn accent (you had to earn it in the womb), and before you could say Mickey Walker, they moved upstate near Albany for a time, but then came back again, Brooklyn, first for vacations, to visit relatives, but then back for good. When she married Colum, he suggested moving to the Bronx, because he was stationed at a Midtown North precinct on the West Side, Hell's Kitchen, and it was hard to get back and forth from Flatbush to there, but soon he was transferred to the Lower East Side, and it cut nearly an hour off his commute. In the summer, he took the boys and girls to Riis Park or the Rockaways, and once he drove them to Coney Island with one of his brothers, then he and his brother, before both took the pledge, got into a fight in a boardwalk bar with two sailors, and the kids were upset afterward, and he did not take them again. The girls dreamed of cotton candy that night, while her sons dreamed of naked women tattoos on their biceps. Gertie tried to smell the sour green grapes in their arbor, but the smell had faded from her life. She remembered that one of her boys played with the first blacks in the neighborhood, two boys whose father was a minister, and they spoke with that British kind of accent from the Caribbean. Oh she didn't always live in Flatbush. When Colum first started on the force, they had a brownstone in East New York and attended Our Lady of Lourdes Church and Colum drank his after-work beers at Grim's Bar and Grill, owned by Eddie Grim's father. (Eddie, Gertie remembered, was a pitcher for the New York Yankees.) People in that neighborhood talked about the Yankee pitcher or about Jackie Gleason, who grew up in that parish and used all the locals' real names on his program and people debated whether Joe the Bartender was really Mr. Grim. Colum called Gleason a phony stage Irishman, but everyone in the family enjoyed his shows, even though Gertie didn't have a TV set in those days. They watched it if they visited relatives with a set or if they were drinking beers in one of the bars on Broadway. Father Williams had shown her a series of photographs, he said, "to jog her mind," but when she looked at Red Hook she told him she thought it was Seoul, Korea, and when he asked if she had ever been to Seoul, she lied, yes, she was a nurse there, but he knew immediately that she was lying. When he showed her a photo of Eastern Parkway, she told him it was Warsaw, Poland, and he said, "You were in Poland, right?" and Gertie nodded, yes. "I guess I told you about that experience already." It was as though Brooklyn were so foreign to Gertie Hopkins that she would need a passport or a visa to reenter it. Besides, she liked Florida, even if she didn't like it when she first arrived. But when she dreamed about Flatbush the other night, she told Father Williams about the dream the next morning. She was walking down Flatlands Avenue when she spotted one of the Jones boys and went over to say hello to him, but he did not seem to recognize her even though he came by their house practically every day as a boy to play with one of her sons. "I'm getting old," Gertie said to the Jones boy, but he kept walking. There were no more reunions in the Knights of Columbus hall or picnics in the summer at the state parks on Long Island or crabbing at night off the Canarsie pier, coffee with doughnuts on a late Sunday afternoon in the basement of the church, her own mother with her brown Third Order scapular, and her beads blessed by the Pope, gone gone, her mother on her ninetieth birthday in the dog days of August, the pitchers of warm beer, Kool cigarettes, setups of Seagrams with 7-Up and ice on each table with stained plastic tablecloths, gone, the bologna sandwiches, the gigantic tomatoes of their garden, the sour green grapes of the arbor, gone, even the smell of those grapes, gone, all gone, the grandparents, the uncles, even some of the cousins, even her own children, all of them, gone gone, World War II, Korea, Vietnam and other catastrophes, hit by a bus, crossing a street late at night, shot down in a bar, of cancer of the lungs, the liver, the penis, the vagina, the breasts, the brain, liver disease, kidney failure, though never any heart attacks in her family, never any heart attacks. Maybe even some of the relatives retired to Florida, or maybe one of her sons or a daughter. They were scattered on the points of the compass, Gertie's seven children, eight, oh hell, she counted their names and only came up with seven, though she remembered that once she counted eight. Names were the hardest to remember. Funerals on Long Island she remembered. Graveyards filled up in Brooklyn, although if you could prove a relationship to Thomas McCann, her great-grandfather, you got a free ride into Holy Cross Cemetery, and she told Father Williams of that, but she could tell that he didn't believe her, figuring it for another one of her stories. Whiskey in paper cups, cigar smoke in the foyer, out in the vestibule, Tromers Beer Garden on Bushwick Avenue, gin mills, Calvary, the Evergreens, Highland Park, filled with their bones, their Brooklyn dreams of upstate houses, fishing boats out of Sheepshead Bay, advancements in the fire and police departments, Wall Street jobs, insurance salesmen, used-car dealers, religious orders gobbled up others, nuns and priests and monks, some even went off to college before moving away, though all of it and all of them now are gone—gone. . . .

What all the remembering and forgetting did for Gertie was to leave that one word, which she scribbled on a piece of paper with a pencil: EVERLAST. And she knew that if she could smell the sour grapes in the arbor, it would come back to her. She heard Colum shouting that word to the boys. His face was red and indignant. "Everlast! Everlast!" he called out with his thick brogue, then he went over and punched one of his sons right in the gut, right on that Everlast label. "Come on, Dad," one of the boys said. It was Robert. Yes, it was Robert, and next to him was the other one, Joe, a bloody mess, and Gertie stood on the back porch, furious at Colum for allowing this to happen. At that moment, Colum seemed to look more like Spencer Tracy than anything else, but this was her mind playing tricks, because Colum never looked like Spencer Tracy in his life. Tyrone Power, maybe, yes, but never Spencer Tracy. Gertie remembered how it felt that day, how she wished she had never married this man. She wished she were anywhere but in that backyard in Flatbush. Colum was teaching the boys how to box. "Everlast! Everlast!" he shouted in their faces, punching Robert in the stomach, right on those words on his red satin shorts. Gertie grabbed her pocketbook and went out the front door. She walked up Flatlands to Flatbush Avenue, and she boarded a bus for downtown and Sis's apartment. Later, Colum telephoned, apologizing, that is, apologizing until he started in again. "They have to know how to defend themselves in this city," he said. Gertie hung up the telephone on him. Two hours later, looking out the window, she saw the old Model-T Ford he restored pull up in front of Sis's building, and that short, big-shouldered, heavy-fisted, furious little man got out. In the back seat, Gertie counted the children's heads, but only came up with seven of them. When she told Father Williams and the girls at the meeting about what she had been thinking the day before, Father Williams said she was blocking out her memories of that eighth child. Gertie felt irretrievable, like trash, like worthless garbage for not seeing the face of that eighth child, because even she admitted that there were times when she swore that there were eight children she bore, not seven. Two bottles of gin every day will do that, she said. But at the next meeting, she had nothing new about the eighth child, and she spoke about Colum again. "Not that Colum was a bad man," she said, "he wasn't bad at all. He didn't drink heavy or smoke or chase women. Oh, he cursed a blue streak, and his temper got him into enough trouble, what his partners called 'taking the law into his own hands.' He was an usher at the eleven o'clock Mass every Sunday. He worked at the Knights of Columbus hall, where all the girls held their wedding receptions because the hall gave Colum a break on the rental fee. Believe me, I never faulted the man but that one time in the yard. He was a godsend." "No secrets," Father Williams said, and, "deny nothing." "What the hell is that supposed to mean?" Maybelle asked. (She was big and black and from Mississippi, and Gertie liked her a great deal.) Sometimes Father Williams was strange and cryptic and the women didn't know what he was talking about. This must have been one of those times, though sometimes the meeting just broke down for no reason, Gertie saying one thing, Father Williams another, Maybelle yet a third thing, while Isabelle or Sarah Ann or Constance had yet other things to say, none of them coinciding. "Gertie's spirit-possessed and borned-again," Maybelle said. "So?" Father Williams asked, as though none of that really impressed him. "You know what I am," Gertie said. "I'm a recovering lying old bag lady who ended up on a street in Tampa before Father Williams found me." "Nonsense," Isabelle said. "Now, now," Cora said. "What the hell are you hiding?" Father Williams asked Gertie and then he lit a Camel cigarette and let the room fill up with smoke. Constance got coffee for everyone, passing the thick, tannish mugs around, knowing who liked it black, who liked it with milk or cream, who with sugar. "Nothing," Gertie said, "I'm not hiding nothing." Father Williams asked Gertie what happened to that eighth child. "I don't know," Gertie said. As Father Williams drifted away from Gertie and over to Cora and Sarah Ann, Gertie tried to remember that time when the police came by to tell her what happened to Colum and how Mayor Wagner showed up for the funeral. There was at least a five-thousand-police honor guard; she wasn't lying about that, was she? She wasn't making that up. Gertie couldn't figure it out, just didn't know what she did with that eighth child, his name, his face, what he did, where he went. He was lost into a black hole of eternity. Two bottles of gin'll do it; two bottles a day. She wanted to cry, but she held it just like she did when she had to pee. She wasn't a delicate flowery woman. She was short-stocky rough with red calloused hands, a florid face with a punched-up fighter's nose turned bluish-red with the years and the weather. Big heart, big bladder, big tits. Not tall, Gertie was still big all over. She could hold it, tears, farts, pee, you name it. Sarah Ann was going on about being a legal secretary in Atlanta, Georgia, that her children went off to college, her husband divorced her, and she took to the bottle. "Fifteen beers a day," she said, "and a couple shots of Wild Turkey to wash it down," but just then Gertie whispered, "Rory," she whispered it so low, no one heard, but she knew what it meant— that eighth child of hers. He was the smart one, the good one, the best and the brightest, a scholarship to high school, a chance to go to college, the youngest and the best-looking, the nicest of the lot, not an ounce of his father in him, nothing of the roughness of his brothers, handsome like a movie star, bright like a Jesuit. Then out of nowhere, Father Williams, his black face glistened over with sweat because the air conditioner wasn't working, turned to Gertie and said, "Everlast." What? Gertie tried to fake him out and started to talk about when she was a nurse in the refugee camps in Thailand. Father Williams didn't usually curse or swear, but he said, "No more bullshit, Gertie," and she understood. No more bullshit. Just the facts. Tell him his name; it was Rory. But Gertie couldn't manage to utter his name publicly. Rory. For the first time in over a year, Gertie wanted a drink so badly, and even if she never was able to remember the smell of the green grapes in the arbor of her backyard in Brooklyn, she never forgot the smell of gin, good old stinking Fuckink gin was her favorite, no pretense at making a martini, no olive, no vermouth, often straight out of the bottle. She tasted the gin on her tongue and felt it go down, burning inside of her like a hot coal, and how her head got dizzy instantly, and she imagined that the others noticed the change, saw her muscles loosen, her tongue go slack, her mouth open, her eyes twirl around inside her skull. Once she was high again, everything would come together. Everlast and Rory. She could be out on the street, without a history, a past, or even without a present or future, just Gertie and nothing else. Without hope, true, she knew that part of the equation, but also a nobody, without a care or woe, without regrets because she was without memory. The booze wasn't all bad in that sense; it had its good side to it, turning her into an irretrievable, they called them, someone or another, maybe even Father Williams himself called them irretrievables, a nice name, like a gang from Brooklyn or Miami, and let her die, dear God, let her end it all. It was a slip, not a slide, only a slip, not a downfall. Within a week, she'd dry out, get back to her purpose, find out about her son Rory and that word Everlast. Gertie had a little money under the mattress back at her monk's cell, and there was a little roadhouse a block or two from the rectory, and she could slip out after dinner, drink a few, get back before anyone noticed. She'd tell the bartender and his customers about the refugee camps at the Thai border, the tents and the flies and the sick children, Mother of God, she'd burn their ears off with her tales. The meeting ended, the group broke up, Father Williams went off to say his vespers, Gertie helped in the rectory kitchen, and afterward snuck out for a breath of air, as she put it, and down the road to the Shady Grove Hideaway. There was only the bartender and a few customers and no one seemed interested in engaging her in conversation since Gertie was at least twice anyone's age in the place, and instead of speech, she listened to a succession of dreary country songs about broken hearts and lost jobs and opportunities missed and suddenly, inches from her face, like a burnt apparition, she saw the face of Father Williams, although at first she wasn't sure if it was hallucination or the man himself. "Everlast!" he spit, and Gertie pulled back. "You're interfering with my right of free enterprise," Gertie told him. "You and your feminine prerogatives," the priest said and ordered himself a beer. "Words," he said, downing the beer, "a mouthful of drunken words." But then this terrible wave of nausea passed over Gertie and she wanted to die. The booze didn't sit right anymore and didn't taste as she hoped it would. She rode in the violent trough of a great wave, and Father Williams reminded her of a black angel, her guardian angel, and she cried on his shoulder. "Your son Rory was a fighter, a boxer," Father Williams said. "I hadn't thought of it before, but I went to the public library and looked up his name in the *Ring Record Book*, his name was Rory Hopkins and he was a welterweight with twenty-three fights when he was knocked unconscious into a coma and never revived, am I right, Mrs. Hopkins, am I right, Gertie? Isn't that your eighth son that you're always forgetting about?" "That wasn't my boy," Gertie lied. "My son never boxed, never did anything wrong. You're thinking of his brothers, his father, even his sisters and me fought more than Rory. He was the baby in the family, my little one. You would have liked him, Father Williams. I always thought Rory might have a calling from God. You'll see what I mean. You go home and call up the Brooklyn telephone directory and they'll get you his number and you can speak with him, find out what he's been doing all these years, ask him to come down and visit his old mother in Florida. Rory'd hop on the first flight down; he was that kind of boy. No, no, no, you have it all wrong, Father Williams, my Rory never had a fight in his life. . . ."

Those in Peril in the Air

■ Alexis Ullmann

A strong literary sensibility is evident in everything Alexis Ullmann writes. His passion for detail and precision of observation are carried with a graceful prose. He is a writer with all five senses open, romantic, nostalgic. It gives me great pleasure to introduce his story "Those in Peril in the Air."

—SUSAN MINOT

*L*ike all nations the French are fond of catastrophe, but there is one kind of tragedy their press dwells on with peculiar relish: the death of the brave and adventurous. *Paris-Match, Jours de France, Le Figaro* magazine, these weekly picture-magazines, imitations of the old *Life*, thrive on the miscarried final exploits of single-handed sailors like Alain Colas and Loic Caradec, rafters of wild African rivers like Philippe de Dieuleveut, or dreamers like Thierry Sabine, the pioneer of the Paris-Dakar Rally. Here is a grinning photograph of the hero preparing for his fatal voyage, one hand on the gleaming metal flank of his machine, the wreckage of which lies scattered across the following two pages; and here are some pictures commemorating past triumphs, and a tender snapshot of the doomed man with his wife or girlfriend. In this frame she has a brilliant smile for the camera, but in the next one, alone, she is looking away from you, and her yellow hair is hidden under a scarf, and suddenly she looks much older.

Adam Harend sometimes came upon such photographs at his job. Neither brave nor adventurous, he worked in an office in Manhattan for the American distributor of a chain of French magazines. Every day at lunchtime he ate a sandwich at his desk, improving his vocabulary as he read of the love affairs and divorces of French movie stars and singers and, occasionally, of violent accidents in wild and faraway places. Thus, one day, he came to read of the death of a young glacier pilot who had been killed in the French Alps while on a mission to rescue a stranded group of climbers. His airplane, a long-nosed Pilatus Porter, had plowed a snowy slope half hidden in a cloud, killing not just its pilot but also the four-man rescue team he was transporting. As for the three climbers, one of whom had been injured in a fall, they were later found to have frozen to death in their bivouac. The pilot had been twenty-six years old, the same age as Adam Harend. The article hinted that his adolescence had been, as the phrase has it, troubled; in fact it had seen him expelled from boarding schools in England, France, and America. His family had witnessed his transformation into a pilot skeptically at first, and then with astonishment: his many projects were usually abandoned half-way. He was the son of an American actress who had been famous in the Fifties and a still-celebrated French director. It was this which had caused *Paris-Match* in particular to single him out among the victims of what it called *l'hécatombe du Mont Blanc*, leaving a vague and fragmentary image—stooped shoulders, a long forelock of black hair—to float in the remoter swamps of Adam Harend's memory.

Normally Adam never went anywhere and never met anyone, but on this particular night, somewhat to his surprise, he found himself in Canada, in the middle of the night, racing across a lake in a small red speedboat. He had a cigar in his hand and a bottle of brandy between his knees. It was early in June, but the moon-light cast a sheen of winter over the treetops on the islands, and a chill stood on the surface of the water. Beside him, at the wheel, his parka zipped up to his chin, sat Peter, his college roommate. They had recently met again at a squash club in New York. In the meantime Adam had grown chubby and acquired thicker glasses, and Peter had lost most of his hair, the remains of which were now fluttering about his ears; the loss had made his nose, always beaklike, seem even larger. Peter was steering with one hand and holding the other out for the brandy. They were crossing the lake in order to fetch Peter's cousin, who had just arrived by car and was waiting by the pay phone on the Yacht Club dock. Her name was Amy, and like Peter she had spent all her childhood sum-mers on Iroquois Lake.

"Listen, I think you're going to like this girl," Peter was shouting over the roar of the engine. "Hell, she could do with some company. Her boyfriend—a French fellow, I thought he was something of a skunk," he shouted apologetically, "totaled himself in a plane crash three months ago."

Just then the light on the Yacht Club dock appeared, sliding out from behind an interposed island. A minute later the dock itself became visible: a wooden pier raised on thick piles, fitted with a streetlamp, under which there now appeared a human form. All this was mirrored perfectly in the still water—a bubble of harsh city light containing a doubled young woman and her duffel bag, floating in the northern night.

Adam dropped his cigar overboard as Peter closed the throttle. A wave surged forward from the bow and died in a luminous curl, sighing, as the hull settled on the lake. They drifted sideways to the pier, the engine gurgling, while above them the girl stepped to the edge.

"Hey, miss," Peter said, looking up at her from the wheel.

Unsmiling, businesslike, she lowered her bag to Adam and clambered down. She steadied herself on his shoulder as the boat swayed under her weight, and then she leaned across him into Peter's arms.

Because she was not as he had imagined her, Adam found her plain at first. She was a small girl and under the streetlamp her face looked pale and slack. "Probably she's tired," he thought.

"God I'm exhausted," she said immediately, settling down between them. It gave him a start.

"That mechanic was a frightening-looking guy," she said as they steered back into the channel. She was holding her hair to her neck, keeping it from flying in the wind. She waved away Adam's offer of the brandy. "And I kept thinking he was going to drive off the road and into the woods and god knows what," she said. "The Stateside mentality—always assume the worst of any stranger. Not you," she added, and she placed her free hand on Adam's forearm.

Peter's house stood on a small island in an archipelago by the far shore of the lake. Across a stretch of black water Adam saw its lights shining in the trees, and then the gables in the moonlight. A bottle-rocket shot up from the island and burst high above them, showering sparks on the water. They cheered. Another rocket went up, and then a third. In the light of the explosions Adam glimpsed Joanie, who was Peter's girlfriend, and Jonathan, another old classmate, waving at them from the deck of the boathouse. When they got there Jonathan proved to be brandishing a half-empty bottle of champagne.

"Ready for a swim?" he asked, crouching to hold the boat fast as they climbed out.

"I dare you," Peter said. "This lake was still frozen six weeks ago."

Amy embraced Joanie and Jonathan. Adam carried her bag up the winding steps to the house, walking ahead of the two girls, while Peter and Jonathan tied up the boat. As he crossed the porch, with its freshly painted white furniture and its boxed petunias, he heard laughter and shouts from below.

"He's going to do it!" Peter was shouting. "I can't believe he's going to do it!"

At the end of the dock Jonathan was stepping out of his trousers. His shoes, his sweater, and his shirt lay at his feet. Standing in his shorts, he bounced up and down for a few moments, his arms swinging at his sides, and then he threw himself off the dock. He surfaced immediately, shook the hair out of his eyes, and set off toward the middle of the lake. A second later a scream rang out, follwed by a tremendous splash, as Peter hurled himself from the roof of the boathouse.

"I don't know if I can deal with this," Adam said.

"Come on down!" Jonathan yelled in from the darkness. "It's as warm as a bath!"

"Yeah. Right," Adam said.

Joanie was tripping down the steps, shedding clothes as she went.

"Jesus Christ," Amy said.

"Animals," Adam said. "Come on inside, we'll have a nightcap and light a fire for those guys."

*   *   *

The lake darkened to a deep blue as the morning wore on. Out on the porch, the flagstones grew hot underfoot. The glare of the white furniture was painful to the eyes. Horseflies flew out to sample the remains on the breakfast plates; bees hovered among the petunias; tanning lotion was applied with wet slapping sounds. The screen door to the kitchen wheezed open and groaned shut constantly. Inside, the refrigerator hummed to itself between visits. Adam had a book in his lap—a swollen summer paperback from the shelves in the den, with sand between its pages—but he couldn't read. The sun was too bright, for one thing, and his head was hazy from the evening's drinking and a restless night in a strange bed. He kept removing his glasses and closing his eyes in order to better savor the unfamiliar embrace of sun and air. It looked as though much of the day would drift by like this. Sprawled in a wooden armchair, Jonathan read through black sunglasses a Xeroxed chapter of a book on marketing strategy, occasionally tapping the eraser of a pencil against his front teeth. Peter, as always, was organizing—calling up the Yacht Club to reserve a court for that afternoon, planning dinner at the Kestrel Inn at the other end of the lake, tracking down the garage in St. John where Amy had abandoned her parents' car.

"He doesn't have the parts," he told her, placing a coffee mug on the table and peeling off his T-shirt. "You're just going to have to fly back with us."

"I hate small planes," Amy answered, looking him right in the eye.

She had a photograph album open on her knees. Adam had looked through some of those albums the night before. Their pages were peopled with brown aquatic children with sun-bleached hair, Peter and his siblings being the focus of the archivisits' attention. Amy—round-bellied little girl, adolescent, incognito behind hair—was recognizable among the satellites. There were entire pages of drenched retrievers with sticks clenched in their crenellated jaws, and an occasional gathering of florid adults in silly paper hats—the men wearing plaid trousers or wild-colored jackets, the women big-jawed and bony—all bunched together for the camera, their eyes hollow from the flash. While in college Adam had suffered shyness and boredom among these people during several weekends at Peter's house in New Jersey. Even the memory of them made him anxious. Once in a while, as she turned the pages, Amy made small noises of recognition or let go a brief, fond laugh that made Adam look at her. She shut the album and closed her eyes, turning her face to the sun. Then she picked up her towel and started down the steps to the dock.

They were climbing up the lawn below the Yacht Club. As he walked Jonathan tossed a canister of tennis balls in the air, making it twirl. Joanie and Adam carried slightly warped rackets they had hunted down in a closet at the house. After a winter of playing squash (he was an excellent player, with a delicate lobbing-and-loping style, a game so sweet it often left Peter as helpless as in a dream) Adam's hand was pleasantly puzzled by the weight of the tennis racket. Peter was looking around him, at the clubhouse with its bright striped awnings, the green lawns sloping down to the lake, the flower beds along the paths.

"I hope she doesn't crack up my boat," he said. "Last summer she managed to have two crack-ups, though I have this feeling that the second time her boyfriend was at the wheel and she covered for him. By then he was already in Dutch with everyone up here."

"What's wrong with that girl, anyway?" Jonathan asked. He caught the canister neatly and sent it aloft again. "How can she resist me?"

"She's not for you," Joanie said. "She needs someone nice."

"But she *likes* shits," he said. "Michel was a prime shit."

"I was kind of fond of him," she said. "Peter couldn't stand him."

"Not true. And I don't want to spend this whole weekend talking about Michel again," Peter said. "It's bad for Amy, anyway."

"She's got to get over this fear of planes," Joanie said. "It's getting to be ridiculous."

Back at the house they swam again, everyone but Adam. He watched them from the mouth of the cavernous boathouse, sipping a beer.

"Is this going to be the weekend Adam didn't get wet?" Joanie called out to him.

* * *

"I know the way home from here," Peter said late that night, taking a cigar from his mouth. They were coming back from dinner in his father's old launch. "Hang on, everyone!" he shouted over his shoulder. He wedged his chart into the angle of the windshield and the dashboard and pushed the throttle open. A girl's scream rang out in the stern. The bow rose out of the water, its green light climbing higher and higher, until Adam had to grab the windshield. Two life jackets tumbled out from under the dashboard and bumped against his shins. They were shooting across the lake in the dark, the old engine roaring and churning, two white waves peeling away from the hull. Adam longed to yell.

Instead, he took the brandy and some cups back to the girls, bending over to walk through the cabin, where Jonathan lay stretched out among the cushions, his hands folded over his chest like those of a corpse. In the stern Joanie and Amy were both kneeling on the bench and leaning out over the transom, watching the phosphorescent wake curl out from under them. Back here the engine was loud and the deck vibrated under Adam's feet. Joanie smiled at him and pointed up at the moon, which would have been full but for a small bite near the top.

"Want some?" Adam shouted, sitting down beside them and holding up the bottle.

Amy accepted a cup and held her hair out of her face as Adam poured. Then Joanie stood up abruptly and made for the cabin, climbing the sloping deck with splayed feet. Amy laughed and nodded in her direction.

"That was subtle," she said.

"What?" Adam asked.

"That was *subtle*," she said, louder.

"What was subtle?" he asked. He was just playing dumb out of shyness. "Wasn't that a fun dinner?" he asked. "I liked that inn." He had to talk very loud and lean into her ear.

"Joanie is going to push you in the lake when we get home," Amy said.

"Really," he commented, not knowing what to say. Then he

added, "She's full of plans this weekend. She wants me in the lake, and she also wants to get you to fly back with us."

Immediately he regretted saying that.

"My boyfriend was killed in a plane crash," Amy shouted.

"I know," he shouted back. "I'm sorry."

"He was a rescue pilot," she explained. "In France. In the Alps."

Then he became excited. "Yes, yes, I know," he repeated. He remembered reading something about this. He had been at his desk in his office; the office had been empty; he had been eating a turkey sandwich and had stained a page with mayonnaise. . . . Just then a name came to him.

"Michel Cirey," he said, risking it.

Amy's eyes opened wide.

"I read about it—about him—in a French magazine," he explained. Like all such coincidences it seemed very meaningful at first, though he couldn't have said why. In his mind he saw a metal airplane seat upended in the snow, the bluish trough carved out of the slope by the disintegrating aircraft—but he wasn't sure whether he had actually seen these photographs or was now inventing it. He couldn't remember if Amy had been mentioned.

"*Paris-Match*," she said.

"What?"

"That magazine you saw. It must have been *Paris-Match*. They got the facts all wrong," she added. She was looking at him expectantly. Realizing what she wanted of him, Adam felt all his excitement drain away. It was typical. He was out on the water in the moonlight with a girl, and he was talking to her about her boyfriend. He put the bottle of brandy down, resting it against the cabinet beneath the bench.

"This was a shirt of his, actually," Amy said, fingering the collar that stuck out from under her sweater. "I just found it today, when I went to check on my house."

Adam nodded. "What plans do we have for tomorrow?" he said after a pause, as though to spare her painful memories.

Once they were docked at the island, he had to climb back on board and enter the cabin to wake Jonathan, who wasn't responding to their calls or their knocking on the porthole. Jonathan spluttered and sighed, as he always had when dragged from his sleep. Goading him slightly, Adam piloted him out of the cabin—after instructing him to watch his head—and over the gunwale onto the dock. There Joanie slipped her arm around his waist and began to walk him up the steps. "Where am I?" Jonathan asked. "Who is this strange woman? Please lead me to my bed." Only after they had entered the house, when Joanie left him to sway in the center of the living room while she switched on the lights, did he change his mind.

"Time for a swim," he said, with finality.

Peter stopped piling logs in the fireplace. "Not again," he said, amazed, delighted.

"Skinny-dip," Jonathan said.

"Right. Skinny-dip!" Joanie said. She was pulling her sweater over her head.

Peter whooped and kicked off his shoes. Amy began to unbutton her trousers. Quite revived now, Jonathan hopped out the front door on one foot, pulling a sneaker off the other. Clothes began to fly.

"All off!" Peter yelled, his voice receding down the path. "Shed the togs! Grease the bodies!"

There was no backing out of this. Naked, blind, and full of dread, Adam stumbled down the stone steps toward the icy lake. Joanie smacked his backside as she flew by, a white blur carrying an armful of towels. He stubbed his toe horribly against a stone. Feet were thumping on the dock. The darkness filled with shrieks and watery explosions. Approaching the dock, Adam reluctantly broke into a run and launched himself skyward. He was convinced he was going to land on someone. But there was only the water. His body was slapped by an enormous hand and forced down, struggling, into a freezing night. His fingers raked along a bed of gravel; mud lodged under his nails. After a great deal of fighting and climbing he was able to free his head of the water and open his eyes. His ears cleared. It was like a bubble around him popping. There were four heads near him on the water, their eyes and teeth sparkling and spray flying from their lips as they spoke—except they could hardly speak for the cold. Mostly they just whooped, and laughed. Adam joined in. He threw his head back and yelled, and yelled again. He couldn't stop grinning, even though it seemed that he couldn't breathe at all.

They straggled off to bed eventually, their bodies tingling from the shock of the lake and the healing warmth of the fire. Adam woke at noon the next day, his head as clear as the sky. A strong wind was blowing through the trees around the house and the lake was broken up with whitecaps, but on the porch, where he ate his breakfast, it was warm and quiet. He had a book with him, but it was far better just to sit, and be. This was their last full day at the lake. Dwelling on the evening ahead, he wondered how he might contrive to find himself alone with Amy; but until now they had done everything as a pack, and there was no reason why that might change on their last night together. Probably he would just have to call her in New York.

Preceded by their voices, Peter and Joanie came out a side door of the house and shuffled down to the dock, where they dropped the towels they were wrapped in. Poised to dive, Peter unexpectedly hesitated, which led to a brief little dance, each circling the other, dodging and feinting. Finally Peter backed himself off the end of the dock and Joanie dived in after him. Only then, looking up at the house from the water, did they see Adam and wave to him. He was in love with them; and also, he discovered, with Amy and Jonathan, who were still asleep upstairs. This was how he should live. He had been wrong to stay in the city so much all these years, wrong to spend so much time alone. He would call Amy. Summer was coming. From now on everything would be different.

They were going to make dinner at the house. In a movie-bright sunset Peter and Adam shot across the lake in the speedboat, leaping off the waves, to buy more onions and cigars at the general store near the Yacht Club. Yelling out of the corner of his mouth, Peter invited Adam back to the lake for the last week in July. Joanie would be coming too—"and a bunch of my cousins.

It'll be hopping up here," he said, his voice jamming in mid-sentence as the hull smacked a wave. "All my cousins. Amy will be at her own house," he added. The matter was settled by the time they returned, drenched, to the island, all of which smelled of the chicken Jonathan was grilling in the fireplace. He looked up at them as they walked in and pointed to the kitchen with his thumb and shook his head.

"They're having this ridiculous argument," he said.

Amy appeared in the kitchen doorway. Her whole body was stiff with anger.

"I'm not going to fucking fly back with you guys tomorrow if I don't want to," she said. She was staring right at Peter, as though he were her main tormentor. "Why?" she asked. "What does it matter if I don't fly?"

"Oh for God's sakes," Joanie said from the kitchen. "I'm sorry, already. I'm sorry."

"Just ignore her," Peter said. "Come on."

"Don't mind me, I'm crazy," Joanie said.

But in the end Joanie won. She didn't even have to bring up the subject again. It happened like this: toward the end of the meal, Peter and Adam and Jonathan fell into telling stories of their days together in college. They soon became convulsed. For some reason each anecdote required more background than the last, and as they filled it in for the girls they kept interrupting each other vociferously, insisting that the best part was being left out and identifying even funnier auxiliary anecdotes that demanded to be told on the spot. Amy and Joanie appeared not to mind. In fact, the three boys laughed so hard as they told their tales—Jonathan would perversely delay a punch line, adding detail upon detail, each one a little bit richer; and, knowing what was coming, Peter would fold in two, one hand across his middle and the other clutching the edge of the table (which made his knife rock back and forth on his plate), while Adam quaked silently and squeezed tears from the corners of his eyes—that the girls too became helpless. It was in the afterglow of all this laughter that Amy, no doubt feeling invulnerable in her happiness (they were all clearing the table and making coffee together, calling instructions back and forth from kitchen to dining room), announced quite spontaneously that she would after all fly back to New York with everybody else. "Fuck it," she added.

"Atta girl," Joanie said, and for the rest of the evening she was very solicitous of Amy and often glanced her way with affection. Draped over the couches by the fireplace, they made their way to the last of the brandy. The fire spat and crackled, licking them with warmth and shadows. Joanie and Amy went up to bed first, and downstairs Peter and Jonathan began to talk about business. Adam's attention drifted away. He tried to remember what they might have talked about on similar evenings in college, but not a single word came back to him.

He picked up his sweater and said good night. Tomorrow was going to be all traveling, back to grim La Guardia airport, back to his cramped and lightless apartment, back to work. He had an impulse to sneak past his door and see if any light was coming from underneath Amy's. His heart began to beat faster as he climbed the stairs. He told himself he was just going in for a chat. He hoped her light would be out.

It wasn't. He reached for the handle—but then drew back, clenching his fingers into a fist. It just didn't seem worth it.

Relieved, cursing himself, he went to his room.

Later he in the night, freezing, with a headache and a great thirst. For a while he lay in the bed, curled up, too cold to leave the quilt, but eventually he forced himself to rise and put on a T-shirt, shorts, and a pair of socks. He crossed the hall to the bathroom. Amy's light was still on. Perhaps she was afraid of the dark as well and couldn't sleep without a light.

He thought of her sudden announcement after dinner and was inexplicably embarrassed for her. Bending over, he drank from the tall old-fashioned tap at the sink. It was lake water, so cold it made his teeth ache. Suddenly he groaned aloud and, straightening up abruptly, banged his temple against the mouth of the tap and drenched his face. He had just recalled his swim of the night before. He had seen himself yelling in the water, yelling as loud as he could in the peaceful night.

As he left the bathroom Amy's door opened, revealing her sleepy head and a length of white nightgown.

"Are you all right?" she asked.

"Yes, yes," he said. "Are you?"

"Yes. I heard you . . ."

"I just banged my head," he explained.

"Ouch," she said. "Will you sleep?"

"Yes," he said. "Good night."

But he was awake awhile longer. It was cold in the room, his hair was wet, and his scalp smarted where he had hit it on the tap. The night was quite still, apart from an occasional scrape and flutter outside his window. Then he heard the very faint sound of a plane approaching in the moonlit sky, slowly growing stronger. It seemed to be searching, turning back, flying over once again, its engine louder all the time. It began to circle, leaving a ring of staggered echoes behind it, and now the noise, which had become deafening, was muffled by the flying clouds, drowned out by the wind, soaked up by the night. It was Amy's boyfriend, searching for lost climbers in the dark. Adam was on the phone too. He wrenched himself out of sleep and sat up. staring at nothing, catching his breath.

The morning was windy again, the lake even rougher than the day before.

"Do you think the plane can land in this?" Amy asked Adam. They were looking out the plate-glass window of the living room, where Amy had been wiping the table clean. A sudden gust boomed in the chimney behind them and rattled the window.

"Jesus," Amy said.

"It may get calmer. I dread this whole trip," Adam said, to make her feel better.

"On the last day of a vacation," Jonathan said, "one should pay a man to come out onto the porch after breakfast with a mallet and deliver a sharp blow to your forehead and ship you home."

They had gotten sand into the rug in the living room. Jonathan had stained the granite bib around the fireplace while grilling his chicken. Countless empty bottles—wine, liquor, beer, and soft drinks—had to be collected in cardboard boxes on the back porch. Peter was on the telephone; the others kept interrupting to ask him where things belonged. They worked steadily for almost two hours, brushing past one another on the stairs and in the hall-ways, carrying objects.

At noon, when the floatplane was due, Adam made sure of the window in his room and then lugged his bag—which seemed to have shrunk, or else his clothes had swollen—downstairs and onto the sheltered porch. Joanie and Jonathan sat facing the lake, getting a last dose of sun. Already it had become strange to see them in long pants. Jonathan had one hand on his marketing strategy Xeroxes on the table, next to a half-full bottle of white wine and its rippling shadow. Joanie had *Windmills of the Gods*, still open at the first page, facedown in her lap.

For a moment they thought they heard the plane, but they couldn't see it anywhere. Searching, they made out among the whitecaps a small dinghy with an outboard motor struggling over from the mainland. It contained a local adolescent, fiercely hung over, summoned by Peter to collect the keys.

Half an hour after the plane was due they spotted it flying toward them from the eastern end of the lake. Adam walked down to the dock to wave it in. The wind was strong down there and the waves were breaking on the rocks and against the boat-house. The dock was wet, its thick coats of paint slick and slippery. The pilot dipped his wings when he saw Adam waving, just before he roared over the house.

He circled the group of islands, the sunlight flashing on his wings. Then he drew away in a long arc and began a steep descent. He disappeared behind a neighboring island, trailing the sound of his engine, which lingered on the air for a moment before dying away.

Turning back, Adam caught sight, on a corner of the boathouse deck, of the empty beer bottle which Jonathan and Joanie had used to launch the rockets on the night of their arrival. He went over to get it, smiling at the memory, and then paused to look out over all that he was leaving. Here the water was rough and the islands seemed to huddle under their coat of pines, but in the distance the whitecaps looked stationary, as peaceful as sheep grazing in a meadow. At the eastern edge of the lake blades of sunlight fanned downward from a tear in a mountain of clouds; in the west gray chutes of rain stood like pillars between water and sky. It was a beautiful landscape but it contained no plane. Adam concentrated and heard only the waves and the wind. Up at the house, the others were hauling their bags out onto the porch. He started up the steps. Everyone was standing around now with nothing to do. Then, inside the house, the telephone began to ring, and Peter went in to answer it.

"He will have flown back to Campbell," the hung-over boy said after a silence. "Too rough to land here."

"We would have heard him go," Jonathan said.

"Can't tell, with the wind like this," the boy answered.

Amy was sitting on the parapet, her arms crossed in a V over her chest. She started to bang the heel of her sneaker against the stone. Adam looked over at Joanie, and Joanie looked away and picked at a white crease in her old blue jeans.

"Kids," Peter said, coming out from the kitchen, "that was Campbell airfield. He's in the channel behind the island and he can't get around to this side, there's too much wind. We're going to have to take a boat over."

"Jesus Christ!" Amy said. "Jesus Christ!"

"Come on, miss," Peter said, holding a hand out to help her down.

They took the largest of the boats and still they had to go slowly. Laden with bodies and luggage, the craft wallowed in the waves; everyone got wet. When they rounded the point and came into the lee of the island, Joanie was the first to spot the plane. Warned by Peter of an extra passenger, the service had sent a larger plane, a Beaver. It was tethered to a dock by a boathouse belonging to another set of Peter and Amy's cousins. A man was standing on the outside float, his head and arms buried in the engine. He was young and blond-haired, with aviator glasses and a very red face. He was wiping his hands on a rag when they arrived, and he was beaming.

"Just checking a line," he said after shutting the cowling. "Just checking a line. There's one more of you than they said."

"No, no, not me," the hung-over boy said. Then he helped them load the bags into the Beaver and shook everybody's hand, even the pilot's.

"Why don't you come with us?" Joanie asked. "Catch a movie in Toronto."

The boy grinned, blushed, and muttered something incomprehensible.

Amy was already inside, all the way in the back. The pilot held the front passenger seat folded over as the others climbed in one by one. The cabin was alarmingly small; folding himself in, Adam had to overcome a moment of claustrophobia.

"You strap yourselves in, eh," the pilot said. "I'm not telling you it's going to be smooth."

He freed the plane from the dock and leaned on the strut with all his weight. As the plane began to drift he jumped onto the float. Hanging on with one hand, he uncoiled the wet painter from the cleat and climbed in with it, slamming his door and latching it shut. It was already stifling inside the cabin. The pilot clamped his seat belt on and looked over his shoulder to make sure everyone else was tied down. He turned a knob on the instrument panel; the radio crackled and hissed; he shut it off, and wriggled in his seat until he was comfortable.

"We're going to let the wind push us back like this for a while," he said. "It'll give us as long a stretch of smooth water as we can use."

It kept getting hotter. They sat in silence, hearing the wind whistle about the wings and the fuselage as the dock, the boathouse, the whole island receded in front of them. The yellow speedboat had reached the point and Adam saw the hung-over boy slow down and stand up at the wheel as the waves came for him and carried the boat up into the air. At last the pilot fired the engine. Flames shot from the pipes along the nose. Everything began to vibrate.

There was an unpleasant moment to weather as the plane took off: one of the floats freed itself from the lake before the other, so that for a time one half of the plane rose through the air while the other dragged along in the water. Adam had been ready for this, remembering it from the flight in, and yet the plane's tipping seemed to go on much too long. It caused an odd queasiness in him, and in the second before the final release it became downright frightening. Not just for him: Jonathan turned and looked at him with amazement in his eyes.

From there on things got worse. Even as it climbed, the plane seemed not to fly so much as stagger about the sky, tripping over invisible objects. Adam's seat would try to leap out from under him, his organs traveled absurd distances inside him, and twice he banged his head on the window and saw stars. His face grew cold under a layer of sweat. He began to sigh deeply, and a monstrous nausea came swimming up through his body. Outside, the wing kept flexing with the shocks; in front of him, the pilot's impassive neck, fringed by a neat blow-dried haircut, began to look like a hallucination. And behind him, Amy moaned suddenly—a strangely sexual sound that startled him—retched, moaned again, and began to throw up profusely into an airsickness bag. Jonathan turned and put his hand on her head, but she knocked it away. Adam looked through the window down at the marshes and lakes crawling by, trying to provide his body with an anchor by fixing his eyes on a motionless point in the landscape. He waited.

When they stepped onto dry land at Campbell airfield, none of them could speak. Adam's legs were shaking. The airport staff—two dry-looking men identical in everything but age, in plaid shirts and baseball caps—kept looking at him sideways, Adam thought. The twin-engine landplane that would fly them on to Toronto was fueled up and waiting for them, but its pilot was busy inside the raised wooden shack that served as an office, filing a flight plan: the weather over Toronto was getting worse and it looked as though he might have to fly in on instruments.

"I'm going to settle the plane tab," Peter said, shuffling up the steps to the shack.

"Let me know," Adam said.

His legs were still weak. He sat down on the grass in the lee of the shack. Jonathan and Joanie were carrying their bags out to the plane. They looked quite recovered: they were grinning out from under their sunglasses, and kidding each other about the coming flight. The wind was so strong, their shirts were flapping on their backs. Amy was walking up and down by the steps, her arms crossed on her chest. She had the same drawn face as when Adam had met her. "Her traveling face," he thought.

"Are you going to be all right?" he asked her.

She didn't answer.

The door of the shack swung open and Peter came out with the pilot. This one was a sweaty middle-aged man with a crumpled pack of cigarettes in his shirt pocket and a five o'clock shadow. He was half bald, but his mustard-colored hair curled over the back of his collar in long greasy strands. Peter raised his chin at Adam and told him how much his share of the planes had cost. It was not an unexpectedly high figure but it was painful to hear all the same.

"Let's move," Peter said. "I don't want to get airport anxiety in Toronto."

Amy, meanwhile, had disappeared into the shack. Adam had assumed she was looking for a bathroom, but minutes went by without her reappearing. They were waiting for her by the plane. All the luggage had already been loaded.

"Oh come on," Peter said.

"Have you got airsickness bags in there?" Jonathan asked the pilot. "She got really sick on the way from Iroquois," he added quickly.

"Here she is," Joanie said. "Poor thing."

"Someone should get in first," the pilot said. "She shouldn't sit in the back if she gets sick."

Jonathan climbed in. Adam followed him up into the wing. He already had one foot in the cabin when he heard Amy ask the pilot if she could get her bag.

"I'm not coming with you," she told Peter. "I'm going to rent a car."

"Oh, shit," Peter said. "Come on."

"I'll pay for my share of the plane," she said.

"It's a half-hour flight." Peter said "We're all sick. You just have to sit through it."

"Stop it. I'm just not coming," she said.

Peter shook his head. "Okay," he said. "Have you got a car?"

"That's not your problem. It's not your fucking problem!" she shouted.

Joanie turned away and looked at Adam, up on the wing.

"Let me up, will you?" she said.

Adam stepped down onto the grass to let her by. Peter's eyes followed her angrily through the window as she struggled to the rear of the cabin and sat down next to Jonathan. The pilot tapped his shirt pocket, carefully extracted a limp cigarette from the pack, and struck a match, which he cupped expertly against the wind. Perhaps, Adam thought, he had seen passengers chicken out before and sensed this was going to be a long struggle.

Perhaps, he found himself thinking, Amy sensed that this plane was going to crash. He caught himself staring at her.

She pointed to the cargo hatch and said something he didn't hear. The pilot, his cigarette dangling from his lip, one eye clamped tight, opened the hatch and started pulling the bags out. The tail of his shirt had come out of his pants and there were rings of sweat spreading under his arms. To Adam he looked like a man who was about to have a heart attack. And why was he smoking around a planeful of gasoline?

"That's the one," Amy said.

"Okay," Peter said. "I'm going to drive with you."

"Don't you dare," she said. "You'll miss your meeting." She sounded as though she were beginning to choke.

Here was Adam's chance to bail out of the flight; but that meant getting stranded on a grass airstrip in Canada with a girl who was about to cry. There was nothing there except a shack, a few parked cars and airplanes, water, and a lot of wind. He couldn't believe how far from home he had strayed.

The pilot had locked the cargo hatch and was headed around to his side of the plane. Peter took his cousin into his arms. She clung to him. Her eyes were shut, her cheeks wet. To Adam this was clearly a final farewell. He had to get himself in the plane quickly he realized, or he too was going to panic. Without saying good-bye he climbed onto the wing, bumped his head on the hutchway, and wedged himself into a seat. He grabbed the two halves of his seat belt and clamped them together. It was then he remembered his dream of the night before, his nightmare flight with Amy's boyfriend.

The memory caused inside him an explosion of terror. It centered at the base of his throat and shot out through his arms and down to his scrotum. He grappled with the clasp of the seat belt in his lap, but his fingers were wild and drunk. Once he had managed to free himself, he lunged upward and banged his head again, violently, on the roof of the cabin. He heard a crack, and a sharp pain ran through his neck and his right shoulder.

"Hey," Jonathan said behind him. "Take it easy."

He heard a knock on the window beside him. He tried to turn his head and almost shouted from the pain. He tried again, slower, and again it proved impossible. Carefully he swiveled his whole torso to the right. Amy's small fist was rapping the plexiglass. Her face was neatly framed inside the rubber-rimmed trapezoid, less than a foot from Adam's: her nose was red and her eyelids and cheeks swollen. She was mouthing a silent good-bye.

But even as Adam answered her, also in silence, he felt that she was looking right through him, at someone else.

She gave him a vague wave of her fingers, and then she started back toward the shack, tilting away from the weight of her bag. Peter had settled into his seat and began to search all his pockets for something. The pilot peered out the window at his wing and rocked the controls, making sure of the flaps. Adam saw a gust of wind whip Amy's hair up and a second later heard it engulf the plane. His hand was pressed to his neck. He felt like crying, and although it seemed like a very long trip, he just wanted to get off the ground and go home, and be alone.

NOTES ON THE CONTRIBUTORS

ROBERT ANTONI's story is an excerpt from his novel *Divina Trace*, for which he has received an NEA and a Michener Grant. Currently holding B.A., M.A., and M.F.A. degrees, he is now a Ph.D. candidate at the University of Iowa Writers Workshop. His work has appeared in *The Quarterly*, *The Missouri Review*, and the Johns Hopkins magazine *Telescope*.

DOUGLAS BAUER was raised in rural Iowa. He holds a B.A. from Drake University and a doctorate from SUNY, Albany. His work has appeared in *The Atlantic*, *Harper's*, *Esquire*, and other magazines. His first book, *Prairie City, Iowa*, was published by Putnam. He is currently finishing *Dexterity*, another novel, to be published by Simon and Schuster in 1989.

PINCKNEY BENEDICT is twenty-four years old. He grew up on a dairy farm in West Virginia, received his A.B. from Princeton and an M.F.A. from the University of Iowa Writers Workshop. He has published one book of short stories, *Town Smokes*, and has written for the *Ontario Review, Southern* magazine, the *Chicago Tribune*, and *Wig Wag* magazine.

STEPHEN COOPER is a writer living in Los Angeles, California.

ANNE U. FORER lives in the East Village of New York City. She has written for *Exquisite Corpse*, among other literary publications. She just turned forty-three, is married, and has a dog.

LYNN GROSSMAN is a writer living in New York City, where she has studied with Gordon Lish. Her stories have recently appeared in *TriQuarterly, Story Quarterly,* and *The Quarterly.*

SIBYL JOHNSTON's story is an excerpt from her novel *"Iris Holmes,"* for which she received a grant from the Keter Foundation. She received a master's degree in creative writing from Boston University and now lives in Middletown, Connecticut.

LOUIS BEYNON JONES is a graduate of the University of California at Irvine Writing Program. He is currently at work finishing his novel *The Counterfeiters.*

MICHELE OWENS is a writer living in New York City.

MIKE PADILLA grew up in the San Francisco Bay Area. He received a B.A. in English from Stanford University as well as an M.F.A. in creative writing. He has written for *Sequoia* and *The Indiana Review.*

MICHAEL STEPHENS is the author of a novel, *Season at Coole* (Dalkey Archive, 1985), and the forthcoming nonfiction work *Heaven, Earth, Human* (Random House), essays on Korea. He has written one play, *Our Father,* which ran on Theatre Row in New York for several years and was produced in Edinburgh and London. He has also written for *Ontario Review, Witness, Fiction, Agni Review,* and *Exquisite Corpse.*

REBECCA STOWE has written for *The Florida Review, Farmers Market,* and *Cottonwood.* She attended the City College writing program in New York.

ALEXIS ULLMANN was born in New York City in 1958. He attended Yale University. Now living in New York, he has worked as a French translator and as an editor and has written for *Grand Street, GQ,* and *Shenandoah.*

DAVID WALTON's 1983 collection of short fiction, *Evening Out,* was published by the University of Georgia Press and was included in the Flannery O'Connor Award Series.

TERESA YUNKER is a writer living in Los Angeles, California.

COLLIER FICTION

Beattie, Ann. *Where You'll Find Me.*	$7.95	ISBN 0-02-016560-9
Cantor, Jay. *Krazy Kat.*	$7.95	ISBN 0-02-042081-1
Carrère, Emmanuel. *The Mustache.*	$7.95	ISBN 0-02-018870-6
Coover, Robert. *A Night at the Movies.*	$7.95	ISBN 0-02-019120-0
Dickinson, Charles. *With or Without.*	$7.95	ISBN 0-02-019560-5
Handke, Peter. *Across.*	$6.95	ISBN 0-02-051540-5
Handke, Peter. *Slow Homecoming.*	$8.95	ISBN 0-02-051530-8
Handke, Peter. *3 X Handke.*	$8.95	ISBN 0-02-020761-1
Hemingway, Ernest. *The Garden of Eden.*	$8.95	ISBN 0-684-18871-6
Mathews, Harry. *Cigarettes.*	$8.95	ISBN 0-02-013971-3
Miller, John (Ed.). *Hot Type.*	$7.95	ISBN 0-02-044701-9
Olson, Toby. *The Woman Who Escaped from Shame.*	$7.95	ISBN 0-02-023231-4
Olson, Toby. *Utah.*	$8.95	ISBN 0-02-098410-3
Pelletier, Cathie. *The Funeral Makers.*	$6.95	ISBN 0-02-023610-7
Phillips, Caryl. *A State of Independence.*	$6.95	ISBN 0-02-015080-6
Rush, Norman. *Whites.*	$6.95	ISBN 0-02-023841-X
Tallent, Elizabeth. *Time with Children.*	$7.95	ISBN 0-02-045540-2
Theroux, Alexander. *An Adultery.*	$8.95	ISBN 0-02-008821-3
Vargas Llosa, Mario. *Who Killed Palomino Molero?*	$6.95	ISBN 0-02-022570-9
West, Paul. *Rat Man of Paris.*	$6.95	ISBN 0-02-026250-7

*Available from your local bookstore, or from
Macmillan Publishing Company, 100K Brown Street,
Riverside, New Jersey 08370*